A TYLER ZAHN NOVEL

HAVOC
TROUBLE ON THE TRAIL

CAM TORRENS

Black Rose Writing | Texas

ISBN: 978-1-68513-687-1
LIBRARY OF CONGRESS CONTROL NUMBER:2025913297
PUBLISHED BY BLACK ROSE WRITING
www.blackrosewriting.com

Printed in the United States of America
Suggested Retail Price (SRP) $21.95

Havoc is printed in Minion Pro

*As a planet-friendly publisher, Black Rose Writing does its best to eliminate unnecessary waste to reduce paper usage and energy costs, while never compromising the reading experience. As a result, the final word count vs. page count may not meet common expectations.

Matt "Dragon" Rossi—this book is for you. Thanks for our time hauling trash in the C-130 but even more for our shared experience on the Appalachian Trail, where you instilled in me the thirst for the thru-hike! Here's a toast, brother! RIP

PRAISE FOR
HAVOC

"The pacing is propulsive. The stakes are high, and the twists are diabolical. This is hands-down the best Tyler Zahn adventure yet."
–Brooke L. French, author of *The Carolina Variant* and the *Letty Duquesne* thriller series

"Tyler Zahn returns for an intricately woven, pulse-pounding mystery full of helicopters, hiking, and hidden assets."
–Darrow Kirkpatrick, author of *Two Sticks, One Path: A Journey Beyond Fear on the Colorado Trail*

"Cam Torrens' *HAVOC* is like *Wild*'s Cheryl Strayed, backpacking deep in the wilderness, stepping into the middle of a battle zone where the swarm of armed "bad guys" lurking along the trail looks just like the army of "good guys" hunting them down."
–Joan Griffin, bestselling author of *Force of Nature*

"*HAVOC*, with its fast-paced action on high elevation trails of the Colorado Rockies, will take your breath away. My favorite Zahn story yet, until the next installment is released!"
–Amanda Jaros Champion, bestselling author of *In My Boots: A Memoir of Five Million Steps Along the Appalachian Trail*

"Pack your gear, lace up your boots, and explore the Colorado Trail with Tyler Zahn. But, be careful–danger lurks around every twist and turn in the best Zahn book yet!"
–Travis Tougaw, award-winning author of the *Marcotte and Collins Investigative Thrillers*

"Torrens put the Cliffs in Cliffhangers! Fans of C.J. Box's Back of Beyond will relish time spent with Torrens' protagonist, Tyler Zahn."
–Timothy Gene Sojka, award-winning author of *Payback Jack, Politikill, 39,* and *Claws*

"Torrens ups the stakes in *HAVOC,* where a mysterious rescue mission turns personal for Tyler Zahn. Gripping, fast-paced, and impossible to put down."
–Gail Ward Olmsted, award-winning author of the *Miranda Quinn Legal Twist* series

"If you're a fan of Tom Clancy's books and Jack Ryan, you'll enjoy *HAVOC: Trouble on the Trail.*"
–Sandra J. Cady, author of *A Game of Luck: A Sam Roma Detective Mystery*

"If you're looking for an edge-of-your-seat thriller that rings with authenticity, this novel is for you."
–A.J. McCarthy, bestselling author of the *Charlie and Simm* mystery series

"In *HAVOC,* the fifth *Tyler Zahn* novel, author Cam Torrens combines his experience as an Air Force pilot and a search-and-rescue volunteer with his love of the Colorado Rocky Mountains to produce a magnificent pot-boiler of a novel."
–Edward J. Leahy, award-winning author of the *Kim Brady Mystery Series*

"Author Torrens does it again! Each *Tyler Zahn* book surpasses the last, proving the series only gets better! What a ride!"
–Lucille Guarino, bestselling author of *Elizabeth's Mountain*

"Full of action, friendship, and family, this story makes you question who to trust as it moves at a fast pace, leaving just enough crumbs for the next adventure."
–Lena Gibson, award-winning author of the *Love and Survival* series

"*HAVOC* delivers heart-pounding action and suspense that will keep you turning pages deep into the night."
–Leah Miles, author of award-winning romantic suspense, *Baby ConSEALed*

"In *HAVOC*, the pulse-pounding fifth installment of the *Tyler Zahn* series, Cam Torrens delivers his most gripping thriller yet. This is the kind of book you cancel plans for. If you haven't met Tyler Zahn yet, now's the time."
–Michelle Caffrey, romantic suspense author

"Every page brings a new twist and turn that you won't see coming. *HAVOC* is a gripping and suspenseful novel that will keep you glued to the pages until the end. Five large stars!"
–LeeAnne James, award-winning author of *The Thin Blue Line* series

"Whether describing a military chopper spiraling out of control or following the cautious steps of a seasoned thru-hiker, Cam Torrens infuses every moment with his signature breakneck pacing."
–Del Blackwater, author of *Dead Egyptians*

"Tyler Zahn battles unknown enemies and rugged backcountry to uncover the truth and protect what he cares about most, his daughter. Smart, intense, and addictive!"
–DL Mitchell, bestselling author of the *Coral Shores Veterinary Mystery* series

ACKNOWLEDGMENTS

The team pulled together again for the fifth installment of the Tyler Zahn series. HAVOC was just a ton of fun to write, and the research for the military scenes took me down memory lane. Thanks to all of you writers, editors, readers, and friends for helping me bring the novel to publication:

My bride, Linda, for continuing as beta reader #1! To my mother, Susan, who always told me I could be anything I wanted to be and now just tells me, "It's the best book you've ever written." I always send it to you first, so I can start with that positive boost. My oldest daughter, Natasha, for early reads of the original manuscript. And favorite sisters-in-law (oh, do I only have two?) Donna and Sandra for their insightful comments.

Thank you to the Central Colorado Writers critique group for tearing the book apart while improving my writing.

The beta readers! The book changed from first draft to final over many months, thanks to your keen observations and suggestions: Mary Riley, Terry Williams, Sue & Ben Paganelli, Alta Beren, Penny Martin, Sarah Greenberg, Kathy Bowen, and Cecilia LaFrance. Fellow writers and my "go-tos" for first reads: Gail Ward Olmsted, Lucille Guarino, and Tim Sojka. Proofreaders Evan "Elvis" Hendricks, Jennifer Irving, Shane Bumgarner, Kristy Beardemphl, Kristin Homer, and Randy "Rudder" Kaufman. And for "The Butcher"—Kay Smith-Blum, many thanks for sharing your superpowers (again).

Retired Army COL Paul Mele and active-duty CAPT Noah Staples for reminding me how important it is to talk to the subject matter experts rather than just making this stuff up. Thanks for educating me on the Army and the Black Hawk. Craig Bissonnette at Colorado's Department of Reclamation, Mining, and Safety for providing information and resources for Chaffee County mines.

The real-world team at the High-Altitude ARNG Aviation Training Site (HAATS) in Eagle County, Colorado. Thanks for the support you give our Search & Rescue teams. You all strengthen our country with your training program and save lives in the mountains on the side! I took huge liberties with your mission in this book. It's fiction!

Thanks, Reagan Rothe, and our team at Black Rose Writing for your support, confidence, and talent!

To my sister, MaxieJane Frazier, who took this book to the finish line with her superb editing prowess.

The title of the book honors the eight-person crew of HAVOC 58 and the Secret Service agent who lost their lives flying out of Jackson Hole, Wyoming, in 1996 on a C-130H. And to their Dyess AFB, Texas squadron mates who still support the surviving families every year during Carry the Load.

Finally, to our readers—thanks for joining Tyler Zahn on his adventures!

HAVOC

1-ZAHN

Buena Vista, Colorado-July 12, 2022

Ferocious winds force a tight two-handed grip on the wheel to stay in my lane, but the county road leading to the SAR bay is clear of traffic today. Fourteen-thousand-foot mountains loom on the right, and snow swirls spiral skyward as Chaffee County Deputy Sheriff Rick Perez's name scrolls across my screen. My daughter, Daria, is out on the Colorado Trail, twenty miles north of here, hiking with my girlfriend, FBI agent Emma Frazier. I mouth a silent prayer that they're below the tree line and mash the *Accept Call* icon.

"Yeah?" I know why Perez is calling. A SAR—search and rescue—alert just lit up my cell ten minutes ago.

"A clusterfuck, Z-man. Downed helicopter. Potential fatalities." Perez's voice comes across at a slightly higher pitch than normal. He's not panicked—I've never seen him lose it. But he's definitely tense. "I'm on my way to St. Elmo. What's your status?"

"Two miles out from the SAR bay. I'll join a ground or helicopter team."

"No one's going in by helo. Winds are way out of limits. Probably why they crashed," Perez says. "SAR might be the first on the scene, but a slew of out-of-state agencies are going to be pouring in. Need you wearing your reserve sheriff hat for this one."

I just graduated from reserve sheriff training two weeks ago and work one day a week out of the sheriff's office in Salida. Uncertain about the protocol for working on off days, I say, "My sheriff's gear is down in my locker at work."

"What do you have with you?"

"My badge, personal weapon, and phone. And my office cell."

"That'll do. Meet me on this side of St. Elmo. Still working the coordinates they gave us, but figure we're going up toward Hancock Lakes or Tincup Pass."

"Got it."

I disconnect, glancing in the rearview mirror before pulling my truck to the shoulder. SAR needs to know I'm not joining them before I turn up the pass and lose cell coverage. I pull off my SAR cap and catch the glint of thinning hair in the mirror. The Active Alert app indicates Becky's running incident command, or IC. If anyone has the personality and temperament to handle an interagency clusterfuck, Becky does.

I hate to call incident commanders when they're just starting a mission. It's chaos—assholes and elbows—at the SAR bay while they try to figure out what happened, how to respond, and what resources are available.

When I place the call, an unexpected male voice answers, "This is Jackson."

"It's Tyler Zahn. Trying to reach Becky. Is she running IC?"

"Yep. She's on the radio with dispatch." Jackson pauses, and I hear loud voices in the background. "And a phone call with the state SAR guys at the same time. Is it important?"

"No. When she gets a moment to breathe, let her know the sheriff's office needs me to work this mission from their end. I won't be responding to the bay."

"Got it. Anything else?"

"Do you have time to update me on what we know so far?" I figure Perez is already out of phone range. Maybe I can bring him the latest info if Jackson knows more than what we do.

"Let me move to the whiteboard." The radio voices fade and Jackson speaks again. "OK. We've got an Army National Guard helicopter, a UH-60 Black Hawk, reportedly crashed at roughly—do you need the coordinates?"

"I've got the ones off the initial call. Any changes since then?"

"Nope. Two hikers saw the helo go down behind a ridgeline, and they activated their GPS SOS button. They guesstimated the coordinates texted to 911."

Daria and Emma couldn't have reported this. When Daria checked in this morning, they were still north of the Three Apostles—way too far north of the crash site to have been the ones to make the call.

"How do they know it wasn't just setting down?"

"Black smoke. They said it crashed. No word on survivors. They're hiking toward the site to see if they can help." Jackson pauses. "You think that's a good idea?"

"Oh, hell yes. Just reaching the crash site with their GPS will be huge. Are you and Becky tracking them?"

"We are." Jackson's voice fades. Becky calls him to her desk. "I got to go, Z-man."

"Roger. This is a biggie."

I hang up and aim my truck for Mount Princeton and the road to the old mining town of St. Elmo. Jackson's description of the helicopter surprises me. The Army runs a high-altitude training school for helicopters called HAATS—High-Altitude ARNG Aviation Training Site—out of Eagle County Regional Airport two counties north. The students stage out of Leadville and sometimes Buena Vista—BV's where I live—on training flights, but I rarely see them in nearby mountains unless they're supporting one of our SAR missions. The school has quite the reputation for attracting elite aircrews. During my time in Afghanistan, I heard plenty of stories about HAATS-trained US Army Black Hawks performing difficult high-altitude extractions in neighboring provinces.

The two-lane gravel road to St. Elmo hugs the cascading Chalk Creek, tall pines standing sentry over the route. The mountain vibe transitions in a matter of minutes from a well-known hot springs resort atmosphere to a decaying mining town so remote residents use shortwave radio for communications with the outside world. Two miles before St. Elmo, I brake at movement on the road's shoulder. A black bear cub scoots across the road and disappears into the woods. I keep my foot on the brake, uncertain if Baby Bear is chasing Mama Bear or the other way around. In answer, a large bear lopes in front of my truck and, without giving me a second glance, vanishes between the same trees.

Perez is easy to find, his Tahoe lightbar flashing amidst the cluster of cabins and storefronts. I park my Tundra and grab my Glock from the glove box. Perez motions from his open Tahoe door for me to join him.

"Any updates?" he bellows. Even in the valley, the wind drowns out a normal voice.

I tell him about the hikers trying to reach the crash site. When I say it might be an Army helicopter, he nods and points to the mountains behind the tiny ghost town.

"HAATS already called us. A Black Hawk is overdue. We know where it's at. Roughly." He clasps his hands over his body armor and stares toward the crash site.

Frustration takes over. "So, what are we doing? SAR's going to be at least another thirty minutes. We need to get up there."

Perez shakes his head. "Slow it up, Z-man."

"What? There might be survivors. This is time-sensitive."

"Right. But your brain is working backward."

What is Perez telling me?

"You're a deputy sheriff now, Zahn."

"Reserve deputy."

"Screw that. You're law enforcement, just like me. We don't wait around for volunteer resources like in SAR. We figure out what we need and tell them what to do. The EMTs I requested are five minutes behind you. If we go running up to the crash site by ourselves, what's our plan? Blow on their owies and pass out Band-Aids?"

Perez is right. I'm thinking exactly like a SAR member trying to find an injured hiker with a twisted ankle instead of a law enforcement officer dealing with a US Army helicopter crash with potential fatalities.

"Sorry—" The word is barely out of my mouth when Perez's eyes shift over my shoulder. I turn and spot the flashing lights of two ambulances. They let out a short siren burst.

Perez says, "Get in."

I buckle my seatbelt, taking in the scent of coffee, gun oil, and flatulence. Perez pulls out in front of the ambulances and leads our small caravan through the town toward Tincup Pass.

"Get dispatch on the shortwave, Z-man. We need an ETA for SAR's ATVs to St. Elmo. Make sure they're sending all of them."

The road in front of us is rocky but drivable, using SAR's Chevy 2500 tech rig and their Toyota Tacoma. I don't see the need to transfer gear to ATVs, but I make the call.

Dispatch reports the ATVs are en route. They relay that SAR plans to use them for the Hancock Lake route and work toward the Alpine Tunnel. Perez bobs his head at their reply.

He starts to speak, but I get it now. "We're taking the road because of the ambulances, but we aren't sure what side of the ridge the crash is on. So the ATVs can cover the south side?"

Perez nods. "Hopefully, we'll know the exact location by the time the ATVs arrive. I've got Cañon City Helitack on the way for a fly-by. No doubt the Army is already on their way."

"I thought it was too windy?"

"Too windy to land. Not too windy for spotting. Turn up the volume on the digital radio. Helitack is on SIMPLEX1. Check on them. Use my call sign."

I follow Perez's instructions. *Helitack, Helitack, this is Chaffee 2 on SIMPLEX1.*

Chaffee 2, we're Helitack 2 about ten minutes out from St. Elmo. Any updates?

I turn to Perez, who nods. *Helitack 2, Chaffee 2 proceeding up Tincup Pass approximately one mile west of St. Elmo with two medical teams. No update on the hikers who reported the crash. No updated coordinates. SAR teams are on their way. Salida Hospital has been notified. How are the winds?* I glance at Perez, who focuses on the road. I figure my radio call must be OK if he's not complaining.

Chaffee 2, Helitack 2 copies all. We're over Salida and the winds suck. If they're any worse from here, then we'll be observation only. No air evacuation capability.

Helitack 2, Chaffee 2 copies.

The shortwave crackles with another call.

Chaffee 2, Dispatch.

Go ahead, Dispatch.

Chaffee 2, the hikers have not moved on the map for the last five minutes. We're thinking they're either stuck on a bad route, or they found the crash site. Are you ready to copy their coordinates?

Chaffee 2 is ready.

We're showing 38.683191 North and -106.400015 East. Read back, please.

I finish scribbling the numbers and hold them up to my reading glasses while Perez seems determined to hit every large rock on the rugged road.

Dispatch, read back is 38.683191 North and -106.400015 East.

That's affirmative. Chaffee 2, standby—we've got a text message from the hikers.

Go ahead.

Text message reads: found the helicopter. No fire. Everyone is dead.

"Ah, fuck," Perez groans.

I say nothing. After more than two decades of military service, this isn't my first rodeo. I've been first on scene at a crash on my home station runway as an Air Force squadron commander and an ocean away on emergency leave when one of my aircrews—flying a mission I ordered them to fly—was shot down near the Iraqi border. It's never easy.

Chaffee 2, got another text.

Go ahead.

Two dead inside helicopter. One dead outside. The outside one was shot in the head.

2-DARIA

Colorado Trail near Lake Ann Pass-July 12, 2022

"Emma!" Daria Zahn's voice competes with the strengthening winds as she breaks above the tree line to the shore of Lake Ann. The figure hiking in front of her doesn't turn. Daria's Achilles tendons beg for a break. They've logged 202 miles on the 490-mile Colorado Trail—or CT—hiking from Denver to Durango. With altitudes reaching up to thirteen thousand feet, the CT is one of the highest hikes in the United States.

"Mud Hen!" she calls. Emma Frazier whips around with a smile, way too excited about the trail name Daria gave her.

Daria picks up her pace to join her. This section of the CT overlaps the Continental Divide Trail. She's had her eyes set on this iconic trek since she moved to Colorado as a kid. If someone had predicted she'd be almost halfway done with the thru-hike accompanied by a thirty-seven-year-old FBI agent her dad has the hots for—a woman Daria had never even met until they rallied at the trailhead on the outskirts of Denver—she would have told them they were a little cray-cray.

Daria's father, Tyler Zahn, was never going to be okay with her hiking this thing by herself. He couldn't have stopped her—she's old enough to vote and legal to drink. He suggested joining her, but her only available start date interfered with his Law Enforcement Academy completion. He knew Daria had her mind made up, so he found someone who could hike with her. It helped that she'd been wanting to get to know Emma better after she started spending more time with her dad.

"You OK with your trail name now?" Daria says, grinning. Her first stab at a trail name for Emma was "Mother Hen." Emma hated it, not wanting hikers thinking Daria was her daughter. Daria tried a day of "Mudda Hen." Emma still wasn't a fan.

The third day on the trail, they met a thirty-year-old ex-Marine with the trail name Smiles. Emma introduced Daria as Little Z, a name totally lacking in originality.

Daria waved her hand at Emma. "And this is Mudder Hen.

"You from Ohio?" Smiles had asked Emma.

"No. I'm from Vermont. Why?"

It was common for hikers to spill their life stories in their brief five-minute conversations. Daria noticed Emma didn't throw her FBI agent, Art Crime Team status out as a conversation starter, not that Daria expected her to.

"I grew up in Toledo. That's our baseball team—the Toledo Mud Hens."

Daria snorted. Smiles obviously misheard her pronunciation of "Mudder Hen."

Emma glared at Daria, then grinned. "I can live with Mud Hen."

Smiles's pace was faster than Daria's, and they hadn't seen him since. Even still, Emma probably could have kept up with him.

A twinge in Daria's heel snaps her back to the present and her hiking companion. With her hair pulled back and her eyes on the mountains, Emma strikes Daria as a woman who has no problem being first through the door and having it held open for her. She radiates confidence.

Emma ignores Daria's question about her trail name. "What's up, Little Z? Ready for a break?"

"Five minutes." Daria's mother gifted her daughter with a warm skin tone and coiling black curls that are challenging to pull back—but she's a runner and in decent shape. In her mind, she should be doing better in these mountains than Emma, who's been working at sea level in Washington, DC for the past year. So far, Emma has outpaced her.

Emma wasn't Daria's choice as a hiking partner, but over the last couple of weeks, they've become close. But not so close that Daria's ready to admit she can't keep the pace.

Emma says. "Let's have a snack. Relax a bit." Daria drops her pack and poles, then digs a small bag of trail mix from her pack pocket and offers it to Emma.

Emma shakes her head. "I need salt. Want some Fritos?"

Daria declines, leaning her head on her pack and surveying the route they've climbed this morning. In the distance, Hope Pass marks the turnaround point for the annual Leadville 100-mile trail race. They crossed it yesterday and spent the night at the southern base. Now they're only a half mile from summiting Lake Ann Pass. Daria twists her head and checks what's ahead of them. They're sitting among the Three Apostles—three thirteen-thousand-foot peaks.

Emma follows Daria's gaze. "This is pretty close to where it happened, right?"

Daria points to the middle peak, Ice Mountain. "In the saddle, just to the left of that summit. Kristee went down the other side during a SAR mission. That's the last anyone saw of her." Emma nods.

Daria knows Z-man—she thinks of her dad as Zahn, or Z-man, just like his friends do—has talked to Emma about the month-long search for Kristee. When he and Emma cracked that art heist last year, Zahn theorized for a while that Kristee might have been involved in it. Kind of crazy. Everyone but Zahn assumes Kristee is dead.

"This whole section is like a walk down memory lane," Emma says, "for both of us."

"How so?"

"When we climbed out of Breckenridge, we saw the Dillon Reservoir, where your dad found those guys trying to mess with the dam."

Daria smiles. The Dillon Dam incident happened before she and her father had reconciled and was his first involvement in a criminal case. Thwarting a major terrorist plot is what pulled him from his post-war funk.

"Now, we're crossing the same mountains where you and your dad lost your friend Kristee. And tomorrow, we'll walk right through the parking lot where the thieves stole the Remington paintings last year."

"Either trouble follows my dad, or you must think there's a whole lot of crazy happening out here."

"Maybe a little of both." Emma eyes Daria's feet. "You tired, or do you have something going on?" Her voice softens. "I thought I saw you hobbling a bit back there."

Daria can't hide her injury. "Something's going on above my heels."

"Blisters?"

"Nope. Like my Achilles tendon—in that area. It only bothers me on the uphills."

"Daria." Emma's voice pitches up.

Daria turns toward the trail winding up Lake Ann Pass, blinking back tears. This journey all started as her idea. Her chance to accomplish something on her own. But to her surprise, Daria discovered she likes Emma. The trail has come to mean so much more as they hike it together. And now, Daria's putting their shared goal in jeopardy.

"It'll be OK," Daria says. "Only a half mile to the top, then the rest of the day is downhill." She uses her optimistic voice but doubts Emma buys it.

"Maybe we should take a day or two in town. We'll be crossing Cottonwood Pass by mid-morning. We can catch a ride down to Buena Vista."

"No." Daria's voice is sharper than she intends. "I don't need a zero-day." They've planned to meet Zahn at a couple spots, but Daria wants him to meet her at the trailhead with a bag of snacks, not cart her out of the Rockies to recuperate at his house. If he sees her taking a break to rest her tendons, he'll assume it's a significant injury and pressure her to either rest longer or get off the trail. Daria doesn't need that kind of help.

Emma says, "You sound like my ex-husband. No. Check that—you sound like my brother. Never would admit to pain. Never would take a break."

Daria meets Emma's eyes, waiting for her to continue. This is the first she's heard about an ex-husband. Her dad mentioned Emma has a twin brother, but he said it was a subject she didn't like talking about. Emma cocks her head at Daria like she expects her to argue.

"It's not that bad," Daria says. "A dose of Vitamin I, and I'll be OK."

"Vitamin I?"

"Ibuprofen." She reaches for her pack. "You ready to hike?"

"Another five minutes. Why don't you send an update to your dad?"

"I'm not going to tell him my heels hurt," Daria says. "Any hint all is not well and he'll come jogging up the trail, checking on me."

Emma nods. She clearly knows Zahn pretty well too. "Just tell him where we are. And tell him I said hi."

"He knows where we are. He's tracking us on the GPS app."

"Daria."

"Got it, *Mother* Hen." Even though she's only fifteen years older, Daria's a bit irked at Emma turning maternal on her. But she enjoys Emma's company too much to make it a thing. "I'll update him. And send him a smooch from you."

"We're not smooching," Emma says. "But a day off in Buena Vista could move things along."

"Eww. TMI." Daria scrunches her nose like she's grossed out, but she's hoping Emma and Zahn work out. Her dad hasn't had the best luck with girlfriends.

Daria unclips her GPS from her pack's carabiner and thumbs through the menu. After selecting a canned message she created before the hike, *On track, on schedule,* she types out a few words to personalize it. *Emma says hi. Thirty minutes from the top of Lake Ann Pass and West Apostle. Thinking of you.* Zahn will know that last bit is about Kristee. He'll be pleased Daria is remembering her.

The GPS dings, indicating the message transmitted. She re-clips it to her pack before slipping her arms through the shoulder straps.

Knowing her dad, she'll probably make it ten steps before he answers, requiring her to stop again.

"You set the pace," Emma says, waving her hand for Daria to take the lead.

Daria's not thrilled about slowing her partner down but understands Emma's trying to help. Twenty steps in, Daria regains her rhythm, the burn in her quads disappears, and she's just left with her nagging Achilles.

They hike past Lake Ann and pause, surveying the jagged peaks to their east. Above the tree line, the wind whips at Daria's shorts. She considers a jacket, but the steep climb ahead reminds her she'll likely be sweating minutes from now regardless of the wind.

Daria jerks to a stop at a loud pop echoing across the peaks. Emma points, and Daria spots a puff of dust and a small cluster of boulders ricocheting above them from the saddle between Ice Mountain and West Apostle—the halfway point of the notoriously difficult Three Apostle traverse.

"Coming our way!" Emma yells. She points to the boulder field at the side of the trail. "We need to get under something!" She unbuckles her pack and drops it.

The cluster of loose rocks gathers steam, collecting larger boulders, as the pops of rock on rock morph into a dull roar. Daria can't tell if the slide will actually cross their path or veer away from where the draw forks. A tug on her arm nearly pulls her to the ground.

"Daria. Now!" Emma screams.

Daria stares at her hiking partner before whipping her head back toward the slope. The cascade of rocks is less than a soccer field away. She nods and rushes after Emma toward the boulder field.

Emma drops behind a large boulder and lowers herself into a crevice formed where the rock leans against another. "In here."

Daria tries to crawl behind her friend, but her pack wedges in the rocks two feet from where Emma shelters. Emma's hand snakes up to Daria's waist and fumbles at her pack's waist buckle. Daria understands and releases her chest strap, wriggling out from under the pack and falling forward onto Emma.

The two women cover their heads and press their legs against each other as an explosive impact jars the boulder above them. A shadow crosses their face as a basketball-size rock flies overhead. A deep rumble of falling rocks continues to echo in the direction from which they ran. Neither hiker says a word.

Finally, the cacophony subsides, replaced with the dull roar of the wind that has chased them all day. Daria's ragged breath drowns out the gale. A faint high-pitched call penetrates their refuge.

"Do you hear that?" Emma says, her voice shaking.

Daria nods. "Do you think it's safe? Emma, I'm so sorry I was slow—"

"Not now—I think someone is out there."

They crawl from behind the boulder, peering out and listening for more rocks before stepping toward the trail. Emma scans the hillside while Daria grabs her pack and joins her. Emma's pack sits untouched by the side of the trail.

Emma points to the ridge. "There. You see the hikers?"

Daria fixates on the saddle from where the rocks might have fallen. The dust she had seen from the initial rockfall is long gone, indicating the winds are also whipping along the ridge. Three figures wave, their muffled shouts incomprehensible. Emma waves back.

"You think they're OK?" Emma says.

"They probably just dislodged the rocks by accident." Daria shades her eyes. "Besides, if they were injured, they'd still be up there yelling or trying to work their way down—not continuing." She points to the hikers en route to West Apostle.

"Their route intercepts ours at the pass. We might see them on our way up."

Daria studies the route the hikers will take. This challenge is just the motivation she needs. "No way. Let's beat them to the pass and wait for them."

3-HAVOC 23

(SIX YEARS BEFORE)

Batman, Turkey-November 18, 2016

The local Kurdish rock band winds down their rendition of Creedence Clearwater Revival's "Bad Moon Rising." Ethan Ward winces.

Shavano and Doubles—aka senior crew chief Sergeant First Class Gary Bissonnette and Chief Warrant Officer Lisa Brumstock—laugh as they stumble from the makeshift dance floor normally used as their UH-60M Black Hawk hangar slot. Shavano's from Salida, Colorado, a town resting under the shadow of fourteen-thousand-foot Mount Shavano. Doubles is the Type-A HAVOC 23 pilot-in-command, or PC, who double-checks everyone else's duties.

"They're terrible!" Ethan yells above the applause and cheers from the crowd of Turkish Army helicopter crews. He turns to HAVOC 23's crew chief-in-training, Sammy "Horse" Ma, for his opinion.

"They suck, Newb," Horse mouths with a smile. Ethan's the most recent addition to the crew. He can't wait for a new call sign and suspects Horse threw the "Newb" onto the sentence just to piss him off. Before Ethan's arrival, Horse was the new guy.

Horse, an immigrant who later became a first-generation Chinese-American, crossed the Himalayas with his family from China to Myanmar—he didn't talk much about what must have been an arduous trek—before they emigrated to the United States. When Ethan joined the crew, Shavano christened Sammy "Horse" after learning that was one of the Chinese meanings of Ma.

Doubles' blue eyes flit to Ethan as she passes, a familiar wild look he's seen before. When their crew rallied back in Albany, New York, for a pub crawl, one shot of tequila ramped her up from the helicopter crew's most gregarious member to the absolute life of the party.

But no one's drinking tonight. The Kurdish-dominated city of Batman, Turkey, doesn't ban alcohol, but it's not readily available either. Doubles tugs on Shavano's hand, coaxing him back to the dance floor.

Shavano cups his hand against Ethan's ear as he passes. "These guys might be terrible. But they're what we got."

Stuck on a Turkish Army post for sixty days, the crew is over five thousand miles from home and living in a Quonset. Not the *crème de la crème* of their Guard unit's routine deployments. In fact, it's not routine at all.

Turkish Aerospace Industries (TAI) has purchased a license from Sikorsky to build the T70 variant of the Black Hawk helicopter for the country's military. TAI still has to build out the infrastructure, not to mention the factory to pump out the helicopters. But that hasn't stopped Turkey, a NATO ally, from requesting US Army Black Hawk crews for mission orientation flights for future Turkish helicopter pilots.

Ethan expected card games and streaming video for entertainment, especially after the deployment commander restricted the crews to the base. That Shavano found a band, arranged their base access, and organized a party—not an easy feat considering the Turkish Army isn't a fan of the Kurds—sort of negates that the band sucks.

Then again, the Colorado native is a legend back in their New York-based 3/142 Aviation Regiment. At age forty-two, he's the oldest crew chief in the unit but still holds regimental records in the bench press and beer bonging. The Albany locals know him for his mad trivia skills at McGeary's Pub on Tuesday nights. Ethan has only been in the regiment for two months, but long enough to figure out Shavano is a force.

The band starts up again, and the four crewmembers eye each other, trying to guess the song.

"*Staying Alive!*" Shavano roars. He grabs the back of Ethan's collar and twists it hard enough for his flight suit top to bunch under his armpits. "I just warmed up your pilot on that last dance, Newb. Go take her for a spin. If you can't dazzle her with your flying skills, maybe you can win her over with your disco moves."

Ethan grins. For a new warrant officer, he's pretty confident in his flying skills, but he hasn't had enough time to showcase his talent to his crew. "What about you? You gonna take Horse out for some extra training?"

"Yeah, Sarge." Horse steps closer. "Teach me some of those Rocky Mountain white guy overbite moves." He clasps his hands together like in prayer. "Please?"

"Fuck off, Horse. No fraternizing between instructors and students. Unless you're offering a ride." He winks at Horse.

Horse makes banjo sounds from the *Deliverance* movie, but his voice fades as Doubles tugs Ethan onto the floor, still glowing from her dance with Shavano.

Ethan moves his hips in time with the music, his hands zig-zagging across his body in a piss-poor John Travolta imitation. Doubles moves like disco never died, her body twisting with the steady beat, hips swinging with the bass. Ethan times his knee bends with her movements, searching for a rhythm that will mask his awkwardness.

He checks over his shoulder, expecting mocking laughter. But Shavano and Horse have their backs to the dance floor and foreheads almost pressed together.

"You got moonshine hidden somewhere?" Ethan shouts to Doubles.

She laughs. "I'm responsible for you hooligans. Why would I be the one breaking rules?"

"You got that vibe thing going like back at McGeary's. I've never seen you with it when you're sober."

Doubles blinks twice and Ethan realizes he might have pissed her off. "I mean—"

"You mean you've never seen me have a good time without drinking?" Doubles' smile returns, like she's moved past Ethan's remark. "You need to get out more, son."

Ethan cringes. When they're flying, Doubles reminds him she's in charge by calling him "PI" for copilot. Calling him son shows she outranks him outside the cockpit as well.

When Shavano pushed him onto the floor with Doubles, Ethan was nervous, maybe because he can't dance for shit, but he hasn't had many opportunities on this deployment to spend off-duty time with Doubles.

Doubles has only been in the unit for five years, but that's four years and ten months longer than Ethan. They've bonded quickly as a crew, but when Shavano and Doubles flip shit to each other over the Black Hawk's intercom, Ethan can detect real affection. Could just be camaraderie from the time they spent in the 142nd together, or maybe they have real feelings for each other.

Ethan spins after his on-beat knee bend, moves to the other side of Doubles, and holds out a hand. She bursts with laughter at his attempt to mock the art of disco. He grins back, but it fades as he peers past her. Two men in flight suits stand in front of Shavano. Horse stands to the side in full listening mode.

Ethan catches Doubles' eyes and dips his head toward Shavano. She turns, and her hips lose their groove. Ethan stops dancing as well.

"That's Major Holmes and the new lieutenant," Doubles says. She steps off the floor toward the group. Ethan follows at her heels, guessing Holmes, the deployment commander, isn't commenting on the quality of the band.

Shavano motions as Doubles and Ethan approach. "You're gonna want to hear this." His voice is loud, competing with the music.

The tallest crewmember in the unit, Major Tad "Johnny" Holmes, was a former post for the Sage College Gators, the local Division-III college basketball team just north of Albany. "We need you guys to fly tonight. Actually, tomorrow. Early."

Ethan expects Doubles to focus on him—to check her copilot's reaction to an expected mission. Instead, she tilts her head at Shavano, who sports a thin smile. Horse shakes his head. Whatever Holmes and his assistant shared before Doubles and Ethan showed up was big.

"Let's take it over to ops," Holmes says. "It's too loud here, and some details are US-only."

Doubles grimaces but nods. "Maybe we can get a couple hours rest before we head out?"

Holmes nods toward his assistant. "LT Perkins is taking care of your flight planning for this one."

If some Turkish general had shown up demanding to fly right away—part of their overall mission—that wouldn't involve US-only information. This mission is something different.

Holmes and Perkins lead the crew to ops. Doubles strides behind, with Shavano at her side. Ethan nudges Horse. "What the hell?"

"Fuck if I know," Horse says. "But they did say we're flying outside of Turkey."

Ethan's heart leaps. He's been flying nothing but training missions since he joined the 142nd. Every crewmember he flies with is a veteran of multiple combat deployments. They've all got stories, repeated *ad nauseam*. When the unit got assigned to this Turkish gig, Ethan's hand was the first raised. Flying wannabee Turkish helicopter pilots around their country was about as far from combat as one could get—but it was the quickest way to get close to a combat zone. This corner of Turkey wedges against the border of three major hot spots. Iran, Iraq, and Syria. If they're going to fly across the Turkish border, then he's going into combat.

They step inside a converted storage container. The mission planning room has two computers and a printer on one wall. A large map of Turkey hangs on the opposite. They huddle around a waist-high planning table with a large-scale map of the Middle East covered by plexiglass.

Major Holmes taps his mechanical pencil on Iraq. "Headquarters contacted us with an emerging situation with the Iraqi Army. As you may know, they've been battling against ISIL in an attempt to retake the town of Mosul."

Ethan nods. He follows the news, but only the headlines. The Islamic State of Iraq and the Levant—or ISIL—has taken over large swaths of Iraq and the Iraqi Army is attempting to get them back. The US is providing intelligence, and some air support, but not getting involved with boots on the ground. First he's heard about the battle at Mosul.

Shavano and Horse nod, Doubles shrugs, but Ethan can't tell whether it's because they've heard all this, or simply an indication that they're listening.

"Two days ago, the Iraqi Army retook the city and surrounding suburbs. Yesterday they retook Nimrud, the ancient Assyrian city forty clicks southeast of Mosul. You guys heard of the Treasure of Nimrud?"

Ethan shakes his head and checks his crewmates expecting the same, but Shavano says, "They've been working on excavating that for years. Tons of relics, mostly large-scale bas-reliefs, but lots of gold, jewelry, and shit. Some big drama after the first Gulf War when the valuable stuff disappeared, but we ended up finding it when we invaded after 9-11, sitting in flooded bank vaults in Baghdad. But the rumor persists that there could be a lot more."

"Should have known Mr. Jeopardy here would know about this. Where do you find the time to learn all this shit?" Holmes's expression is disbelief.

"It's a hobby. Don't even get me started on Egyptian tombs."

Holmes shakes his head. "The Iraqi Army took casualties at Nimrud, including six dead soldiers. They loaded them up in body bags onto one of their helicopters to return them to Baghdad," he traces his finger southeast on the Tigris River, "but then cut south toward the Euphrates River—"

"And crashed," Shavano interrupts.

Holmes whips his head to Shavano. "What the hell?"

"Not rocket science, Johnny."

Ethan's eyes widen at Shavano's casual use of the major's call sign. Shavano is enlisted. Holmes is an officer. The two men must go way back.

"But it's not online yet. How did you hear?"

"I didn't. You're sending us to Iraq to help with something. You're briefing an Iraqi helicopter route. We already know their pilots suck and their birds are shit. I'm making an educated guess."

Holmes purses his lips. "The Iraqis flew a drone over the crash site. Looks like no survivors. You're going in to help."

Doubles pipes up. "What if there are survivors? We're not medevac equipped. Why not the special ops folks in Iraq? And who's flying formation with us?"

"You guys are flying single ship. Our spec ops guys are going in for the helicopter crewmembers, dead or alive. They're already moving out."

"Then what do you need us for?"

"Morgue duty. You're picking up the guys that were already dead back before the helo took off. There are six dead Iraqi soldiers in body bags that need to be moved to Baghdad."

Mosul, Iraq-November 19, 2016
The Black Hawk approaches the recently liberated Mosul airfield low and hot. Dawn is still an hour away, so the crew wears night vision goggles. Doubles flies while Ethan backs her up, monitoring the arrival path. Shavano and Horse scan for threats from the open rear windows.

They touch down on the pre-planned refueling spot, but the fuel support personnel Major Holmes arranged are nowhere in sight. Shavano shuffles to the fuel station, dragging his intercom cord behind him.

"Padlocked," Shavano says. "I'm unplugging to go knock on some doors." He points toward the nearby hangars.

"Bullshit you are." Doubles barks. "We'll work it by radio. Who's to say ISIL didn't take the field back?"

"Don't want to hang here too long, Ms. Doubles," Shavano reminds her. He does a three-sixty, scanning for signs of life.

"PI, get on the HF to Major Holmes and have him make some calls."

Ethan blindly broadcasts on the oldest radio on the aircraft to no avail.

Shavano growls over the intercom. "We're sitting still too long."

Doubles holds firm. Ethan keeps trying. A bloom illuminates his NVGs as a vehicle emerges from between the hangars. Shavano turns toward the lights.

"See?" Doubles says, "Radios and patience."

"I don't think that's what got them out here," Shavano replies.

"Why?"

"Got four bars of cell service. I just called Holmes and told him to light a fire under these guys' asses. He gave me updated coordinates for the crash site."

Doubles turns toward Ethan, rolling her eyes. "I guess I don't have to tell you to have your weapon—" She stops and raises her NVGs. Ethan does the same.

Shavano pantomimes instructions to the Iraqi unlocking the fuel hose.

"Who the fuck is running this crew?" she mutters.

Airborne with a bag of gas, Ethan loads the Iraqi helicopter crash site coordinates into the GPS. A hint of dawn brightens his side of the aircraft.

"Huh." Ethan says over the intercom.

"What?" Doubles replies.

"I'm looking at where they went down and where Baghdad is. It doesn't line up."

"Explain."

"The shortest route would be southeast. Pretty much down the Tigris River. These guys flew straight south and crashed due west of Baghdad. Close to the Euphrates. Burned a lot of extra gas by taking the long way."

"Probably got lost," Shavano pipes in from the back.

Ethan finishes inputting everything he can into the navigation system, pausing between waypoints to scan outside. Dawn illuminates the taupe-baked desert floor, but the thing Ethan notices are the shadows. Instead of flat sand, he traces the black smudges of shadows fingering across the desert. Jagged cliffs at least three hundred feet high line both sides of their route. Doubles doesn't have the aircraft dragging in the river bed but she's definitely down in the dirt.

"Holy shit," Ethan says.

"Ain't the route your mama takes on a Wawa coffee run is it?" Shavano says. "Did I ever tell you about the canyons back in Colorado?"

"The map at ops didn't show mountains here." Ethan turns to Doubles.

"There aren't. Everything within a hundred miles is so flat it makes these plateau walls between the streambeds look huge." She flicks her eyes at the instrument panel. "We're ten minutes out. Before Landing Checks."

Ethan drops his head to the electronic map. "The crash site is on top of the plateau to your right. West side. You'll need to pop up and fly unmasked for a half mile."

"Got it. Call when we're parallel with the site, and I'll pull up." She darts a glance at Ethan. "We're going to ease out of this canyon like we're peeping in someone's window, OK? Let's get a feel for what we got before we go racing into the bedroom."

Doubles cracks him up, the way she talks like a man, walks like a lady, and runs the show. Well, mostly. Doubles' comment about Shavano going renegade back at the fuel pit was only partly tongue-in-cheek.

Everyone knows when the shit hits the fan, Shavano has the most experience under pressure. But he knows when to pull back on that dominant side and let others think they're in charge. Ethan isn't sure if that's because he respects Doubles or wants to sleep with her.

"Two minutes," Ethan calls, and Doubles eases back on the airspeed. "Ready, ready, abeam." She pulls the cyclic back and lowers the collective, using the airframe as a brake while holding altitude. As the helicopter settles, she adds collective and left pedal, pivoting ninety degrees until the plateau floor fills the windscreen.

Creeping forward toward the coordinates, the crew scans for threats again. A quarter mile in, Ethan picks up the glint of metal in the distance reflecting in the morning sun.

"Crash in sight," he calls. "Eleven o'clock low. See the flash?"

"Got it." Doubles pivots the helicopter thirty degrees left. "Left seat, Right seat, scan the approach."

"Clear left," Shavano calls.

"Clear right," echoes Horse.

Doubles drops to a hundred feet off the deck. A quarter mile from the site, she does a clearing three-hundred-and-sixty-degree orbit around the downed helicopter. Ethan looks past Doubles to the mangled mass of metal below. The field of debris he expects to see is missing.

A collage of helicopter parts, contained within twenty yards of the aircraft, looks like it dropped straight down. A ribbon of sand shows between the main body and the tail section where the aircraft has split in half.

"Crash site's clear," Shavano calls. "I might have a visual on body bags on the tail side of the main fuselage. Some unidentifiable shapes near the fuselage on the south side. Put her down when you're ready."

"I'm going to land nose-to-nose with the wreck," Doubles announces over the intercom. "Looks clear of vegetation. Don't see anything in our way. PI, what do you think?"

Ethan cranes his neck to scout out Doubles' planned landing zone. "Looks good."

Doubles accelerates outside her loop a hundred yards then teardrops back toward the crash, descending until the wheels make contact with the plateau's surface.

"Wheels down," calls Shavano.

"Looks like the spec ops guys haven't been here yet," Doubles says.

"How do you know?" Horse calls from the back.

"Because the pilot and copilot are sitting right in front of us." Ethan's voice is soft over the intercom.

Spiderweb cracks distort the opacity of the downed helicopter's windows, but the slumped human forms face the crew. A splash of red paints the copilot's window preventing a view of his head. The top of the pilot's helmet points straight at HAVOC 23.

Shavano calls, "Request clearance to exit."

Doubles says, "Scout the wreckage for the body bags. Should be six. Once you've got them located, come back for Horse and Ethan. Copy?"

"Copy."

"Look for the rest of the crew's bodies. So we can pass it on to the spec ops guys if we talk to them."

"Jesus, Doubles. I got it. Am I cleared?"

"Shut it. You know what to do. But I still have to say it. You're cleared. Out."

Shavano exits the right side of the aircraft, unplugs his comm cable, and disappears around the crash. An uneasy feeling washes over Ethan. What happens if Shavano doesn't return? In a perfect world, Shavano could have uncoiled his intercom cord to maintain comms, but the distance between their landing zone and the back side of the crash is too far a stretch.

Doubles must be as nervous as he is. Ever since the US pulled out the majority of its troops, it's been difficult to get a read on the actual threat level in Iraq. Ethan's chest vibrates with the throb of the helicopter's blades. The ten minutes that pass before Shavano returns feel like thirty.

Shavano approaches the door, waving at Horse to pass something to him.

"Tell him to plug in and tell us what he found," Doubles calls to Horse.

Ethan twists in his seat. Horse thrusts the comm cord toward Shavano who is throwing a medical duffel over his shoulder. Shavano waves the cord off, but Horse pushes it at him again while pointing toward Doubles. Shavano lowers the duffel on the door sill and plugs in.

"What's up, Ms. Doubles?" Shavano pants.

"What did you find? And where are you going? You're not hauling those bodies back by yourself."

"Nope. I've found them all—including the crew chiefs. They're wedged in the back of the main fuselage. The body bags are all on top of each other, spilled out the back end. I've got one bag that's tore up though. I'm using the med kit to fix things up so we can carry it back."

"What, like Betsy Ross? You think you're going to sew it?"

"Ms."

"I'm serious."

"Since you asked, bodily fluids everywhere. I'm going to use the stuff in the bag here to staunch it. Then I'll come back for Horse and Mr. Ward."

"Gross. Just do it quick."

"Roger." Shavano unplugs again and trots back around the back side of the crash site.

Less concerned about this round of waiting, Ethan relaxes. Shavano returns minutes later and slings the medical bag over the sill of the doorframe. Horse reaches for it, but Shavano waves him off, jumps onboard, and stows the bag in the same place he retrieved it from. He plugs in.

"OK. Mr. Ward, Horse, you ready?"

Horse nods. Ethan turns to Doubles. She nods as well.

"Roger," Ethan replies over the intercom.

Ethan unplugs and hops out, ducking under the rotor blast. He is boots on the ground in a combat zone. He follows Horse out from under the blades.

Shavano skirts the wreckage, Ethan and Horse close behind. Ethan steels himself for what lies on the back side of the crash, prepared to be stoic facing a dead body for the first time. His preparation is unnecessary. Shavano waves toward a mound of what looks like blue tarps. As Ethan nears, he distinguishes the cigar-shaped rolls. These are the body bags.

Shavano points Horse to one end, then indicates for Ethan to move to the other.

Ethan motions for Shavano to come closer. He cups his hand near Shavano's helmet. "Which is the one we're supposed to be careful with?"

Shavano gives him a hard stare. Ethan's uncertain if it's because he's wasting time with his question or because Shavano thinks he's questioning the veteran crew chief's actions.

Shavano motions Ethan to follow. He rounds the opposite side of the wreckage from their approach and points toward the nose. A tangled strip of shredded blue interlaces with what looks like strings of intestines. A piece of tail rotor blade lies next to the mangled mass of flesh. Ethan understands on some level that this is what remains of a human body, but the only thing he can identify are things that should be inside the body. No head is visible. No feet show. Just a six-foot-long strip of guts.

His stomach heaves, and he vomits down the side of the helicopter wreckage. The bright yellow stream trickles onto packages of bandages, a splint, rolls of gauze, and other first aid supplies—the stuff Shavano needs to "staunch" the dead man from leaking. The pungent scent of burned fuel scorches his nostrils, but it's the subtle, coppery reek of blood that pushes him over the edge. He wipes his mouth and twists to look at Shavano.

Shavano shrugs and yells, "I'm trying." He moves closer, cupping his hands again. "You and Horse start moving those other bags. I'll keep working on this one."

Ethan convulses again, this time avoiding the first aid equipment. He's dreamed of this—the combat zone, adrenaline racing, getting the mission done under enemy fire. No one's even shooting at him and he's puking down the side of an aircraft, immobilized by the most gruesome sight he's ever seen.

"Yo, Newb!" Shavano yells.

Ethan stares wide-eyed at Shavano while holding his vomit. He opens his mouth, but no sound emerges.

Shavano cuffs him on the side of the helmet hard enough that Ethan has to stagger to keep his balance.

"What the fuck?" Ethan wrinkles his nose as Shavano advances on him again.

"Snap the fuck out of it. You and Horse move the other bodies now."

Ethan pauses for a moment, catching up with Shavano's directions. He locks eyes with the crew chief before turning to where Horse unstacks the body bags.

"Mr. Ward!"

Ethan whirls, his hands in the air in case Shavano throws another blow in his direction.

Shavano grins. "Bring me some of those big black trash bags from behind the rear seat. And duct tape."

The first body bag takes forever to move. They shuffle to the aircraft, Horse walking backward and Ethan making head movements in the direction they should move. When they get to the helicopter, Horse adjusts his grip forward on the bag, twists, and shoves the feet across the floor. He hops into the rear seat compartment and drags the body inside while Ethan pushes.

While Horse moves things around to make room for the remainder of the bags, Ethan plugs into Shavano's cord. He keys the mic. "PC, PI's up."

"What's the status?" Doubles says.

"We got four more bags like the one we just loaded. Then the torn one."

"How much time you think?"

"Maybe ten minutes. The last one's going to take longer it's, it's…"

"What?"

"It's going to be like hauling a bag of soup."

"Shit," she says.

Ethan grabs the trash bags and Horse grabs the tape. They hand both off to Shavano who is elbows-deep stuffing vomit-stained absorbent gauze around the body.

The next four body bags prove easier. Ethan and Horse swap back and forth on the walking backward duties. They stack the first two bags on the helicopter floor forward of the rear bench seat, head near the right door, feet near the left. The next bag goes between the two beneath it, like a mini pyramid of corpses. The fourth goes on the web-backed seat and the fifth angles between the pyramid top body and the seat body.

Horse plugs in and points toward Shavano's comm cord for Ethan to do the same.

"We're gonna have to tie them down. They won't stay in that pile without something holding them," Horse says.

Ethan keys his mic. "Right. Let's get the one Shavano's working on and throw some tie-down straps over the whole pile."

Horse grimaces. "That's gonna be like strapping down hot fudge on a sundae."

They circle around the back side of the wreckage. Shavano has the body's top and bottom halves inside the garbage sacks. A strip of bloodied clothes, intestines, and torn blue tarp remains across the middle of the corpse where the sacks weren't long enough.

"I cut a bag open for the middle," Shavano yells. "You two roll him and I'll wrap it around."

Ethan moves to the head end. Horse positions himself at the feet. Shavano twists his wrist in the direction he wants them to roll. Ethan nods at Horse and lifts the body's right shoulder. Horse is slow to react and Ethan's end of the ripped body makes a full twist while Horse's remains in position.

Horse mouths, "oops," and rolls his end. Shavano tucks the plastic in place and they roll the body back in unison. Reaching under the corpse, Shavano pulls the plastic through.

"Now you roll, and I'll tape," Shavano bellows.

Horse and Ethan find their rhythm, twisting and turning the corpse while Shavano works the tape. Like a Mayfair moving team, the body they pack is a tightly rolled Turkish carpet.

They finish, and Horse crouches at his end of the body preparing to lift. Ethan squats too.

"Hold on," Shavano raises his hand, and moves around to a space between the fuselage and the body. He reaches inside a broken window.

"Saved these for you guys." A gray blade extends from an ornate hilt in one hand. Shavano unclenches his other hand to reveal a dull gold ring and a bracelet.

"For us?" Horse says, barely loud enough to hear. "Awesome."

"Hell yeah. How else are you two newbies going to remember your first combat mission? Pick the one you want. I'll give whatever's left to Ms. Doubles."

Horse doesn't hesitate, grabbing the gold ring and dropping it in the chest pocket of his flight suit. Ethan reaches for the knife, then pulls his hand back.

"Problem?" Shavano says, tilting his head.

Ethan looks from the knife to Shavano, expecting a taunting sneer at his reluctance to take the knife. Instead, the crew chief wears an expression that looks like bewilderment. Like this is normal, and what kind of warrior wouldn't want a small token to remember his battle by?

"Is it from the body?" Ethan says. The pieces don't appear new, almost like they are family heirlooms or something.

Shavano pauses before answering. "No. I found them right after we touched down when I was scouting. Set them to the side. They're not valuable, Newb—just souvenirs."

Ethan's nausea disappears. They are minutes away from finishing the hardest part of the mission. Does he want something to remember it by?

He reaches for the knife.

4-ZAHN

St. Elmo, Colorado-July 12, 2022

Everything changes the moment dispatch radios "shot in the head." This is no longer solely a SAR mission. The presence of possible shooters in these mountains means it's an active crime scene.

Perez skids the Tahoe to a stop. I instinctively check my passenger side mirror, bracing myself in case one or more of the ambulances rear-ends us. Paramedic reactions must be sharp because both vehicles sit angled on the road behind us.

"Go tell the medics what's happening," Perez says. "I need to talk to dispatch."

The wind almost rips off the Tahoe door as I jump out. I jog back to the first ambulance and signal to the driver in the second emergency vehicle to join us. The other driver stays in his vehicle and sends his teammate, slight of frame with ebony hair pulled back into a braid. She joins us at the first driver's window.

"What was that call about gunshots?" she says.

The ambulance is tuned to the mutual aid channel.

"Stop the SAR teams at St. Elmo." Perez's voice booms, but it's directive rather than panicked. "Send a message to those hikers on scene. Tell them to back away from the accident scene and take cover. Switch frequencies for the remainder of this call. I'm going to Blue 3 now. Talk to you there."

The first driver raises his eyebrows. "What the fuck is Blue 3?"

I ignore his question, although I understand his frustration at being left out of the loop. Blue 3 is the code word we use for an internal sheriff frequency we can talk on when we don't want everyone listening in on sensitive information.

I raise my voice over the wind, "Did you copy the previous radio calls? The hikers found the helicopter. Everyone's dead. A possible gunshot wound?"

Both EMTs nod.

"It doesn't necessarily mean it's true," I continue. "We don't know how qualified these hikers are to recognize bullet wounds. But they could probably tell if there were any survivors. And it sounds like there aren't."

The EMT from the other vehicle shifts her weight from side to side. "We need to get up there and confirm that."

The first driver glares at her. "You and what army? We need to stay the fuck away until these guys figure out what happened."

"You're both right," I say. "Someone will need to examine the bodies. But no one is going up there unarmed until we determine if there's a threat in the area."

"Z-man, I need you." Perez yells from the Tahoe.

"Just stay here for now," I tell the EMTs.

Perez hunches over the laptop screen in the center console.

"You got service for that thing up here?"

Perez shakes his head. "We don't need it. The maps are already downloaded. I just input the updated coordinates the hikers gave us. Look at this—we're here." He points to a spot on the road to Tincup Pass, then shifts his finger left an inch. "The crash site is here."

I study the map. We're only a half mile from where the helo went down, but a 1300-foot ridge sits between us and the helicopter. "If we went up from right here, we could climb through the trees on this side, crest the ridge and descend diagonally to the aircraft without intercepting this rock face." I run my finger across the route that makes the most sense.

"Agreed. You've got your Glock?"

I pat my shoulder harness under my shirt.

"You heard me tell dispatch to freeze SAR and have the hikers take cover. When I switched to Blue 3, I told them we were going up to evaluate the crash site. You down for that?"

"Why are you even asking?" I say, hoping he's not flashing back on our first mission together. The time I said no. "We're not on a SAR mission. I'm ready."

"OK. I'm taking the shotgun and my sidearm. Grab a medical pack from the guys behind us and tell them what's up. We'll talk through our plan while we're hiking."

The talk-while-hiking strategy fails. With no trail in sight, Perez and I bushwhack our way up the steep slope, grasping at rocks and tree branches to pull ourselves forward. Every two steps forward results in one step back, the soft dirt and pine needles hampering our efforts. The shotgun doesn't have a sling, which means Perez is tugging at trees with one hand. I've got both arms free but am carrying twice the weight with my personal pack on my back and the medical bag strapped in the front.

My legs burn from the lactic acid buildup, inevitable above ten thousand feet when hiking a thirty-degree slope from a cold start. The saving grace of these Rockies is that they don't go up forever. Our highest peaks top out just higher than fourteen thousand feet—that's why we call them 14ers—so you always know that eventually you will stop climbing. I use this knowledge to ignore the burn.

This scramble isn't the first time Perez and I have climbed at this altitude. With nothing to prove to the other, we pant in pain together, the wind disguising our gasps.

An electronic ding from my pack stops us both.

"I need to check this."

"Thank God," Perez wheezes. He takes a minute to catch his breath. "Who's GPS texting you? The SAR teams aren't even out in the field."

"It's Daria."

Perez knows Daria. "She ended up hiking the CT with your FBI girlfriend? Right?"

"Shhh." I hold up my hand while checking my messages as if his voice prevents me from reading. The truth is I'm not much of a multitasker.

Emma says hi. On track, on schedule, I read. *Thirty minutes from the top of Lake Ann Pass and West Apostle. Thinking of you.*

I let out a breath. *On track, on schedule.* That's all I needed to hear. Well, the *Emma says hi* makes me pretty happy too. I thumb the words *Love you* and hit Send.

"Everything OK?" Perez says.

"Yep. They're at Lake Ann."

"Like the Three Apostles Lake Ann? Where…"

He's going to say something about Kristee Li disappearing out there and I can't deal with that now. "Yes, it's the Lake Ann you're thinking of, and I don't have time to process that. What's our plan for this?" We haven't talked about how we'll tackle the helicopter only hundreds of yards away.

Perez nods. "When we approach the helicopter, I want you to hang back."

"Why—"

"Let me run the whole thing by you first. When I'm done, if you have a better idea I'll listen."

I nod. Perez values my opinion.

"I'm in uniform and you're not. If I approach the helo, there's a chance the hikers might come out of hiding. They'll recognize me as law enforcement. I'm concerned about the hikers exposing themselves—in case bad actors are up there. Perch yourself in the best position to survey the accident scene and cover the hikers. Does that make sense?" Perez waits.

"It does." And I don't have a better idea.

"I'll check for survivors and evaluate the hikers' gunshot claim."

We crest the ridge where a thin spattering of trees blocks our view of the open rock face. We move twenty yards along the crest for higher ground. Perez stops and points, the roaring wind and threat of a shooter preventing conversation. I pull up next to him, my eyes following his finger. Halfway down the slope rests an olive-green helicopter, the tail rotor and rear fuselage only a football field from us, separate from the main body further away and slightly downhill.

I move forward, scanning for a route to the wreckage, as if I might still save them, but can't. Just like I couldn't save my crew in Iraq.

The wind forces the wreckage smoke into a horizontal stream below us. No flames are visible.

"There," Perez says. "See between the tail and the main body? That patch of green? That must be the one they said was shot. I'll go check it out, then move to the crash. You stay high and keep these boulders between you and the wreck."

"Got it."

Perez starts down, shotgun at the ready. I work across the ridge, not quite in a low crawl, but using the larger rocks for cover. Crossing a boulder field is like a microcosm of hiking a mountain range. The crevices between the rocks are so deep that each boulder turns into a separate obstacle. I peep over the top of each rock as I traverse, checking for a shooter. The journey to where Perez directed me takes longer than I expected. When I peer from the rock protecting me, Perez is already examining the body we spotted from the ridge. I train my Glock above Perez's head even though the handgun is virtually useless at this distance. Perez asked for cover. I'll do my best.

My VHF radio crackles, the tactical one we use for person-to-person communication in the field. "Z-Man, you up?" Perez says.

"Roger."

"The hikers were right."

Perez doesn't need to elaborate. The body he's examining was shot. I survey the accident scene from above again, now more certain of a threat in the vicinity. The question is: what's the threat doing? Are they retreating because their job is finished, or are they hiding? Waiting for us to evaluate the site and bring in help. The worst case would be an ambush: they know we're coming and they're waiting for us.

"I copy. What's the plan?" I'm honestly curious about what the next move will be. Nothing in the Law Enforcement Academy trained me for this.

A whistle pierces through the wind. I whip my Glock toward the western side of the slope where the remainder of the helicopter rests. In my peripheral vision, Perez pokes his head from the crevice hiding the body and points the shotgun in the same direction.

The whistle blows again and this time it's accompanied by movement from the gaping hole in the helicopter fuselage where the tail section used to be attached. Two men emerge from the wreckage, the lead blowing a whistle for the third time. Both wear shorts, their bare legs visible. The second man has two hiking poles and as soon as he clears the helicopter, he crosses them above his head, yelling toward Perez. "The other two are in here." The hiker thrusts a pole toward the fuselage.

"Z-man, hold your position." Perez's voice comes across the radio.

"Roger."

Perez cups his hands and yells at the hikers. "Get back inside the helicopter!"

The two men freeze, staring in Perez's direction.

"Get back. Take cover in the helicopter." This time Perez waves the shotgun toward the men.

The first hiker turns to the other for less than a second, then both men scramble inside.

Perez's voice comes across my VHF radio. "I'm going to join them in the helo. If you don't see a response from anywhere else within five minutes, then join me."

"Roger."

Perez steps across rocks from his position, moving toward the wreckage. While shifting my eyes between Perez and the rocks in front of me, I pick my way closer to the accident scene. Perez told me to hold my position, but he also implied I should cover him. I can't do that with a handgun from this distance. I work my way to the crevice where Perez examined the body and—after a quick glance at the bullet hole in the back of the young man's head and the resulting blood stains seeping from what must be left of his face—set up with my Glock pointed toward the helicopter. Perez has disappeared inside.

I count to a hundred before giving up on Perez's five minutes, then climb from the rocks to follow his route. Halfway to the wreckage, I spot movement from the back of the helicopter. I cautiously raise my weapon, recognizing it's likely Perez or the hikers, then lower it when Perez beckons me forward.

I step out of the wind and under the jagged metal in the rear of the helicopter. The two hikers are scrunched as far back from the cockpit as possible. I look from them to Perez. He nods toward the front end.

"It's pretty messed up in the front seats. Too windy to stay outside. I don't blame them," he says, shifting his eyes back to the hikers. "Meet Shane and Michael."

The hikers nod at me but remain silent.

"I need you up there with me for a look, Z-man. I want a second opinion."

I'm unsure what I can offer but figure I can wait until we check out the bodies before asking. We step through the tangle of the rear seat aluminum and webbing until our shoulders are wedged between the two pilots.

I avoid looking at the bodies right away, instead focusing on a grease pencil inscription scrawled on the front windshield. HAVOC 23. I point it out to Perez. "Probably their call sign."

He nods toward the right seat. "Check out the bodies."

Even wearing a helmet, I can tell the pilot is female. I'm not surprised—we've had women helo pilots in all services for over thirty years. What focuses me on this one is the fact she's dead. I've seen my share of dead bodies before, but none of them have been women. The scene before me twists my gut—not an ache but a burn. I've always treated women as equals, but there are times in crisis when I feel an instinctive need to protect them. A different feeling than what I would have for a man. I don't talk about it much because, well, it's just not the correct thing to say these days. But for me, that doesn't make it any less true.

The woman's helmet is cleaved down the front, and it's obvious a blow to the head contributed to her death. She slumps forward in her shoulder harness. I reach forward to pull the helmet back and examine her face, but Perez grabs my hand.

"Lean in and look up at her face. Let's avoid touching anything until the accident team gets here."

I lower myself to my knees and extend my torso further between the two pilots. I glance to the left while edging forward and my stomach heaves. The copilot in the left seat has no face. There's red flesh atop a neck framed in a helmet. I assume the crewmember is a "he" based on the shape of the rest of his body. But there are no eyes. No nose. Just bulbous flesh and a yawning hole where a mouth would be expected, flecks of white inside where one might find teeth, but so haphazard it looks like someone tossed white gravel into a fresh deer carcass. His flight suit is saturated with blood, his nametags unreadable.

"Focus, Zahn."

Perez's voice snaps me from my paralysis, and I turn my head back to the dead woman in the right seat. Whatever killed her did not mar her face. Her eyes are closed, and her expression remains unblemished. In the span of seconds, I think *she's beautiful, she's talented, she's gone.*

"What do you see?" Perez's voice is soft behind me, and for the first time, I notice how the wreckage has blocked the howl of the wind.

I twist in his direction. "Blunt force to the head. You can see the crease in the helmet. No other injuries above the neck, although I think you'd need to take the helmet off to confirm. Plus, we can't tell if she has a neck injury with her hanging in the harness like this."

"What about bullet wounds?"

It dawns on me what Perez was asking for when he mentioned a second opinion. It wasn't to confirm these crewmembers were dead. The hikers already reported that. Perez confirmed it when he initially examined the bodies. He wants to know if the crash killed these two or if they died by gunshot like the other crewmember.

I scan the pilot's body from the neck down, searching for bloodstains. The patch on her right breast is soaked with blood, but I recognized stitched wings and the name Doubles embroidered into the fabric. Her right knee is soaked in blood, but so is the shard of metal poking from it. It's not a gunshot wound.

"I don't see any indication of a bullet wound on her."

"OK. How about him?"

Reluctantly, I shift my head to the left. I'm already certain I won't know if he took a bullet to the face because there is no face. I push myself upright and examine the back of his helmet. No entry or exit wound. Then I perform the same scan I did on the woman—neck to shoes—searching for other wounds. His left hand, sliced from front to back, has stopped bleeding. The dirt stains on his knees appear to match what has entered the cockpit as the wreckage lodged into the side of the mountain.

"I don't see anything. Nothing that indicates firearms."

"Let's move outside," Perez says. We scoot back out of the front of the helicopter and crawl past the two young men. "Stay here for a minute," Perez directs.

The two hikers nod.

We step from the helicopter into the howling wind and move toward a flat rock. Perez still holds his shotgun. I've holstered my Glock.

"What do you think?" Perez shouts.

I'm at a loss. I know people get shot. I know people crash aircraft. I've never encountered the two things happening at the same time. "It's like the helicopter crashed. Someone on the ground saw it happen. They came to the crash site and finished off the survivor."

"Could be," Perez nods. "Could be."

I'm confused by his response. "What else could it be? I don't see any other options."

"How many people are on a Black Hawk crew?"

I've worked with Black Hawk crews in Iraq, hitching rides back to base after meetings at other bases. Realization hits me like a first-date slap after a botched attempt at a kiss. "Three minimum. But often four. A pilot, copilot, crew chief, and a door gunner. We've only got three here."

Perez says nothing, shifting his eyes from the main fuselage wreckage to the tangled metal a hundred yards away to which the tail rotor was attached.

"You thinking the people who did this took the other crewmember?" I suggest.

"No. I'm wondering if the other crewmember is the one responsible for all this."

5-DARIA

Colorado Trail near Lake Ann Pass-July 12, 2022

"Thank you." Now that they're hiking again, Daria is comfortable saying what she tried to say while they were crouched among the rocks.

"You're welcome. I didn't do anything but point to the rock."

"I froze. I was more concerned with trying to anticipate which way the rocks would go than I was with looking for shelter. I'm not sure how long I would have waited if you hadn't pulled me."

Emma nods. "It'll be interesting to find out from those hikers what happened."

The Apostle hikers reach Lake Ann Pass first. Emma could have beaten them there if Daria wasn't slowing her down. But Daria knows her partner won't leave her. Two switchbacks from the top, they intercept the three-person party graciously waiting at the side of the trail to allow them to pass before they continue down.

Based on the challenging off-trail traverse and light packs, these aren't Colorado Trail thru-hikers. Daria's surprised when the lead hiker lowers his pack and sits. Normally, only fellow thru-hikers take the time to stop and talk.

He addresses Emma. "Hey. Sorry if we scared you with the rock. I'm Rob." His eyes are hidden behind wide-lensed running sunglasses. He hasn't even looked Daria's way.

"We saw a fire or explosion or something to the south, beyond Cottonwood Pass," Rob says. "When we moved up the north ridge to get a better view, Rachel stepped wrong. Launched that boulder over the edge. Damn lucky she didn't fall with the rock." He turns toward the woman and shakes his head. "It's windy as hell when you crest the pass."

Rob's narrative rubs Daria wrong. He still hasn't made eye contact, and he's "mansplaining" the falling rock, implying he would never have slipped. And if he thinks all the falling rock did was scare Daria and Emma, he has no clue about the severity of the rockslide.

"What about the fire? Could you see it?" Daria launches her question over Emma's shoulder, trying to keep her tone light.

"Not the actual flames," Rob replies. "The smoke roiled up like it was going to be a big mushroom cloud, but the wind blew it toward the Arkansas River valley before it could form." He waves his hand toward the trail.

Emma lowers her pack to her feet. "Did you call it in?"

The hiker between Rob and Rachel leans forward. "No cellphone coverage out here even on the ridge. And we don't have anything with satellite like your GPS there." He nods toward Daria's pack.

"We can send an emergency signal," Emma offers. "Fires are no joke out here."

"Your call," Rob says. "The smoke disappeared pretty fast. By the time we hit the pass, it didn't look like much was burning."

Emma shoulders her pack, steps past Rob, and aims for the next switchback. "We'll check it out. Have a good hike down."

Rob's eyes widen as Emma walks away. He glances Daria's way, then back at his hiking partners. "Nice talking to you."

Emma either picked up the same vibe from Rob that she did, or she's pissed about his nonchalant attitude toward the fire. Daria likes her reaction. Rob's concerned about Rob.

"See you." Daria shoots a grin at Rob and his friends. Emma is already past the next switchback and walking opposite Daria about twenty yards uphill. She tosses her head toward the pass's summit, a visual cue for "Let's move out." Daria nods.

Daria crests the pass minutes after Emma, the wind buffeting her as soon as the ground levels off. Emma has dug a fluorescent green shell from her pack to layer up. Daria lowers her pack to grab a microfleece pullover. Emma gazes south. Daria spots no sign of smoke.

"See anything?" Daria shouts because the wind drowns out normal conversation. She almost loses her pullover trying to run her arm through the sleeve whipping in the wind.

Emma shakes her head without turning.

"Should we call it in?"

"Those guys made it sound like a big fire—at least initially. But I don't see anything." Emma turns, hands on her hips, and looks down. "If it was sustained, we'd see smoke. Even in this wind. What do you think?"

Blue sky, and snow-tipped ridges as far as Daria can see, with a howling wind as the background music. "I vote no. I'm not saying they didn't spot something. But it's either burned out or too small to worry about. And if we hit 911 and screw up the texts on the GPS, they'll send people out to look for us."

"I agree. We can ask around about it when we catch a ride into Buena Vista tomorrow. How are the tendons?"

Daria doesn't remember committing to taking a day off in town—just agreeing it was something they could consider. Her tendons feel better, especially after combining a dose of ibuprofen with the psychological boost of reaching the high point of today's leg. Or maybe it was the adrenaline of surviving a rockfall. Emma's acting like stopping in Buena Vista is a done deal.

Emma came through Denver for a conference last fall and spent a couple of days in BV with Zahn. Daria's not sure where Emma slept. And she's not going to ask. They're two great people who deserve each other. She's happy for her dad. Not so happy that she's going to rearrange her hike for the two lovebirds, though.

"My legs are good," she strokes her calf. "Tendons are better now that the uphill is done for the day. Why don't we plan on heading into BV tomorrow but make the overnight decision when we get there?"

Emma tilts her head toward the trail and raises her eyebrows. As they start down the south side switchbacks, she says, "Sounds like a plan. Should we give your dad a heads-up?"

Daria buries a smile. The talk about heading into Buena Vista is about more than resting Daria's feet. "I'll send him a message at our next break. How far to the campsite?"

"About two miles down to Texas Creek," Emma waves at the creek basin below us, "and another three upstream. So five total." She traces her finger from the creek below to a high point in the distance. "See that? That's Cottonwood Pass—about a five-mile climb tomorrow. My guess is we'll be looking for a ride by nine in the morning."

By the third switchback, the wind dies to a gentle breeze and they can talk without yelling, but they don't say much. Daria is still processing the rockfall and how Emma saved her. When you add their near-death experience to all they've shared over the last several weeks, the sudden reprieve from the wind's roar doesn't seem awkward.

Normally, afternoon thunderstorms would be building in the west and rolling their way, but high pressure has kept the buildups at bay. The view stuns Daria. The surrounding mountains pop in crystal clear contrast to the sky, the horizon defined by jagged crests in all directions. Capitol Peak near Aspen looms in the distance, with Crested Butte nearby. The entire Collegiate Peaks Range runs in front of them. The last fourteener in Chaffee County, Mount Shavano, is just visible, and Pike's Peak juts skyward a hundred miles away.

They descend below the tree line and the views are replaced by dense conifers and sporadic patches of green aspens biding their time until their autumn color bursts. Unlike last summer, when the lack of rain turned the forests into tinderboxes waiting for a spark, this summer's thunderstorms have kept the dead, pine beetle-infested underbrush moist. The fire danger hasn't peaked above MEDIUM yet.

The two women stop at a stream runoff crossing the trail to refill their water bottles. Emma uses a filter—hanging a two-liter plastic sack of creek water in a tree and running it through surgical tubing to a four-inch filter and into her clean bottle. It's a foolproof system, as long as the dirty water bag and clean water bottle don't get mixed up. Zahn taught Daria that adding a drop of bleach to the water does the trick, but Emma thinks it makes the water taste like a swimming pool. Daria has two liters of water filled and is ready to go while Emma's still trickling water into her bottle like slow-drip coffee.

Daria grabs a seat on a log near the stream and pulls her GPS off her pack. She owes her dad an update.

Hey, we're taking a run into Buena Vista tomorrow morning for resupply. Haven't decided if we'll stay the night or not, but if you're around, we wouldn't mind seeing you. Especially the "E" part of "WE." Get it? Sheesh—your dad jokes are rubbing off on me.

She doesn't tell him about her tendon issue. Or the rockfall. Wise. Prudent. Conservative. Dad.

No one would ever accomplish any life goals if they followed that advice. Taking a break might work for a middle-aged man who takes longer to heal, but Daria doesn't have time. It's July. Her social services job starts next month and part-time grad school in September. If she's going to finish the CT, she needs to do it now. Leaving the overnight in BV option ambiguous also serves Daria's tight schedule—even if it means less time with Zahn for Emma.

Emma finishes filtering, she slings her pack over her shoulder and points at the trail with a grin. "Lead on, O Captain, My Captain."

They've alternated the lead every day since they began the Colorado Trail, but today is Daria's first day of dealing with real pain.

Daria returns the grin. "Try to keep up, youngster." She throws on her pack, cinching the waist belt while on the move.

Another hour and they hit the flowing creek Emma spotted from the top of the pass. The wind dies to a whimper. The water runs high, not because of any precipitation today, but from the thunderstorms of the previous week. The CT turns in the opposite direction of the current, up the valley. They'll camp where it crosses the creek. In the morning, it should just be a two-hour hike to Cottonwood Pass where they'll thumb a ride into town.

Daria's GPS alerts her to an incoming message. She calls to Emma over her shoulder. "It's Dad. I can check it at our next break."

"Stop and read it. I don't mind."

Daria swallows a laugh. Of course Emma doesn't mind. Daria thumbs to the message page without disconnecting the GPS from her pack.

Good to hear from you. I'm on a SAR/sheriff mission south of you, close to St. Elmo. I'm not sure whether I'll be able to meet you two tomorrow or not. The mission will be multi-day. But I think coming into town is a good idea. Plan on spending the night.

"A multi-day SAR mission?" Emma says, when Daria shares the news. "That means it's something big, right?"

Daria studies the message and rereads it while answering. "Most missions are a day unless they're looking for a lost hiker." She pauses. "Haven't heard him call it a SAR/sheriff mission before, though." She glances at Emma. "And I don't understand why he says to spend the night if he doesn't even think he will be there."

Emma frowns. "And 'will be a multi-day mission' instead of 'could be.' A lost person they could find in the next ten minutes. He sounds certain they'll be out for multiple days."

"I have an answer he'll appreciate." Daria thumbs a reply into her GPS and hits send. "He uses it on me all the time."

"Show me." Emma reaches for her GPS.

Daria twists the GPS on its carabiner so Emma can read it.

"*Roger.*" She laughs. "He's going to love that."

An hour from their planned campsite, the trail abruptly disappears at one of Texas Creek's hairpin turns. Normally, there would be rocks or a log or something to work their way across and pick up the trail on the far shore. They find nothing.

They hike north between the river and Waterloo Gulch. The gulch forms the backside of the saddle between North Apostle and Ice Mountain, the site of last year's landslide. Kristee disappeared that day. Broken branches and muddy footprints next to the gulch's creek indicate other hikers have searched for a crossing in this area. They bushwhack up and down the bank to look for their own. The tracks peter out and they decide to backtrack to the original point where they lost the trail.

"Ahhh—Jesus!" Emma screams.

Daria whirls. "What's going on?"

Emma barrels toward her, waving her hands. "Bees! Get out of here."

Emma whips by and Daria follows close on her heels. A shadow flits by, then another. They emerge from the thick underbrush lining the river bank at the original spot where they lost the trail.

"You OK?"

Emma pirouettes, turning her calf in Daria's direction. A large welt juts from her leg like a mini volcano. A red circle the size of a quarter surrounds the sting. "Not a bee. Yellowjackets. Those things hit you like a taser, but the pain goes away pretty quick."

"Need my first aid kit?" Daria carries ointment and an antihistamine. The sting looks bad.

"I'm not allergic. By tomorrow, it'll be itching instead of hurting." She glares at Daria. "What the hell, Daria? Between your tendons and this, it's like someone is telling us it's time for a break or something."

Emma isn't angry at her. But she's not wrong. Everything went smoothly until today. But Daria isn't sure the answer to trouble is a day off in town.

6-HAVOC 23

(SIX YEARS BEFORE)
West of Baghdad, Iraq-November 19, 2016
"Aircraft twelve o'clock low," Ethan calls.

Doubles follows Ethan's line of sight. "Got it." She pushes the helicopter down the quarter-mile gap between the plateau they just left and the next one.

"Iraqi?" Shavano says.

"I couldn't tell," Doubles says.

"We're on the rescue-common frequency. Should we ask if it's our guys?"

"I got a better idea." Doubles maneuvers the helicopter lower in the wadi and turns so they point perpendicular to the oncoming helicopter. "Let it fly over us first."

They hover at the wadi's bottom drifting forward and waiting for the traffic to pass above. Horse crowds behind the pilots scanning the sky.

"Get your ass back here, Horse," Shavano calls. "The pilots got eyes on the front. We need you scanning back here so no one sneaks up on us."

Horse disappears just as the helicopter flies overhead, the number "57" taped on the window forward of the Black Hawk's tail boom. The 160th Spec Ops uses this method to identify their aircraft in flight.

"Looks like our guys," Doubles says. "Make the call, PI."

Ethan pulls up his commo card and checks the radio frequency. The call isn't one he practiced in training. How to verify a friendly aircraft in a combat zone when uncertain who is supposed to be there.

US aircraft approaching Iraqi crash site, US aircraft approaching Iraqi crash site, this is HAVOC 23 on departure.

Doubles' head bobs up and down in approval.

Shavano's voice comes over the intercom. "Nice call, Newb. Didn't tell them where we were departing from. Didn't tell them how far—" Shavano's compliment is interrupted by a radio call.

HAVOC 23, this is GHOST 57 on crash common. We're on arrival. How copy?

The call sign is special ops. They're not giving up too much detailed information either. Ethan keys the mic to answer. Doubles keeps the aircraft below the plateau wall.

GHOST 57, we've got you in sight.

Doubles laughs. "Nice. Unless they saw us when they flew over, that's going to piss them off. Give them the report."

Ethan senses Shavano listening to his every word since it's mostly Shavano's observations Ethan has to report. *GHOST 57, we've retrieved the six body bags and are delivering them as planned. We also identified four crew members. All deceased. Two in the cockpit, two in the rear of the main compartment. How copy?*

HAVOC 23, GHOST 57 copies all. Safe flight.

Ethan double-clicks his mic in acknowledgment.

The flight to the Alsklat Army post in Hosseinia on the north side of Baghdad takes forty-five minutes. Doubles pulls max continuous power and flies nap-of-the-earth. Thirty minutes out, Ethan uses the HF radio so Major Holmes can phone the Iraqis to prepare for their arrival.

As the crew enters Baghdad airspace, Ethan switches to Baghdad Control and announces HAVOC's position. According to Shavano, the country's capital is no longer the free-fire zone it was at the turn of the century. Baghdad International is back to welcoming commercial aircraft. The residents sell their wares on the city's streets with no more fear of a drive-by shooting than tourists in Iowa.

Doubles follows the controller's instructions, climbing to one-thousand feet over the northwest quadrant of Baghdad, and flying direct to their destination.

HAVOC 23, welcome to Alsklat. Please establish a right base as if you were landing Runway 20 and land in the designated distinguished visitor spot on the tarmac just south of the control tower.

Ethan says, "Sounds like we're getting the DV treatment. Think they'll have lunch?

Doubles smacks Ethan's arm. "Not for us. It's for their fallen soldiers. Tell them we got it."

Baghdad Control, HAVOC 23 copies landing instructions. Will comply.

"Fuck lunch, Newb," Shavano says. "We land. Offload the bodies. We get the hell out of this country."

Theoretically, Doubles should make that call—not Shavano. But he's right. The crew shouldn't loiter any longer than they have to. The question is whether Shavano's concern is for their safety or because prolonged ground time might increase the risk of the Iraqis discovering their souvenirs from the crash site. And what the heck did Shavano take for himself? It doesn't make sense that he would find three items and give them away leaving nothing for himself. He had to have grabbed something. Is he really going to give that bracelet to Doubles? She doesn't come across as the war trophy type.

Doubles sets down fifty yards from the red carpet leading to the base of the control tower, as close as she's willing to get with the engines running. Parallel rows of Iraqi soldiers form a gauntlet to the building. Shavano pulls the door open. Two soldiers in camouflaged uniforms approach the aircraft, slicing their hands across their throats in the universal aviation signal that means "shut down your engines."

"PC?" Shavano's voice is droll over the intercom. "They want us to shut down. I'm telling them no."

"It's a ceremony, Shavano." Doubles keys back. "Can you imagine if the Russians swung by Dover, kept their engines running, then started offloading a dead American wrapped in a Hefty garbage bag?"

The first Iraqi points through the rear compartment to the far side door and makes opening signals, while the second keeps signaling to cut the engines.

"Ms. Doubles? Not only is shutting down our engines on this mission against the guidance we were given on departure, it's also a stupid, fucking idea. Do you really want to put another American crew in jeopardy to come fix us if we can't start our engines again?"

Ethan turns to Doubles. She isn't going to like Shavano questioning her commands. Not wanting to give her the impression he's taking sides, he shifts his gaze toward the instrument panel.

Shavano doesn't wait. "They want us to close this door and use the far side one to offload. I don't got a problem with that. Recommend that be our compromise. We'll let them choose the door. We choose to keep the engines running."

Doubles exhales before answering. "Roger. Make it happen."

The two Iraqi soldiers jog back to the senior officers lining the carpet and stop at the first one in line. The two young soldiers endure a tongue-lashing while Shavano and Horse close the door facing the carpet and maneuver to the other side of the helo. The senior officer raises his arms pointing first at the young men, then at the helicopter. The soldiers remain frozen. The senior officer walks down the carpet toward the tower and stops at the last man before the door, a tall Iraqi soldier with medals weighing down the right side of his chest. The second officer, more senior than the first, shows no emotion. He points toward the building and sweeps his hand toward the helicopter.

When the building doors open, two men push a coffin on a gurney out onto the carpet and aim for the helicopter. The soldiers don't want the distinguished visitors inside to see the body bags. They want the coffins loaded on the back side of the helicopter so only the coffins are visible when they pass in review on the red carpet. Thus, the compromise.

A young Iraqi officer replaces the original soldiers who came out to the helicopter. He follows the gurney around to the far side door. Shavano and Horse have unbuckled the tie-down straps in preparation to move the garbage bag-wrapped body.

The officer waves his hands at the sight of the black plastic.

Doubles has Ethan clearing for people and obstacles out the front of the helicopter while she observes the happenings in the back. "What's the deal, Shavano?"

"They sent their English speaker. He wants to know why this one's in garbage bags and the others are in body bags. He says they're all supposed to be in body bags."

"Did—"

Shavano cuts her off. "Yes. Now he's asking if we touched the body before we put it in the bags."

Ethan recalls he and Horse rolling the corpse back and forth. Of course, they did.

"Aw fuck. He wants to see the body before they accept it."

Ethan turns to Doubles. "That's a bad idea."

"I don't think we have a lot of choice," she says, twisting to look in the back. "Shavano?"

Shavano nods. Ethan watches him huddle with the Iraqi officer, cupping his hand against his ear before stepping back and gesturing from the body to the group of people outside. Shavano pulls his knife, slices through the trash bag, and motions for the officer to inspect the body. The officer pauses at one point, steps back and stares at the senior crew chief, then nods. He grabs one of the soldiers and points to the control tower. The soldier runs inside.

Ethan's heart pounds. Did something the officer saw inside the garbage bag clue him into the fact that they had robbed this man or others of their personal possessions? There was no way Shavano just found the items. They had to have been with one of the bodies. Suddenly, he feels less like a seasoned combat veteran and more like a gun for hire. A mercenary who does a job for spoils on the side.

"Crew chief, where's that guy going?" Ethan points to the soldier.

"Our officer sent him in for another body bag."

Ethan slumps in his seat, the reaction so visible that Doubles turns to him and tilts her head. She keys her mic. "So, everything's OK then? They're not pissed about the garbage bags?"

Shavano says, "I told him what happened. We had a choice to bring their comrade home like this or leave his body alone in the desert. We chose to bring him home."

"Nice—and true," Doubles says. "Classy, Shavano. What did he say?"

"He called us heroes. He said we're his brothers now."

A warm glow spreads through Ethan's chest. Pride in bringing a warrior to his final resting place. Before he opens his departure checklist, he touches his hand to his heart. The Iraqi knife nestles in his flight suit pocket.

7-ZAHN

St. Elmo, Colorado-July 12, 2022

I tuck into the helicopter wreckage next to the two impatient hikers to avoid the howling wind. Perez radios Deputy Jesse Sanders who just arrived at St. Elmo.

Chaffee 4, this is Chaffee 2.

Go ahead.

The accident scene is clear. I detect no threat in the vicinity.

Chaffee 4 copies. I thought that was a bogus call.

Negative Chaffee 4. Hiker reports are accurate. Someone used a weapon up here. That someone no longer appears to be in the immediate area but that is not confirmed. Dispatch recovery teams only with an armed escort.

Perez shoots an annoyed look my way. I nod. We can't compromise the safety of the recovery teams. But this scene needs to be analyzed before anything moves.

Chaffee 2, Chaffee 4...I copy. I'm sure you already know this, but we don't have the resources—

Perez cuts in. *Jesse, you're not getting it. We've got a federal asset down with three fatalities, one by gunshot. This thing will be at the federal level within an hour. The Army's probably en route. Get on the radio with Chaffee 1 right now and communicate that someone was shot without creating a panic among every yahoo with a scanner out there. Can you do that?*

Sanders doesn't answer right away. Chaffee 1 is Brad Larkin, the Chaffee County Sheriff. He already knows a helo is down. He likely heard the hikers report the fatalities. But this will be the first confirmation that a crewmember was murdered.

Got it. Sanders finally replies. *I'll get Buena Vista and Salida to send up police while we organize the big guns.*

Perfect. Let me know when you have a team on the way.

The four of us head out into the wind. The wreckage on the slope's narrow shelf appears stable. The impact location can't have been an accident. The pilot didn't have enough control to keep from crashing into the side of the mountain but she must have had enough to choose where on the mountainside she wanted to hit. The almost-level terrain will simplify the body extractions when the teams arrive.

The hiker who introduced himself as Shane turns to Perez and raises his voice over the wind. "Are me and Gonzo cleared to leave?"

I smile. This must be the trail name thing Daria told me about. "You got a trail name too?"

Shane doesn't return my smile. "Dragon." He turns back to Perez. "We've told you all we can. Unless you need us to help with anything, we're going to work our way back to the trail." He points to the west. "Same way your search helicopter headed."

"What search helicopter?" Perez's voice is sharp. He glares at the hiker.

"About halfway here, while we were hiking in the trees, a helicopter flew right over us. Small. Red and white. We waved at it, but don't think it saw us. We figured that's how you got here so quickly. Because they told you where the wreckage was."

Perez shakes his head. "Not one of ours. How many minutes after the crash did you see it?"

Shane turns to Michael. Michael scratches his nose and takes a step forward. "Maybe ten minutes."

Perez raises an eyebrow at me.

I don't want to alarm Shane and Michael. Dispatch only referenced the report from these guys. Nothing else. So I say, "You want me to check with Chaffee 4?"

Perez nods. I step a few feet away from the group to make the call, as Perez continues talking to the hikers.

"You two aren't leaving this site until someone walks you out. I cleared the immediate area, but we're still uncertain of the status beyond that. We'll hike you out the way we came in. Give you a ride to town."

Michael mutters, "Dude." He stops, recognizing he might not have chosen the best address. "Sir, I mean, we're thru-hiking the Colorado Trail. We can't just ride back with you, then join the trail somewhere else. We have to get on the trail exactly where we got off, or it doesn't count."

People complain about the twenty-something generation, how they're slow to find work, all about experiences rather than possessions, and living seasonally between their vans and their parents. But Daria's smart, driven, and willing to work for what she wants. Dragon and Gonzo might sport dreadlocks and basketball shorts, but someone who doesn't want to miss a single step of a meticulously planned 490-mile hike doesn't sound too aimless either.

Perez shuts Michael down. "You can figure it out after we get you out of these mountains. No disrespect, but this thing is bigger than your hike."

Sanders knows nothing about another helicopter and says he'll run it through the back channels to track it down.

I say, *Heard anything from the Army or the HAATS training program yet?*

HAATS has another helo on the way. About ten minutes out, Sanders reports. *They say an Army unit from C Springs is mobilizing and will probably be there in an hour.*

I key my mic. *Find out if the HAATS team is armed.* Perez and I can't leave this site until the approaches to our location are cleared or someone relieves us in place. The HAATS training program might not have the assets to do that, but it's worth asking.

· · ·

The HAATS helicopter calls from the air. Wind gusts prevent them from landing on the same shelf as the Black Hawk wreckage. They manage to put down about a half mile up the road from where Perez parked his Tahoe and radio their plan to hike to our position. When the armed three-man security team scrambles over the ridge and joins us, Salida Dispatch radios the inbound Army team from Colorado Springs not to land at the site either and to use the same ground route as the HAATS team.

Both our SAR teams radio that they are still working their way up to the site. One team is approaching with a litter on the same route Perez and I took. Another is coming in from the south, also packing a litter. The idea is for each team to assess their route to see which is easiest if the winds don't die down and we have to evacuate the bodies by ground egress. Both teams are accompanied by law enforcement.

I know the SAR teams are hoofing it as fast as they can, and I worry they will get here too soon.

Perez must sense my frustration. "What're you thinking, Z?"

"What are the SAR teams going to do when they arrive?"

"Package the bodies. If the winds die down, we'll call in lift and air evac them out. If they don't, then we'll do it the hard way and carry them down to where the emergency vehicles are." Perez surveys the steep southern approach. "If we have to move them on the ground, I'm guessing the route you and I took will be easier."

I shake my head.

"What?"

"It's more than a crime scene."

Perez wears a determined scowl I've seen before. He says, "I'll snap pictures myself. If you're thinking we need to wait for the state and feds before moving the bodies, I disagree." Perez will work with the higher-ups but likes to do it on his terms.

"It's also a military aviation accident," I say. "There'll be the FAA, the Army's Combat Readiness Center, and other federal looky-loos rushing in to analyze what happened. I'm not sure they're going to let you move the bodies before their arrival."

Perez holds my gaze. "Wrong, Z-man. When an airplane runs off the runway at a major airport, they don't leave the bodies out there for multiple days until the investigation is over. Photo documentation is adequate. And—"

Chaffee 2, Chaffee 4. Perez's radio interrupts his lecture.

Perez grabs his hand mic. *This is Chaffee 2, go ahead.*

Roger, Chaffee 1 wants you back at the office. Wants an ETA.

Perez rolls his eyes at me before answering. *Chaffee 4, he knows where I'm at, right?*

Affirmative. The interagency guys are already rolling in, and Chaffee 1 asked for you and Zahn to hand over the site to the Army team that HAATS brought and return to headquarters. Told me to go too.

"What the fuck?" Perez's eyebrows arch as he waits for my response.

I shrug. "You got me." I'm not too surprised at this turn of events. In the Air Force, when something happened that was so big it attracted outsiders, your boss could be more worried about looking good for the visiting generals than for the actual incident itself.

Chaffee 4, Chaffee 2. I'm not leaving without pictures. Need twenty minutes, plus an hour to get back to the Tahoe. Another hour to get back to headquarters. Pass that along, please. Around 2.5 hours.

Uh, Chaffee 2—he's not going to be happy.

Perez stares at me as he answers. *Copy.*

"Between me and you, Z-man? Our boss is losing sight of our priorities."

"Sheriff Larkin? If this thing turns out half as huge as you predict, he's going to be neck-deep in more help than he needs. Probably just trying to get ahead of the inevitable."

Perez shakes his head. "Would you pull your team off an active crime scene while bodies lie dead at the site?"

"Probably not."

"He's got some stressors at home." Perez hesitates.

"Like what? Kids? Wife?"

"His mom's sick. She refuses to move to where she can get treatment and he's been paying out of pocket to bring doctors to her."

"That can't be cheap."

"If he didn't have his posse helping him out, his mother probably wouldn't be alive."

"His posse?"

"That's what us deputies call them. He's got a half-dozen guys with money he hangs with. You know, shooting at the range. Hunting. Jeeping."

I know from my previous interactions that the county as a whole respects Larkin. He holds an elected position. "Sounds like he's lucky to have them."

Perez looks like he's thinking about what I've said. "Maybe. His mother's still alive."

After giving Michael and Shane a heads-up that we'll be leaving soon, we divvy up photo duties. We each use our department cell phones to document the accident scene. Perez takes the tail section and the gunshot victim. I'm back in the main wreckage—a place I'd hoped not to enter again—taking photos of the aircrew and the cockpit. I try to avoid looking at where the copilot's face used to be, but my stomach lurches as I focus my camera on the scene. I work through the cockpit as quickly as possible, then move outside for exterior shots. As I exit the wreckage, the Army team crests the ridge above us.

When we finish, we hand over command of the site to the Army, briefing them on how the SAR teams should perform upon arrival. The Army specialists agree with Perez. If a helicopter can land close to the wreckage, we should package the bodies and get them out of here.

We grab Michael and Shane and scramble across the ridge and up to the crest. We stop briefly at the top to regroup, Perez and I huffing and puffing. Our two thru-hikers' chests hardly heave.

Downhill is faster than uphill, but this slope is so steep on the downhill we're grasping onto aspens, logs, and roots, just to keep our descent under control. Halfway down, a yell pierces our muttered complaints, and I catch a flash of red through the trees. A SAR team of four and a BV cop I've known for a couple of years, Officer Linzmeier—not one of my favorite members of local law enforcement—appear.

"We almost to the top?" The lead hiker, Gina Pursche, a former ultrarunner turned SAR volunteer and a county commissioner, grins at me.

"Sure." I tease.

Perez claws his way over to Linzmeier to discuss the accident site security. I address the rest of the SAR team who have caught up. "You heard on the radios. The helo's wedged into a flat spot near the boulder field. Three dead. Two in the aircraft that look like they died on impact. Another one about fifty to seventy-five meters from the crash. Dead from a gunshot wound to the head."

The guy behind Gina pokes his head out, the frame of the litter strapped to his pack. "What's the plan for us?"

I recognize the raspy voice first, Tom Poore, a local pilot who usually sticks to driving ATVs and snowmobiles when not flying.

"Package the bodies like a patient. Hopefully, the helicopters can get up there in this wind. But if the winds don't die down, you'll be bringing them down there." I point toward the Tahoe at the bottom of the steep slope.

"Ah, shit," Poore mutters.

Gina nods at us and continues up the slope. Poore shakes his head and follows.

As Perez and I approach the Tahoe, my GPS pings with an incoming message.

Daria.

Perez glances back at me. "Take it." He nods toward Michael and Shane. "We'll load our packs. I'm going to check in with dispatch on the shortwave. They already pulled Sanders back from St. Elmo."

I scroll through the incoming message, my hand squeezing the GPS. Daria and Emma are over Lake Ann pass and into the Texas Creek basin. Still a long day's hike from here, and I'm not happy with the fact they are walking toward the accident site while the shooters are still unaccounted for.

They're coming off the trail tomorrow—hitching a ride from Cottonwood Pass into Buena Vista. My grip slackens and I let out a breath. One less thing to worry about. Plus, Daria made a joke, hinting that Emma wants to see me.

I text back, telling her about the SAR mission but withholding the details. I know from experience that when I come on too strong with Daria about safety, she tends to do the opposite of my recommendation. She's confident in her ability to take care of herself. I close out the text: *Good idea coming into town. Plan on spending the night.*

I can't help thinking about a chance to see Emma. We've been talking to each other by phone once a week—and it's about more than work. I sense Emma might be ready for us to move forward in our relationship. I'm gun-shy about commitment after my last experience, so it's somewhat ironic we've grown closer over the last year. I'm anxious to hear how it's going with Daria. Her infrequent texts make it sound like they're becoming fast friends. Not that their hike is a litmus test, but if they don't get along, it would be tough for me to pursue Emma. If the Sheriff keeps us working overtime with this inevitable interagency nightmare, I'll be lucky to get home at all tonight.

Perez has swung the Tahoe around so he's pointed toward the river valley. Michael and Shane take the rear seats. I climb into the passenger side.

"All good?" Perez says.

"They're coming off trail for the night. That's good."

"Where's she sleeping?"

"Daria? At the house." I know Perez isn't asking about Daria. Perez gives me a look.

"Look, I like Emma a lot. But I'm not sure our first sleepover should be while my daughter is in the house."

"Good thinking, dude," says Shane from the back. "Can't imagine my dad bringing home some hot gal for a—"

I cut Shane off. "Thanks for the input."

Perez mocks surprise. "Wait. First sleepover? You mean—"

"That's enough from you too," I say, my tone light. "She stayed in a motel last visit." I'm not really pissed. We dealt with the horrible things we saw in the military by flipping each other shit to distract ourselves from the sick feelings weighing us down.

I'm happy to get my daughter and girlfriend out of the mountains and down to safety. Now I need to figure out how to duck out of work and see them.

8–DARIA

Colorado Trail near Texas Creek-July 13, 2022
Daria layers up before crawling from her tent. The basin has kept them out of the wind, but even in July, the early morning chill at ten thousand feet reminds her of the Colorado Rockies' secret. The mountains veil their dangers with beauty, and more than one search and rescue mission every year involves hypothermia in the summer.

Emma boils water on her gas stove, her morning coffee a necessity. "How's the wasp sting?"

"Like it never happened," she says. "A little itchy, but pretty much a non-event. How're those tendons?"

Daria hasn't even thought about her feet since waking.

"Good." She grins and steps off to a tree in the distance the opposite direction of Texas Creek to relieve herself. A tea drinker, she doesn't require a hot drink for a morning startup or even breakfast before breaking camp. A snack of trail mix during mid-morning breaks works.

They pack their gear, then walk the twenty yards to the stream. A log rests on the bank at the obvious crossing point, and they sit to remove their boots while surveying the current. Some crossings have rocks or logs forming a primitive bridge, but not here. Daria ties her boot laces together and drapes them over her neck, then uses her poles to keep from slipping on the rocks strewn across the river bottom. Halfway across, her feet are so numb from the frigid water they burn. Emma splashes behind her.

They dry off with yesterday's hiking shirts and tie their boots. The trail switchbacks up the south side of the basin, and ten minutes in, both women are breathing hard.

"I'm not sure it's the full night's sleep or that Texas Creek water reducing the swelling," Daria says, "but my feet feel great. The tendons too."

"Hopefully, it was just the pass yesterday."

"Maybe we don't need to go into town," Daria offers. "We've got food to keep going."

Emma's voice from behind carries a smile. "How about we wait until we get to the top of Cottonwood Pass before we decide?"

The trees diminish in size and give way to willows as they leave the forest. This flat basin before the final climb to the pass is alpine swampy with pools of standing water on both sides of the trail. The wind picks up the higher they climb, forcing them to raise their voices to talk to each other.

Daria turns to warn Emma to watch for moose but freezes in her tracks. Now that the trees are behind them, the south side of the Three Apostles—the mountains they skirted yesterday—pop against the blue sky like the thousand-piece puzzles Daria's mom used to get her for Christmas.

Emma's eyes follow Daria's and she pivots. "Wow."

"Right?"

"You asked me why I'd be willing to drop everything and hike with a gal I barely know? Don't get me wrong, Daria—I already love you. But I wanted this."

Daria grins. "Me too."

At the far end of the basin, the CT zigzags up a steep slope before crossing the highway. Three hikers work their way down the trail toward them.

Twenty minutes later, the trio steps aside to let Daria and Emma by. A woman who looks about Daria's age leads the group. Another woman, who appears to be the age of Daria's mother stands next to her with a man of similar age.

The younger woman asks, "You guys doing the CT or Continental Divide?"

Daria smiles. "How do you know we're not day hikers?" she teases, pleased the woman automatically assumes they are thru-hikers. Probably the grizzled look after their two weeks on the trail.

"Day hikers don't carry any more than they have to. You guys are loaded up."

Daria nods. "We're doing the CT. I'm Little Z. This is Mud Hen."

"Nice," the woman says. "I'm Fainting Goat. This is Quaker and Cold Brew." The older man and woman wave. "We're CT-ers too. Northbound." Fainting Goat flushes. "Obviously."

Emma pulls up next to Daria. "Do we get the trail name origin stories or are you all in a hurry?"

Quaker chuckles. "Everyone wants to hear the backstory on Fainting Goat."

Fainting Goat laughs. "You tell yours first."

Quaker shrugs. "I eat oatmeal on the trail for breakfast and lunch. I add it to my freeze-dried meal at night. Generic, but everyone started calling me Quaker." He turns to the woman beside him. "My wife likes to get on the trail early. As soon as the tent is packed, we're moving. So we soak our coffee the night before and drink it cold. Cold Brew."

"Bor-ing." His wife smiles.

"These guys gave me my name the second day on the trail out of Durango," Fainting Goat says. "I was exhausted after climbing a ridge and resting after a switchback. I didn't hear them coming up the trail. They scared the shit out of me—and I passed out."

"Lucky she didn't hit her head," Cold Brew adds.

"We've been hiking together ever since," Fainting Goat says. "Just got back on the trail at Cottonwood Pass after a zero-day in Buena Vista."

Daria's tendons and feet are still feeling good, and she's chagrined at the reminder about going into town. She wants to stick to their original schedule.

Emma says, "Beautiful town, isn't it? Where did you stay?"

"Best Western," Quaker says. "We ate good. Slept good. Things were hopping though."

Daria laughs. "Sorry. My dad lives there. I've never heard anyone call BV busy before unless it's the Fourth of July."

"No. Because of the helicopter crash," Quaker says. "Ambulances galore, Sheriff's vehicles blocking streets, search and rescue trucks everywhere."

Emma's voice is sharp. "Do you know what kind of helicopter it was?"

Quaker shrugs. "Not sure. Our ride up the pass told us it crashed just west of St. Elmo, pretty close to where you'll be tomorrow or the next day if you stay on the trail. Rumor is no one made it out."

"That explosion those guys on West Apostle said they saw." Emma shoots a look at Daria, her voice even, thoughtful. "That must have been it."

Fainting Goat shifts her stance, and Daria senses enough chit-chat. Time to hike. They say their goodbyes and crest the ridge overlooking Cottonwood Pass a short time later. The parking lot before them is half-full, tourists scurrying from cars to take pictures from the second-highest paved road in the United States before dashing back to get out of the wind.

Emma grins and sticks her fist at Daria for a bump. Daria bumps, then wraps Emma in a hug. Emma squeezes back. "How you feeling?"

"Good." Daria glances down at the parking lot. "Let's keep going. I mean I know you probably wanted to see my dad—I do too—but we've got that rendezvous with him planned by Monarch, and that's only three days away, right?"

Emma shrugs with a grin. "Sounds like Z-man might be busy with that crash, anyway." She studies her phone. "I've got two bars. Going to text your dad. If your wheels are good, then let's move out." Emma points south. "Hike on! I'll catch up."

9-HAVOC 23

(FIVE YEARS BEFORE)

Albany, New York-November 19, 2017

The 3/142 Aviation Regiment doesn't use hard crews—the same four people flying together for every mission—outside of deployments and special missions. Available personnel man day-to-day missions. While hard crews foster teamwork under the pressure of real missions, mixing personnel up for training helps crewmembers learn from each other, and discover who are the good pilots and who are the "not-so-good" ones.

After HAVOC 23 returns from Turkey, Ethan scores several temporary duty stints in Ft. Huachuca, Arizona, and another in eastern Georgia. None last longer than two weeks nor inspire the same camaraderie he felt when he flew with HAVOC 23.

Ethan's Turkey deployment and combat support mission to Iraq make his new-guy experience in the 3/142 brief. He's promoted to CW1—a chief warrant officer. Shavano spreads the word that the new PI, has hands of gold and is cool under pressure. If Shavano likes you, everybody likes you.

What Ethan can't figure out is why. Is it Ethan's sparkling personality, wit, and charm—doubtful—or because Ethan knows how to keep his mouth shut? It still gnaws on Ethan's conscience about the Iraqi knife. Instead of prominently displaying it with his growing coin collection and his shot glasses from every country he's flown in, the knife remains stuffed behind his socks in his top dresser drawer. The more military experience he gains, the more uncomfortable he is with the knife.

The Uniform Code of Military Justice, or UCMJ, makes it pretty clear: he could be court-martialed for Article 103-Pillaging or Looting, Article 121-Theft or Larceny, Article 134-Maltreatment of the Dead, Smuggling, Customs Violations. Some of these are Geneva Convention violations. Some can be tried in civilian courts. All can ruin Ethan's life.

He considers discussing it with Doubles, but he's uncertain Shavano gave her the bracelet. If he did, then Doubles might say she doesn't see anything wrong with it. But if not, what will she think of Ethan?

Ethan's uncertainty about Doubles' and Shavano's relationship disappeared when the two moved in together shortly after their return from Turkey. The timing is no coincidence. Obviously, they hooked up during their overseas mission.

Shacking up together surprises him, though. This kind of officer/enlisted relationship—even though warrant officers aren't commissioned—would be an actionable UCMJ offense in the active-duty force, and against the rules in the Guard, as well, but Ethan expects their tight-knit unit will just look the other way. Part of him is jealous. He's a warrant officer. Shavano isn't.

But Doubles takes the awkwardness out of the situation. She's always asking how many flight hours he's accumulated, or checking on his timeline for pilot-in-command upgrade. She badgers him to find a long-term girlfriend, but he can't tell her the woman he wants is living with someone else.

On an early morning two-ship flight to Bangor, Maine, Ethan's assigned to fly with Horse. The PC on the other helicopter is Doubles. A dead minivan battery delays Ethan's pilot's arrival. This morning's flight is a positioning leg—moving the helicopters to Bangor so they're ready for tomorrow's exercise support. Doubles pushes the takeoff time later to allow the other pilot to square away his car and join them for planning. The three HAVOC 23 veterans grab a coffee.

"Happy anniversary," Doubles says, looking from Ethan to Horse.

"Uh, we're not even dating," Horse deadpans, sliding his eyes toward Ethan.

"Not even close. Horse is a left-side of the bed kinda guy and so am I. Would never work," Ethan adds.

Doubles starts the theme song for a show that tugs at Ethan's memory. "Na-na-na-na-na-na-na, Na-na-na-na-na-na-na,…?"

"Batman," Horse and Ethan call out in unison.

"One year ago today, boys. The Iraqi mission."

Ethan glances from Doubles to Horse trying to gauge the direction of the conversation. If she wants to talk about Ethan's first and only combat support mission, he's game. But if Doubles has decided to discuss their illicit souvenirs, Ethan's less than excited. He and Horse haven't talked with each other about what happened.

Ethan says nothing.

Horse's return glance at Ethan is just as blank as the one Ethan gave him. He answers Doubles with a smile. "Those were the days, Ms. Doubles."

Doubles stares at Ethan, then turns to Horse. "That's it? We fly low level into a combat zone, pull out dead bodies and deliver them to the Iraqi Army, then get nominated for the humanitarian mission of the year—and all you got for me is 'those were the days?'"

She whirls back to Ethan. "Which is more than you offered." She shakes her head. "What's the deal? Shavano won't talk about it either. When I press, he heads to our garage and works on that damn Vette he bought when he got back."

Ethan winces at "Our garage." The possessive pronoun—Ethan was an English major as opposed to his twin sister who favored criminology—hints that Doubles' and Shavano's relationship leans more to the permanent nature than the temporary.

"I figure it was the dead bodies that got you guys. That's the only thing different about your experience than mine, right? Was it really that bad? Most of them were in body bags."

"All but one," Ethan says. "And that one was pretty bad. We came back to the aircraft for trash bags, remember?" He turns to Horse, who nods in agreement.

"And that memory trumps celebrating the mission?" Doubles swivels her head between the two men. "Nothing else you want to discuss?"

Horse shakes his head. Ethan follows suit, then realizes how guilty it looks if they are both staring at Doubles. His eyes sweep to the far wall covered with souvenirs crews have brought back from overseas missions. A small restaurant billboard from the island of Crete. An autobahn sign from Germany.

Doubles didn't earn her call sign for saying one thing and meaning another. She got it for being meticulous. But Ethan can't tell what she's after with her questions. Is she trying to get them to talk about the gifts Shavano gave them? Did Shavano give her the bracelet and not mention the gifts he gave Ethan and Horse? Maybe the same kind of guilt wracks Doubles as Ethan.

"What kind of memories do you have?" Ethan ventures. Maybe she wants to get something off her chest. Who knows, maybe Horse will start talking too. Ethan has no idea how the crew chief feels about the ring.

"I feel proud—like we were part of something bigger than ourselves. We weren't just showing the Iraqi Army what America stands for; we were embodying the bond between warriors. When our fellow warfighters couldn't retrieve their fallen, we stepped in to help. It was about having each other's backs, no matter what." She shakes her head then lowers it like she's embarrassed. "I know it sounds all patriotic and stuff. But I'm proud of what we did." She raises her head, zeroing in on Ethan. "And it pisses me off that the three soldiers I flew that mission with don't seem to feel the same way. Every time I bring up Iraq with Shavano, he slinks away like he's embarrassed about something. Now I bring it up with you two—and you give me the same shit. So I'm asking one more time. Anything you'd like to discuss?"

Ethan doesn't dare look at Horse. Doubles has indirectly answered Ethan's question about whether Shavano gave her the bracelet or not. Ethan has been wondering how the woman he respects so much would be willing to take a memento from a dead Iraqi soldier. Based on her speech, he has his answer. She probably doesn't know about the bracelet—or any of it.

The discussion Doubles is so interested in can't happen. "No, ma'am. I got nothing," he says to Doubles.

She puffs air like she's disgusted before turning to Horse. He doesn't meet her eyes, picking at something on his finger.

Doubles stands. "Have a great fucking day, gentlemen."

10-ZAHN

Salida, Colorado-July 12, 2022

Perez drops me at my truck in St. Elmo, and I follow him and the hikers to Salida's only hostel, a large building that looks like a poor man's bed-and-breakfast, five blocks from the sheriff's office. Perez takes Michael's and Shane's contact info.

He shakes hands with both. "Thanks for your help today. You didn't have to go to the scene. The fact that you found the wreckage, passed on the coordinates, and remained there until we arrived, well, that says a lot about your character."

The two hikers seem nonplussed. Michael nods.

Shane says, "We're going back out, you know." He turns toward the hostel. "We'll spend the night, but we're hitting the trail tomorrow."

Perez says. "It's not like we're clearing out the entire wilderness. But it wouldn't hurt to call our office tomorrow morning and get a status check. Just to be safe."

"Right," Michael says, looking like it's the last call he plans on making.

"Hike on," I call out my window as I pull out behind Perez. I park my Tundra in an outer lot at the Sheriff's Office and lock my personal Glock in the glove box before heading inside. Perez waits for me in the hallway. Robin, who runs the front desk, stands in front of the conference room holding a cardboard box and what appears to be a forced smile.

"Work phones, personal phones. Your radios too. I'll get them back to you after the meeting," she says. "Sheriff Larkin's orders."

Perez shakes his head, drops two phones and his radio in the box, and enters the room.

I give a collegial smile to Robin, surrendering my phones. "Sounds like this one's going to be a big deal."

Robin's smile disappears, but she doesn't speak.

The conference room is internal, with windows looking out to the other offices and the front desk rather than outside the building. Someone already closed the shades. Sheriff Larkin sits at the head of the table, facing a projector screen. Larkin catches Perez's eye and nods to the empty chair on his left. The office has been down an undersheriff since Deputy Adams retired, and Larkin hasn't filled the position. Perez is the county's next senior law enforcement officer. The remainder of the chairs around the table are filled. Jesse Sanders sits at a laptop at the opposite end of the room from Sheriff Larkin. Scott Powers, the only other reserve deputy on the team, occupies a folding chair on the room's perimeter. I grab a seat next to him.

"Who the hell's out there keeping the county safe if the entire Sheriff's Office is in here?" I whisper.

Scott opens his mouth, then stops as his eyes focus on something over my shoulder.

"You got a problem with the way I'm running this, Zahn?" Sheriff Larkin's voice is quiet but firm.

My humorous take on a serious question has fallen flat. Larkin's a good boss, and in our interactions over the past couple of years, he's shown mutual respect. This is the first time I've heard him call out one of his deputies like this.

"No, sir. I apologize for interrupting. Just not used to seeing all of us in one room."

Larkin sighs. "I've got Buena Vista and Salida police picking up our coverage while I've got you in here. I need to get us all on the same sheet of music before we get back out there."

Perez glances at me, but I can't read his eyes. If BV and Salida police are covering our normal duties, then who the hell is up in the mountains containing the accident scene, escorting the rescue teams, and searching for the perpetrators?

"I just got off a teleconference call with the Colorado Bureau of Investigation, the Federal Aviation Administration, and an accident investigator from the Army Combat Readiness Center. Before I tell you their thoughts, I'd like Deputy Perez to give us a brief on the scene. Rick?"

Perez steps to a large wall map of Chaffee County. Without notes, he walks through the timeline of events, throwing in the word "approximately" whenever he needs to refer to a time. When he gets to the hikers calling in a gunshot wound on one of the bodies and follows up with the words "which we later verified in person," eyes shift around the table. Hearing this salient point out loud from a member of their own team ramps up the tension.

We were always going to get more help than we needed from the feds on this one—the crash happened on federal land with a federal asset, with an Army guardsmen aircrew under another state's administrative authority undergoing federally mandated training. A bureaucratic maze that would take hours if not days simply to confirm who was in charge.

But the murder adds a criminal aspect that involves the Colorado Bureau of Investigation—also known as CBI—and probably the FBI.

Perez wraps up the brief by reiterating that he and I would still be out in the field if not recalled for this briefing—a not-so-subtle jab at his boss that maybe huddling your assets at the beginning of an ongoing investigation, when your culprits are still at large, isn't the best idea ever.

"Thanks, Rick." If Larkin's pissed at Perez, he's covering. "Questions?"

The deputies at the table exchange glances. Perez keeps his eyes on Larkin.

"Alright. Now that we're on the same page, CBI is waiting for an update." Larkin nods toward Deputy Sanders at the opposite end of the table. "Jesse, connect us up."

Jesse Sanders taps on a laptop in front of him and glances at the screen behind him. Nothing happens. He taps again, then turns. Nothing.

Powers shifts in his chair next to me. Jesse stops pressing buttons. Larkin sighs from the other side of the room.

"Mind if I take a look?" Char Flores offers. Flores is our newest addition to the office, but has already established herself as our IT guru.

Jesse shrugs, pushing back from the table.

Flores kneels next to Jesse and pulls in the laptop. Instead of tapping, she stares at the screen. She stands and shoves a hand in her right pocket, and does the same with her left. "Forgot, no cell phones. The laptop's not connected to the Wi-Fi. Let me grab my phone outside to see if it's a problem with the computer or with the building's Wi-Fi."

"Fuck." Larkin scowls. He leans forward and mashes a button on a small plastic console with a wire coming out of it. "Robin?"

The intercom is silent.

"Robin?"

No answer.

Larkin scans the room and stops at me. "Zahn. Go ask Robin to check the Wi-Fi, would you?"

I pop to my feet. I'm probably the second or third oldest deputy in the room, but also the most junior. If Sheriff Larkin told me to go brew a pot of coffee, I'd ask how he takes it.

When I turn the handle, nothing happens. I turn harder. The door is locked. I check the button that locks the door from my side, but that's not the problem. A keyed deadbolt is visible through the crack in the door. I was the last person to enter the room. There's no way to turn that deadbolt from the inside.

I turn to Larkin. "Door's locked. From the outside."

Larkin flushes. "What the fuck?" He pushes the intercom button again and takes a breath. Losing his temper in front of his subordinates is not part of Leadership 101.

"Robin?" His voice is even. "Thank you for securing the room. We're having Wi-Fi issues. Could you please unlock the door so we can check it out?"

Silence.

Sheriff Larkin isn't the only one frustrated. By all rights, Perez and I should be out in the field controlling the accident scene and doing things instead of spending our time trying to reboot a Wi-Fi system and engage in a Zoom call. We've got our entire sheriff's office crammed in a small room, our local police forces covering our normal duties, and minimal law enforcement covering the largest incident this county has dealt with in years.

And this is just my brain screaming at me. In the back of my mind, is the niggling certainty that the longer we take to organize this operation with the state and feds, the more likely we're going to be working straight through the night. This means the odds of me seeing Daria and Emma tomorrow are dwindling. After years of war, family tragedy, and chaos, I'm the king of compartmentalization. The helicopter aircrew are dead. Nothing I can do about that. Our team should be containing the area of operations to find the people responsible for the murder of at least one member of the crew. My boss doesn't agree. Nothing I can do about that.

Now I just want a hint of organization added to this mission so when I leave this meeting, I can see my daughter and girlfriend—even for a few minutes. More importantly, I need to tell them why they should spend at least one night in BV. Possibly more. Whoever shot that crewmember might still be in the area and Daria and Emma are hiking right toward their last known position.

"Shit." Larkin's attempts to hold his temper fail. He slams his fist on the table and pushes back his roller chair. He strides halfway across the room between the table and the seats where Scott and I sit. A ring dangles from the blackout blinds keeping our room invisible from outside observers.

Larkin tugs the ring, then releases it. The shade springs upward with a clatter revealing cubicles on each side and a corridor leading toward Robin's desk. Robin sits in her chair.

Instead of facing toward the building's entrance, Robin's chair is turned toward the room we occupy.

"What the—?" Larkin's voice is low. Everyone swivels their chairs.

Robin's eyes are wide. Her hands are clasped between her legs. A man wearing a black ski mask stands next to her. An AR-15 barrel touches the side of her head.

11-HAVOC 23

(THREE YEARS BEFORE)

Salida, Colorado-July 2, 2019

Shavano died last week. Everyone expected it. The venerable crew chief had been diagnosed with multiple myeloma early in the year. From the time word got out, Ethan never talked to his crewmate again, relying on updates from Doubles on his condition.

Although Shavano took his last breath in the Albany Medical Center Oncology Wing in New York, his final resting place was never in question. Over two hundred people journey to the small town Shavano never stopped talking about—Salida, Colorado—to mourn the loss of a man who lived a life larger than anyone Ethan has ever known.

A convoy of vehicles rolls from the highway through Fairview Cemetery toward the gravesite. Ethan walks alongside the rest of the mourners on a trek from the main cemetery's entrance overwhelmed at the number of guests he recognizes. National Guard coworkers he's only seen in flight suits or jeans back in New York sport crisp Class A uniforms like himself, medals dangling from their chests.

Despite the Arkansas River's twisty route through this mountain valley, the land is yellow, rocky, and arid. Pockets of trees line the river and sparse cottonwood groves mark irrigation canals. A water source connects to Fairview Cemetery somewhere because both coniferous and deciduous trees tower over the rows of graves.

Ethan spots Horse between two stands of trees, surveying the mountains overlooking the western side of the valley. Horse turns as Ethan joins him.

"When did you get here?" He hasn't flown with Horse in almost six months. Ethan should have reached out when people started making arrangements to attend the service.

"Last night. You?"

"Drove in from Colorado Springs this morning. Sorry—I should have asked you about splitting a rental. Or sharing a room."

Horse's gaze returns to the mountains. "I stayed with his mother again."

Ethan tilts his head at Horse, then follows his eyes to the mountains. He's unsure which words surprise him the most. That Horse knows Shavano's mother, or the "again" implying he's been here before. "How—"

Horse's points straight ahead, interrupting. "That's Shavano. Right there."

Ethan's chest tightens. He turns to Horse to check his expression. Is this a joke?

Horse's finger aims at the largest mountain on the valley's edge and Ethan suddenly gets it. Shavano. Mount Shavano. Gary "Shavano" Bissonnette's namesake, the majestic fourteen-thousand-foot peak that dominates the town of Salida and overlooks the cemetery.

"Can you see the angel?" Horse's voice is quiet. He doesn't drop his finger.

"What angel?"

"The Angel of Shavano. Look at the snow from bottom to top. See how it channels up the ravine on the approach to the mountain, then spreads into wings near the saddle?"

As soon as Horse explains it, Ethan gets it. A thin white body with delicate arms spreading wide as if embracing the valley below. "I see it. But how did you?"

Horse drops his hand and faces him. Ethan didn't intend to sound mocking; he's just surprised at a new side of Horse.

"No, man. It's a thing. The Angel. Shavano told me about it last summer when we climbed the mountain."

Ethan flinches, then looks back at the mountain. "After he got sick? You and Shavano climbed that thing?"

Horse nods, and glances at his watch. "Hey, it's getting ready to start."

A crowd is gathering about a football field away.

"I went and saw him at his house one day back in Albany," Horse continues. "Doubles was off on a mission. Shavano mentioned you hadn't been around. I just wanted to talk about that Iraq stuff. Do you know what I mean?"

The memories of what they did still haunt Ethan. Not so much that he can't sleep at night. But enough that he, too, had considered talking to Shavano. But he never did. "So, did you talk?"

"Sort of." Horse smiles. "I wanted to talk about the ring he gave me."

Ethan nods. How could he forget?

"And Shavano didn't want to talk about it. Instead, he said if I really wanted to understand what happened in Iraq, I needed to understand where he came from. And we climbed that mountain." Horse tosses his head toward where they had admired The Angel.

The two men stop behind the rear row of guests. A priest works his way from a small group of people to the lectern.

Ethan whispers, "What did he tell you?"

Horse tugs Ethan to step back from the row of people and lowered his voice. "Not a damn thing. We summited, then he collapsed about halfway down the mountain on the way back. Exhaustion. After all the chemo and treatments, the climb ended up being too much. Fortunately, one of his friends with us was on Search and Rescue. She called her teammates, and they wheeled him off the mountain on a litter. After he recovered and returned to New York, we didn't talk about the ring. He was dying. Trying to put his affairs in order."

"I'm surprised his mother is still talking to you. Did she blame you for letting him overdo it?"

Horse laughs. "She knew what he was like. No one tells Shavano what he can and can't do." He nods toward the front row of chairs. "That's her."

Ethan follows Horse's gaze to the frail woman sitting alone in the front row. A tall man with silver hair approaches and leans forward, extending his hand. Shavano's mother jerks her head at the man, ignoring his hand. The man nods and walks away. He slides into the next aisle beside a young Asian woman.

"Wonder what that was all about?" Ethan turns to Horse.

"That's Shavano's half-brother," Horse replies. "Met him at the hospital when SAR brought in Shavano off the mountain."

Ethan studies the man, noting his cropped hair and broad shoulders. "Military?"

"Not sure if he was. He told me he's law enforcement. There's something between those two—Shavano and his brother. Obviously, Mrs. Bissonnette doesn't like him much either."

"I take it they share the same father, then? Not the same mother?"

"That's what Shavano told me." Horse nods toward where the man sits. "And the gal he's sitting with is Kristee Li. She's the SAR team member who climbed with us. I guess she's friends with both brothers."

Ethan spots Doubles sitting three rows back wearing her military uniform and sitting with other members of the 142nd. As if she can sense his presence, Doubles turns to Ethan and Horse, then nods toward empty chairs at the end of the row.

"We've been summoned," Ethan says, moving forward. He turns to Horse. "Why isn't Doubles in the front row? The girlfriend and all."

Horse shakes his head.

Ethan stops. "What?"

"Where have you been?" Horse's smile is thin. "They haven't been dating for a couple of months. He pushed her away after the symptoms started."

Ethan's embarrassed by the surge of joy at Horse's words. What kind of selfish friend is he, celebrating the fact that his dead crewmate is no longer dating the woman he craves? Horse stops to hug Kristee before joining Ethan and the rest of their unit.

The priest opens the ceremony in prayer and presents a completely impersonal eulogy. Shavano's attendance at the local high school, his military career, and how proud the community is of his service to his country could have applied to anyone from this part of Colorado. The generic tone pisses Ethan off. The Shavano he knew was so much more than that.

Before the interment, the priest offers the lectern to anyone who might want to share their memories of Shavano with those in attendance. A moment of awkward silence ensues as no one comes forward. Ethan doesn't feel as if he knew Shavano well enough to speak. He shifts in his chair and spots movement at the end of the aisle.

Doubles strides to the lectern. The priest steps to the side and Doubles adjusts the microphone.

"Good morning. My name is Lisa Brumstock. I served with Shavano—Gary Bissonnette—in the 3rd of the 142nd Aviation Regiment out of Albany. We flew the Black Hawk together. Me sitting up front doing the flying, Shavano in the back running the show."

A couple of Ethan's friends chuckle, recalling what it meant to have the unit's most experienced crew chief on one of their missions.

"We called Gary, 'Shavano.' Did you know that, ma'am?" Doubles pauses as she focuses on Shavano's mother. Mrs. Bissonnette nods her head, but the rest of the locals don't seem to recognize the call sign.

"He chose his call sign because it reminded him of home." Doubles points at the mountain behind the attendees. "He never stopped talking about this place. All of us in the unit probably know more about Colorado and Salida than we do about our own homes."

Everyone in Ethan's row laughs out loud, and Ethan joins them. Shavano wouldn't shut up about Colorado.

"Normally you don't get to pick your own call sign. But we let Shavano have it. Do you know why?" Ethan shakes his head. Doubles continues. "Because he was big like a mountain—not just physically, but his personality too. Like the currents you have in your river out there." Doubles opens her arms wide to the river valley. "When you got sucked into his sphere, it was hard to get out. And you didn't want to."

"Shavano and I were in a relationship for the last several years." Doubles' voice goes up in pitch, and Ethan worries whether she'll keep it together. "I loved him." She pauses. "We fell for each other on a support mission to Turkey—a mission that turned dicey when we were sent into Iraq to support the Iraqi Army. Shavano's courage carried the day for us. I was scared. The crew was scared."

Doubles fixes her gaze on Ethan and he nods almost involuntarily.

"But he got us out of there. And I'll never forget that." Doubles chokes on her words, before continuing. "He wasn't perfect, though. He suffered from the same worldly wants and desires as all of us. But Shavano was brave, kind, and served our country well." Doubles wipes a tear from her eye and turns to the casket. She calls over her shoulder, "Battalion, tench hut."

Ethan rises with his unit. Doubles renders a salute and holds it. The rest of the unit follows suit. Ten seconds pass. Doubles drops her salute. Ethan lowers his hand. Doubles turns to her battalion members and dips her chin. Everyone standing sits.

Mrs. Bissonnette sobs as Doubles returns to her seat. Ethan's crewmate's gesture—taking the lectern when no one else would—saves the funeral for a silent crowd who seemed to know Shavano but failed to grasp the full measure of the man.

As the priest returns to the lectern, the silver-haired man stands and steps forward. "I'd like to say a few words about my—"

Mrs. Bissonnette calls out, "No."

The man stops, raising his hand toward the lectern indicating he has something to say.

Mrs. Bissonnette shakes her head. "That pilot's words were enough." She glares at the priest. "Bury my boy."

Horse lets out a low whistle.

"What's going on here?" Ethan says.

Horse mutters, "Small towns."

12-ZAHN

Salida, Colorado-July 12, 2022

The reaction in our meeting room could be a case study of paradigm shifts. I'm locked in with seven men and one woman, all law enforcement officers, and appropriately armed…except for me. At this moment, we may be the densest concentration of firepower in the entire county.

The blind spools up, and Larkin mutters in disbelief. The reaction of the rest of the room is almost synchronous. The deputies rise from their chairs, draw their weapons, and move to the window as one.

Robin's head tilts to the side as the barrel of the automatic shoves harder into her skull.

A voice crackles behind us from the table intercom. *Put your weapons down. You are to remain in the room. Any attempt to interfere with our operations will result in the death of your coworker here.*

I pivot between the intercom and the window. The commands are not coming from the man holding Robin. Her intercom connection is behind her desk, which means at least two individuals are involved in this. Jesse and Scott secure their weapons and cup their hands against the windows, peering into the outer office area.

The voice continues. *Yes. You all are—how should I make it clear—in our crosshairs.*

Flores and the remainder of the deputies still hold their weapons, although everyone points them down. I can't tell if their compliance is in the hopes the gunman will pull the barrel out of Robin's ear or because they realize we don't have a lot of options.

Flores turns to Sheriff Larkin. "Sir?"

Larkin still stands by the window. I'm unsurprised he didn't react to the gunman. When you have seven personnel working for you that react in less than a second, you can take some time to contemplate the next steps.

"Stand down," the sheriff says, moving back toward his end of the table.

Sanders turns to our boss. "Sir, I don't think—"

"Sanders, shut the fuck up. Put your weapons away. Robin is out there with a gun to her head and we're sitting in here like fish in a barrel. Zahn, close that blind."

I follow Larkin's instructions.

"Turn out the lights," Larkin commands. He reaches for the intercom transmitter and gathers the cord so he can move with it. Flores flips the switch, and the room goes semi-dark, with a dim glow from the edges of the blinds and a steady red light emitting from the intercom. "We need to find out what the hell's happening here. Unless they got in here and bugged this room, we should be able to talk. Get down on the floor and spread out while I contact them. We need to figure out what they want."

I move past the door, bumping into Sanders as we make our way to the far side of the room. No one is going to hang out near the windows facing the armed men.

"This is Sheriff Brad Larkin. Explain yourselves." Larkin's voice is firm, and I assume he's using the intercom. Probably from the floor.

Nice job with the lights, Sheriff. Night, night.

"Identify yourself. What are your intentions?" Larkin's voice is louder as if volume will prompt a response.

No one answers.

Larkin's last transmission carried both the mistaken belief that he has any sense of control and a trace of emotion. He tries again.

"We are standing by for intent."

Silence.

•   •   •

The intercom remains silent for the next twelve hours. We spend the first hour assessing our resources and options.

"If they don't talk, then we don't know motive or intent," Larkin says. "Let's think about how to either get help or get out. Anybody?"

Perez takes the lead on the discussion. "Comms. Let's do an inventory of what we have to communicate with."

Powers' voice is first. "No phones. No radios. We put them all in Robin's box."

Flores says, "I'm guessing flares and a signal mirror aren't going to do us any good. Not like we can run off anywhere and send a smoke signal."

"Run…run," Perez says. "I got my GPS watch. It's no smartphone, but I can connect through to my fitness app."

"Can you send a message on it?" I say.

"No."

"We don't have to tell anyone," Sanders says. "They're going to figure it out within the next couple of hours."

Larkin nods. "Unless those guys are forcing Robin to answer the phone, people are going to know something's wrong here when their 911 calls go unanswered."

"Then what?" Powers says.

"Then every county and state resource will be piling into Salida. When's the last time you heard of a hostage situation in a public building outside of Denver?" Larkin says.

No one speaks.

"Which brings me to my next news. You all aren't going to like this, but we're not breaking out of here." Larkin's voice sounds resigned.

"We don't even try?" Flores says.

"We can brainstorm all we want. It'll be good to have an option if the opportunity arises. But as long as they have weapons trained on us and a gun on Robin, we're not risking it. Not when we know trained hostage teams will be on site soon."

Our unsuccessful planning session complete, we turn to more immediate problems. Like where to relieve ourselves. Again, Larkin attempts to contact our captors through the intercom, citing food, water, and bathroom necessities. We receive no answer.

When Jesse Sanders informs the rest of us he plans to pee in a corner, I suggest the coffee urn. We dump the remaining coffee in the corner and use the eight-cup brewing pot.

I drift off to sleep with no expectation of a full night's rest. I wake with a stiff neck, but seven hours of sleep under my belt.

•   •   •

"We're pissing in the coffee pot, and we got two people ready to shit in the corner. If you're still listening to this, we could use some help." Larkin shakes his head and turns to Perez. "How do we know they're still here? They might have taken Robin and just left last night."

Perez shrugs. "I'd say this is an emergency. Let's work on the door and see what they say. If they're still here and heard your last transmission, then they know why we would try to get out."

I assume that a bunch of cops should be able to work the deadbolt free of the doorjamb but it takes a good amount of time just to decide which tool we should use.

Flores explains that if we take the knob off, we'll have better access to the deadbolt. She wants the screwdriver from one multi-tool combined with the blade from another. Sanders is convinced the seam between the door and the frame is the answer and we need to be prying instead of picking.

"Fine. Play with the knob," Sanders says. "I'll stand by with my blade."

Although the room remains dark, we've been trapped inside long enough to acquire night vision. Sanders's silhouette is visible on one side of the door. Flores kneels in front of the doorknob. It's too dark to see the screws, so she works by feel.

She whispers, "There's one. Now I just need to—"

The sound of automatic fire rips through the building. Sparks fly through the ceiling above Flores. Her shadowy figure tumbles backward. I scramble toward her and reach her side as Sanders approaches from the other direction.

"Are you hit?" I say.

The bullet holes above us glow yellow from the outside lights, providing just enough illumination for Flores's eyes to shine. "No." She releases her breath. "That scared the fuck out of me."

Sheriff, I thought I told you all to sit tight? The intercom blares from the table. A figure moves toward the device.

Larkin answers. "We've been calling. We need—"

A squeal interrupts Larkin's transmission. He must have released the button because our captor speaks next. *I'll tell you what you need and don't need. We heard your bathroom complaints. We're going to open the door now. You will receive two plastic five-gallon buckets. One has food. The other toilet supplies. Don't mix them up.*

A loud thud-thud echoes on the meeting room door.

That's your DoorDash calling. Before they open the door, you move your personnel to the opposite end of the room. The delivery team is armed with the same weapon that put the holes in your ceiling. Any false moves mean more holes.

We wait for Larkin to respond, but when he speaks, it's obvious he's talking to the room.

"You heard him. Flores, Zahn, Sanders—move back here."

Flores scrambles to her feet and moves toward Larkin. Sanders and I follow.

Larkin presses the intercom. "We've moved away from the door."

From outside the meeting room, a muffled yell is just audible. "They're clear. Open the door."

At the opposite end of the room, a wedge of light appears as the door swings halfway open. I wait for the doorknob to fall off and our escape efforts to be discovered. But the knob holds fast.

The plastic buckets hit the carpeted floor with a soft thud, and the door slams shut. A metallic click indicates our captors haven't forgotten to deadbolt the door behind them.

"That's it?" Perez says in a low voice.

"Zahn, go check what they gave us."

I move to the end of the room and grab the buckets, dragging them under the small bullet holes still allowing beams of light to enter our space. I pry off the lids. Two rolls of toilet paper sit inside the first bucket.

"The first bucket is our new toilet," I report to Larkin.

The remaining bucket is stuffed with sub sandwiches—the kind you'd find in the deli section of a grocery store—and bottles of water.

"Perez won't be happy with the food," I say.

"Let me guess, a bucket of ground beef?" vegetarian Perez replies.

"Nope. Ham sandwiches."

The room is silent. We've been stuck here for almost twelve hours and have reverted from planning to escape to worrying about our basic survival needs.

"I call your ham," Sanders says. "I'm starved."

13-DARIA

Colorado Trail south of Cottonwood Pass-July 13, 2022

Four miles past Cottonwood Pass, Daria regrets skipping the Buena Vista stop. The altitude isn't the issue—they're descending from over eleven thousand feet, the air thickening with every step—but her Achilles tendons scream for a break.

Daria debated wearing hi-top hiking boots but went for trail runners instead. Most hikers she's met have made the same choice. Boots are out; low-cut running shoes with decent cushion and thick knobs for traction are in. Daria's feel great—except for the heel collars, which rub against her tendons.

She drops her pack and sits next to Emma. "This part right here." She lifts her shoe and points to the offending piece. "The bane of my existence."

"Should we have your dad bring new shoes?"

"Maybe. Or maybe I can fix these."

"How?"

"Cut off the piece that's rubbing."

Emma tilts her head. "You going to do it now?"

"I'm not walking another step without trying it first."

Emma checks her map app. "We're like a quarter mile from a stream crossing." She taps her water bottle. "I'm out. Do you mind if I hike ahead and start filtering?"

Daria loves this idea. She doesn't need advice on how to slice up her $150 shoes. She'd rather make her mistakes all on her own. "Knock yourself out. I'll catch up with you in ten minutes or so."

She unclips the small pocketknife from her pack and pulls off her right shoe. Several minutes of slicing later and the offending material is gone. She tries it on, walks a few steps. Better. She repeats the process with the left shoe, stuffs the scraps in her pack—leave no trace—and sets off.

The trail crests a rise that her map app identifies as Wander Ridge. Wind whips her face as she takes in the view. Before her is a draw feeding into the distant Mineral Basin. A mountain lake rests halfway down, rockslides paused at the banks as if afraid to touch the water. The vibrant green of the willow thickets provides a sharp contrast to the iron-stained orange and tans of the surrounding ridges.

This vista is no more spectacular than yesterday's Lake Ann Pass panorama, but she is literally standing on the Continental Divide of the United States. The basin in the distance carries water that flows into the Mississippi River, and on to the Gulf of Mexico, to become part of the Atlantic Ocean.

She turns around and stares west. Taylor Park Reservoir shines blue like a giant opal slipped from the sky's pocket. That water flows into the Gunnison River, to the Colorado River, and on to the Pacific. Not many people get the opportunity to straddle the high point of the continent.

A distant throb draws her eyes to the horizon. A black speck—a helicopter—moves the same direction they are hiking. Maybe it's part of the mission her dad is on.

The trail switchbacks like a shoelace down into the draw. Daria shades her eyes and traces the path, searching for Emma. At the rockslide, a flash of blue—Emma's jacket. She's not alone.

Water stops are common meetup points, but Daria quickens her pace. It'll take a few minutes to reach Emma. The stranger must be a NOBO—a northbound hiker—or a day hiker heading back to Cottonwood Pass. No way they caught up with any SOBO hikers.

Emma waves as Daria rounds the last bend before the stream. Daria lifts her hand in response, sizing up Emma's newest companion. He's Emma's age, his hair cropped short. Her first guess is middle-aged, but then she remembers Emma is only thirty-seven and wouldn't appreciate that label.

Daria loosens her pack, assessing the man's tan Frogg-Toggs rain jacket, popular among budget-conscious thru-hikers. She has a similar blue set stuffed in the back pocket of her pack.

Emma turns from filtering her water and points at the man. Her hand quivers slightly, probably from the icy mountain water. "This is Moldy Beans. Moldy—or should I call you Beans?—this is Little Z, my hiking buddy."

Moldy Beans glances at Emma. "Beans works." He turns to Daria. "Hey, Z. What's up?"

Daria smiles. "Do I even want to know the story?"

Beans shakes his head. "Tried to DIY freeze dry my food. So I could avoid those ten-dollar backpacking meals. I had fellow hikers watching when I opened up my rice and beans special. It was—"

"Moldy?"

Beans grins.

"NOBO?" Daria gestures behind her.

Beans flicks his eyes toward Emma.

Emma says, "SOBO. He's hiking in our direction."

"We didn't see you in front of us on the ridgeline," Daria says. "You must have been here a while."

"Yeah, mid-morning nap. When Em—Mud Hen, sorry, started splashing around, she woke me up."

Daria looks at Beans. "So, the helicopter crash? Know anything more about it?"

"Yeah, she told me," Beans says, his eyes widening. "No survivors?"

"That's what we heard. Mud Hen and I figure we'll be walking pretty close to the site tomorrow. I saw a helicopter flying in that direction just ten minutes ago."

"Where was it?" Beans says.

Daria points. "About ten miles away."

Beans follows her finger and stares in that direction. Finally, he turns back. "How far are you two hiking each day?"

Daria glances at Emma. "Around fifteen. A little less the last couple of days." She doesn't mention her injury.

"You want to hike along with us?" Emma says. She raises her eyebrows at Daria, who can't tell if she's apologizing for asking Beans the question without Daria's consent, or if she's checking for her approval.

Beans seems to pick up on their non-verbals and turns to Daria. "That OK with you?"

Daria doesn't mind hiking with a stranger. That's what thru-hiking is all about—meeting new people, having new experiences, embracing change. But she doesn't want to slow Beans down. "As long as our pace doesn't mess up your schedule."

"Sweet. I'm tired of hiking alone."

Daria and Emma have crossed paths with dozens of hikers on this first half of their trek. Emma hasn't invited anyone to join them before and Daria's not sure how she feels about her dad's girlfriend inviting a man of her same age to join them.

14-HAVOC 23

(TWO and a HALF YEARS BEFORE)

Albany, New York-January 10, 2020

"What do you want to do, Ethan?" Doubles' head bends close so Ethan can hear her over the buzz surrounding their back table at McGeary's. The rest of the company huddles around a dartboard set between two pool tables or bellied up to the bar.

Her suggestion for them to grab a table had been so unexpected that Ethan hadn't considered conversation. Now he has no idea how deep Doubles' question probes. What does he want to do tonight? What does he dream about doing with Doubles? Or what does he want to do with his life?

"Talk. I want to talk with you. It seems like we just pass each other in the hallways at ops and never get a chance to catch up." He studies her eyes, trying to decipher if his answer is right.

Doubles grins. "My question was more existential, Ethan." She pauses and reaches for his hand. Ethan checks to see if anybody in his unit is watching. No one pays attention to them. "But you're right. We need to catch up. I've been preoccupied." She pulls her hand back.

Ethan wishes she hadn't. "I know. It's hard to believe it's only been six months since the funeral."

"That's not been the problem." She sighs. "It was already over when he died. Yes, I was torn up about it. I loved him. But it wasn't like I lost a soulmate. There was a reason we broke up. Do you want to hear about it?"

"No." The last thing Ethan wants to do is rehash Doubles' and Shavano's relationship—good or bad.

Doubles blows a puff of air. "You don't care."

"I care too much."

"I didn't know you and Shavano were so close."

"We weren't. Damn it, Lisa…you know why I care."

"Then why don't you do something about it, Ethan? Where's the man I met in Turkey? Cutting loose on the dance floor. First to raise his hand on a combat mission to Iraq. Where's the pilot who volunteered to put his life in danger to do the right thing by those Iraqi soldiers? When I think of you—and I think of you more than you know—that's the man I remember. Not the polite 'we never get a chance to catch up' man."

Ethan's face flushes. "I'm right here, damn it. I'm just waiting out of respect for what you and Shavano had. Look at it from my point of view. If I ask too soon, you might never give me a second chance."

Doubles' hand returns to Ethan's and squeezes it. "If you don't ask tonight, you might not get another chance."

Portsmouth, New Hampshire-July 10, 2020

"Want to share secrets, handsome?" Doubles' sultry voice freezes Ethan in place. He grins, glancing right and left as if ensuring she hasn't mistaken him for someone else. Their sister crew clusters around a table at the opposite end of the Portsmouth bar, Horse spinning another "back when I was in Iraq" tale. Both crews landed less than an hour ago, rushing to check in so they could hit the bar before the bottle-to-throttle cutoff time for tomorrow's mission.

Ethan opens his mouth to deliver a suave reply but ends up gaping at his girlfriend like a fish wondering how the hook got stuck in its mouth.

"What's the matter, Big Boy? You look a little flustered."

That's an understatement. Six months after Shavano's funeral, Ethan asked Doubles out on their first date. Another six months have passed, and he still can't believe they're an item. And now, she has that glow in her eyes just like when she stepped off the makeshift dance floor in Batman, Turkey. Except now he's part of the moment.

"Here? What about them?" Ethan nods to the other table. "And Horse?"

Doubles smirks. "I'm not that kind of girl, Ethan. Not into multiple partners and all."

Ethan flushes. If he leaves with Doubles, the crew will know. But Doubles already seems to know what he's thinking.

"Do you really think the whole *us* is a secret? There's no way in the 3/142nd that a crew romance goes undiscovered," Doubles teases. "Besides, I had to tell Horse."

Ethan hesitates, then sits again. "Why? Not that I care, but why?"

"I let it slip when we were doing Shavano's estate stuff. Right after you and I started seeing each other."

Ethan hasn't given a thought to Shavano's house, furniture, or personal possessions. "Why was Horse involved? I get you—you and Shavano dated for so long. But why Horse?"

"Shavano put it in his will after they got back from that glory days trip to Colorado. The one where they tried to climb the mountain with that search and rescue woman, and Shavano had to get his ass carried down by her teammates? They must have bonded because as soon as Shavano got back, he appointed Horse his executor in his will."

"And you?"

"He left me something too. That's why I was there."

Ethan's first thought is Shavano's Corvette. "The car?" But he's only seen Doubles drive her BMW.

"No. Got any other guesses, Ethan?" She gives him a knowing look. The bracelet.

If he brings it up, she'll wonder how he knew. Unless she already knows. Shit.

"No idea," he lies.

"Oh come on. Take a stab at it."

Ethan stares at Doubles. Her choice of words is no accident. Her grin has narrowed to a thin smile. He realizes they're not leaving for her bedroom without having this conversation.

"A bracelet." Ethan makes it a statement rather than a question. He knows that's what Doubles is talking about.

Doubles nods. "A bracelet." She points at Horse across the bar. "A ring." She turns back to Ethan. "A knife. The only difference between what he gave you and Horse and what he gave me is timing. Why do you think he waited until he died to give me the bracelet?"

Ethan knows the answer to this question, but it shames him to say it out loud. Shavano gave Horse and him the Iraqi soldier's possessions because he knew they would take them. "He probably thought you wouldn't accept the bracelet if he gave it to you while he was still alive? I don't think you would have."

"You're spot on. Now that I'm stuck with the thing, I have to figure out what to do with it. How to make it right."

Ethan's face flushes more than it had when she'd invited him to bed. Why hadn't he considered this when Shavano died? It was bad enough that the knife has been sitting in his underwear drawer for four years, a dagger of guilt hiding among his personal possessions. Now Doubles has highlighted the obvious. Why not figure out the name of the dead soldier and see about returning these possessions to his family?

"I could help with that," Ethan says. "I've felt guilty about it ever since he gave it to me. If you decide to return the bracelet to the Iraqi soldier's family, I'd like to be a part of that. To give the knife back." Ethan nods toward Horse. "Horse might too. I haven't talked to him about it, but maybe we could give all three things back to his family."

Any semblance of a smile drops from Doubles' face. "Ethan. What are you talking about? What Iraqi soldier?"

"The torn-up body bag. These things had to have come from the remains of the guy in the bag. Where did you think Shavano got the bracelet from? You mean you didn't know?"

Doubles shakes her head. "You're missing the big picture here. We're not talking about one Iraqi soldier. We're talking about a country's heritage. I tried to explain this to Horse, but he won't get involved with returning anything. You know why?"

Ethan shakes his head in confusion. *A country's heritage? What is she talking about?*

Doubles says, "Because he sold the ring."

"What? He pawned off a dead soldier's family ring for cash?" It was one thing to keep the memento. Another to profit from it. Add another to the list of military offenses Ethan is a part of.

Doubles moves closer. "For a hundred thousand in cash," she whispers, just loud enough to be heard over the music. "And he got taken."

"What do you mean by taken?"

"He found out the guy sold it on an auction site the next week for $1.1 million. The buyer was advertising it as part of The Treasures of Nimrud." Doubles forms air quotes with her fingers.

"You mean—"

"I got my bracelet appraised. The jeweler told me it's about 3,000 years old. He told me to go to a museum. That he wasn't qualified to put an estimate on it. But he did say it couldn't be worth less than $2.5 million. Probably more." She shakes her head. "These aren't personal possessions of a dead Iraqi war hero, Ethan. These are artifacts from the Assyrian Empire, looted from the archeological site where Iraq fought ISIL. Who knows how much your knife is worth?"

Portsmouth, New Hampshire-July 11, 2020

The next morning they pick at rubbery eggs and packaged muffins while rain lashes the breakfast bar windows. Both crews are on a weather hold.

Doubles says, "This stuff isn't ours, and I'm not going to be the Army warrant officer accused of stealing a country's treasure. Do you see where I'm coming from?"

Relief washes over Ethan. He's spent four years wrestling with guilt, but Doubles sees the bigger picture—the reputation of their unit, the Army, and their country.

She continues, "We don't know if Shavano knew what he was giving us or not—whether he thought it was a dead man's possessions or if he knew it was from the site. Did he tell you anything?"

"No. We never talked about it. Horse said they were going to talk on that Colorado trip, but it never happened. I don't think Horse knows the stuff is treasure. We talked about it belonging to the dead guy."

Doubles cocks her head. "Did you hear me when I told you he got taken when he sold the ring? He knows. We've talked about it. He's way more worried about losing the $100K he's already got when I raise the flag and try to give the stuff back. And he's still pissed he didn't get the million."

"What's your plan? Our plan? And why did you wait so long to tell me?"

Doubles glances around the empty breakfast bar. Report time isn't until ten a.m. and the other crew is probably sleeping off their late night. "First, I wanted to make sure you were on board with returning our relics. The bracelet and the knife."

"Yes." Ethan doesn't hesitate.

"I thought so. We'll talk about how we do that later. But right now, I need your help with something Shavano left behind." She reaches into her flight suit pocket and grabs her cell phone. She taps a button and hands it to Ethan.

Ethan uses his thumb and forefinger to expand the picture. "This is an instrument chart." He moves closer to the screen. "An L-13. These are all electronic now. How did you get one?"

Doubles smiles. "Not everyone is one hundred percent digital. I mean yes, the Guard is. The airlines are. But if you're a charter airline or private pilot and can't afford the redundancy of our electronic flight bags, then you might have one of these."

"OK." Ethan doesn't say anything more. It's not like Doubles to play guessing games, so he assumes she'll tell him the significance.

"Shavano wrapped the bracelet in this flight chart like a Christmas gift or something."

"Are you suggesting it means something?"

"I didn't think so at first. My dad was a pilot too. Fixed-wing. He used to save his charts like these when they expired and use them for wrapping Christmas and birthday presents. These white charts meant the gift was going to an adult. He'd use expired VFR sectionals, you know, with yellow and green for the kids' gifts. So I didn't think it was too weird."

"Until?"

"Until I opened Shavano's gift to me. And read what was inside."

"I thought you said it was the bracelet?"

"It was. When I handed it to Horse to look at, I saw writing on the inside of the map. On the L14 side."

Ethan waits.

"It was a note from Shavano. It said, 'Now you have what is yours. If you want what is mine, use our crew. Our mission to take those fallen soldiers home added to the 3/142nd's history. I'm proud of that. And proud of you. Consider this a token of my appreciation. M1981199.'"

"What the hell does that mean?"

"I have no clue. Until I saw the note, I hadn't considered the fact that Shavano probably took something as well. Why would he give something to us and not keep something for himself?"

"What did Horse think? Any ideas?"

"That's the thing, Ethan. When I opened the package, I didn't even know about Horse's ring and your knife. He hadn't told me yet. I just had this feeling that something was wrong about all this." She lets out a breath. "Shavano? Dropping clues? WTF? I *still* haven't told Horse."

"Don't you think we should? Shavano made it sound like he wanted it to be a crew effort."

"Stop it. This isn't a *Pirates of the Caribbean* thing where we band together for a treasure hunt. I told you because I knew you'd want to do the right thing. When I mentioned to Horse that I was returning the bracelet to the Iraqi government, he went ballistic. The guy doesn't have a sliver of integrity when it comes to money." She shakes her head. "We don't have to throw Horse under the bus for this. We'll send my bracelet and your knife back anonymously. When we get whatever Shavano had, we'll return it the same way. I'm OK with letting Horse's ring go. Hell, he didn't know what he was doing." Doubles scans the room again. "But I need you to help me solve this." She taps her phone. "Sound good?"

Ethan nods. He's loved this woman since the moment he walked into the unit. Fate ended Shavano's life. But it's also brought him and Doubles together.

"Beyond good, Lisa."

Doubles' eyes widen. Ethan only calls her by her given name behind closed doors.

"I love you," he says.

15-ZAHN

Salida, Colorado-July 13, 2022

Something's not sitting well with Sheriff Larkin. A few minutes after we finish our sandwiches, Larkin begins wheezing. The bullet holes in the ceiling allow enough light for us to distinguish each other. Larkin leans sideways at the end of the table.

Flores moves toward him. "What's up, Boss?"

Larkin claws at his collar. "Breath. I can't catch it. Heart…"

"He's choking," Powers says.

"Not if he's talking." Sanders, one of two EMT-certified members in our office, joins Flores. "Get him on the floor. Loosen his collar."

I glance from Larkin to the door. Maybe this is an opportunity.

I crawl to Perez. "We need to use this to get out."

Perez shakes his head. "Even if those guys out there give a shit, do you think they're going to drop those weapons when they pull him out?"

"No. But what if they don't know how many folks we got? They took over the building after we were already in place." I point to the ceiling tiles. "You could go now. Use Larkin as a distraction to get out of this place."

Perez's gaze follows my finger. "Not your worst idea. But I'm the number two guy in the office. Don't you think they'll figure out I'm gone?"

Sanders shouts, "Get those guys on speaker. Pulse rate's elevated. He's hyperventilating. We need to get him out of here."

Flores scrambles toward the intercom.

I say, "They probably don't know about us reserve deputies. Powers or I could go."

"I can't quite picture Scott crawling across the ceiling tiles," Perez whispers.

"Right."

Flores's voice is high-pitched, but firm on the intercom. *This is the meeting room. We have a medical emergency. You need to get him out of here.*

"Rick, if it's going to happen, I need to get up there now."

"They'll shoot first, Z-man. You sure?"

I'm not. Daria's old enough not to need me. But I need her. And I'm scared as shit. But they could start picking us off one by one until they get whatever they want. I can't wait to find out.

We don't even know if the outside world is aware of what's happening here. If not, I can sound the alarm. I glance toward Larkin, but all I can see are the squared toes of his regulation cowboy boots.

"I'm sure." I snag a chair from the table.

Who's sick? The sarcastic voice drawls through the intercom.

Sheriff Larkin. He can't breathe.

Perez says, "I need to let Larkin know—"

"Rick, you can tell him when—if—they bring him back." I step on the chair and onto the table. "Hand me the chair."

Perez hoists the chair onto the table, crawls up next to me, and braces it in place. I push a ceiling tile straight up and slide it to the side. Two pipes run a foot-and-a-half above the tile ceiling, one above the other with a six-inch gap.

Neither Flores nor Scott moves to help.

Same deal. Back away from the door unless you want to get shot.

"Get back from the door. They're coming," Flores calls.

Perez shouts over Flores, "Moving everybody your way."

We understand. We're moving everyone now.

"I need another six inches," I tell Perez. "Brace that thing. I'm using the armrests."

Perez straddles the chair for support. I place my right foot on the right armrest, balancing myself on the thin metal framework, and step up, stabbing my left foot toward the other armrest. The chair twists slightly, but I'm high enough to grab the pipes. With a pipe in each hand, I pull my feet toward my head.

My abs scream. I wasn't good at gymnastics as a teenager, let alone approaching fifty. I tuck my feet through the hole like a WWII pilot climbing into the belly entrance of a B-17. My feet clear the hole, and I extend my left leg, wedging my ankle between the two pipes.

A crash sounds below me. Perez has knocked the chair off the table. He rights it and joins the others surrounding Larkin.

I drag the panel back across the opening below me. Three loud raps on the door below echo through the roof tiles.

"Back away from the door."

Everyone below has worked their way toward the two men tending to Sheriff Larkin. Lights flash against the ceiling tiles closest to the door, sending pinpoints dancing onto the pipes above me. They're using flashlights or headlamps, so we can't see their faces. But it's difficult to take attendance with a flashlight in the dark.

"Move it, move it, move it!" The voices below boom with precision rather than panic. Like boot camp drill sergeants, they only raise their voices to add tension to the scenario. I have no idea how many of our captors have entered the room. Probably more than two, simply because they wouldn't want to risk being overpowered.

I move across the ceiling space but freeze when my butt brushes against the flimsy tile below me. Whether our captors take Larkin away or not, they will eventually leave the room. I need to wait. Upside down, my arms and legs clinging to a pipe, my abs ache like I'm in one of Ruth's community center yoga sessions. Both forearms twitch, and a burn radiates toward my shoulders.

Namaste, my ass.

16-DARIA

Colorado Trail near Emma Burr Mountain-July 13, 2022
Daria's shoe surgery works. Three minor mountain passes remain between the hikers and the road to Tincup Pass where they plan to camp, but on the toughest trail day so far, her heels don't hurt.

When they reviewed the trek back in Denver, she and Emma glossed over these elevation bumps, paying more attention to the big climbs. But bouncing between eleven- and twelve-thousand feet all day long, a 500-foot climb is plenty to take her breath away and make her legs burn like 400-meter intervals in high school track practice.

They stop for lunch, and Daria does a double take at Beans' menu choices. He's got a package of Sour Patch candy wedged between his legs while he shakes a miniature bottle of Tabasco sauce over a four-inch cracker.

"That's lunch?" Daria says. "Candy and hot sauce?"

Emma glances up from her stove. "Really, Beans? Get a cup. I'll split mine with you."

Beans flushes. "My first long hike. I didn't exactly do a lot of research. The trail was kind of a last-minute, impulse decision."

"What do you have planned for dinner? Twizzlers and hot chocolate?" Daria grins but she's not kidding. "What about your tent and your sleeping bag? What do you have?"

"Little Z." Emma's voice pitches up at the end like she's reprimanding Daria.

"What?"

"Weren't you complaining about all the so-called experts asking us about our gear so they could tell us what we should have brought?"

One out of every three conversations with thru-hikers inevitably turns to gear. How heavy is it? How warm is it? Or how waterproof? And it's guaranteed that whoever is offering advice isn't going to listen to Daria's answer and say, "Oh, that sounds perfect." More likely she'll get a five-minute briefing on the other hiker's wise purchase of the latest technology.

"Busted," Daria says. "Sorry, Beans."

Beans appears relieved Daria isn't going to make him empty his pack out for inspection. "I'm still getting the hang of the food." He points at Emma's freeze-dried meals. "I might try those next."

"Where are you planning on resupplying?" Daria senses Emma's eyes on her. She turns to Emma and mouths, "What?" Not an unreasonable question if they're going to hike together. When she looks back at Beans, he's looking over her shoulder like he's trying to spot a grocery store.

"Maybe Gunnison?"

Daria glances at Emma, who's messing with her stove and doesn't meet Daria's eyes. Gunnison is an hour's drive west from their next paved road crossing. Turning east to Salida is half the distance. Beans might be the most clueless hiker Daria has met on the trail so far.

•   •   •

By mid-afternoon they've topped the last pitch before their descent to the Tincup Pass road. The trail arcs in front of them in the shape of a "C," skirting a 13-er named Emma Burr, before disappearing over a saddle. Daria's phone app shows the path from the saddle to the river valley below will switchback like the "Z" in her last name on repeat. The wind whips at these mini-summits, so the hikers descend a hundred yards to a flat rock for a break.

"All downhill from here," Beans says with a grin.

Beans is clueless about all things Colorado Trail. Daria considers calling him on what lies ahead but stays silent. Emma already thinks she pokes Beans too much.

"How're the tendons, Daria?" Emma doesn't use her trail name, a hint that she's serious about her question. Or maybe she expects a serious answer.

"Good. Cutting up my shoes made all the difference. I think the heel collars aggravated my Achilles." Daria scrolls her map app. "Good thing. We've got like twenty miles to Monarch Pass tomorrow."

"There's an out at the bottom of that valley." Emma points at the distant saddle. "If you hike down Tincup Pass, you'll run into St. Elmo."

"Isn't that a ghost town?"

"They evacuated St. Elmo during that fire last summer. Fifteen to twenty people. But tourists come up this time of year to feed the chipmunks. We could probably get a ride to Buena Vista if we needed it."

Emma wants to see Zahn. Daria wants to get miles in while her tendons are feeling good. Beans watches them both.

Daria says, "I'm good." She glances Emma's way and catches a flash of movement behind her friend. Two northbound figures trudge their way.

Emma notices Daria's reaction. "What?"

"Hikers coming our way."

Emma follows Daria's gaze. Beans shades his eyes.

Hikers are drawn to all things human. Sure, they talk about the beauty of the silence and communing with nature. How nice it is to escape civilization. But give most hikers a couple hours of wild, and most of them crave the familiarity of society. When they cross rivers, they look for a bridge. When they stop for lunch, if there's a flat spot that looks like a table, they use it. New faces provide excitement for the day.

"Maybe they can update us on the helicopter." Daria stands. "Let's see if we can beat them to that cliff." She points to the midpoint of the trail's C-shape.

Beans rummages through his pack. Emma stands and shoulders hers. Daria takes ten steps down the trail before pausing to check on Beans. "You coming?"

Daria tilts her head. Beans wears a neck gaiter around his head and a pair of sunglasses.

Beans must notice her reaction. "Sun's burning me up."

Daria tracks the progress of the approaching party. The closer the unidentified hikers get, the more she studies them. And the more she checks out their gear, the less the two men look like hikers. Small packs. Maybe thirty liters as opposed to Daria's fifty. Neither man uses trekking poles.

The lack of poles isn't that surprising. Using a hiking pole in terrain like this can twist a shoulder if a pole tip wedges between rocks.

Or they're carrying their poles. The pointed silhouette of what appears to be a single pole juts above each man's head. But at fifty yards away, Daria's positive they're not hikers. Their pants are pulled up from their ankles and either tucked into their boots or bloused like her dad used to do when he wore his Air Force camouflage uniform. The boots look military too. Both men wear vests, and she can spot items dangling beneath their pack straps.

And the item she thought was a hiking pole. It's not. These men are armed.

Weapons are the norm in Colorado rather than the exception. The government allows open and concealed carry. The number of people taking advantage of Colorado's liberal gun laws depends on what corner of the state one visits. Daria's dad told her most of the people out here own guns. Most don't open carry. He said he doesn't know how many carry concealed, but suspects plenty do.

They're probably not hunters. No camouflage, no vests, and who hunts on the Colorado Trail?

"Ladies. Sir." The lead man steps to the side of the trail. Technically, Daria and her friends are hiking downhill, even though this section barely has a slope to it. She and her hiking partners should be moving to the side. This guy is polite.

Emma says, "What's up with the guns? You guys don't look like thru-hikers."

The man in the rear turns and faces the way they've come. He's not the talker.

"TSA," says the first man. "We're on an assignment."

"You want to check our bags?" Daria blurts. She's inherited her warped sense of humor from her dad. Sometimes it just spills from her mouth before she knows it's coming. Beans tugs on Daria's pack from behind. Daria turns, and he gives her a slight head shake. When she turns back, Emma is already taking over the conversation.

"What's TSA doing on the Colorado Trail?"

"Did you hear about the helicopter crash?" the man says.

Emma and Daria nod.

"Standard procedure to have teams out looking for debris or clues to the cause. We're the north team."

"I thought the helicopter crashed near St. Elmo. This is a long way north."

"It's a pretty mysterious crash. We might end up scouring the whole route if we don't find anything soon." He leans to the downside of the trail so he can see past Emma to Daria and Beans. "You guys talk to anybody about the crash? Hear of anybody finding anything?"

Daria shakes her head and glances at Beans. He does the same.

"OK, then. If you don't mind, I'll grab your names and phone numbers so when you run into our other teams, we'll know who we've talked to and who we haven't."

Daria steps forward. "Daria. Daria Zahn. My cell—"

"Hang on here," Emma interrupts. "How about you show us your credentials first? Just so we're all straight about what's going on."

The second man stiffens but doesn't turn. The first man peers at Emma as his smile disappears. "Maybe I wasn't clear. We're federal law enforcement officers investigating the loss of a federal and state asset. Are you implying you won't cooperate?"

"I'm not implying anything. I'm asking you to follow protocol and prove you have the right to ask these questions."

"Because you're an expert on law enforcement protocol?"

Daria waits for Emma to drop the bomb. The FBI probably trumps security line screeners when it comes to prestige.

But Emma doesn't. "I watch a lot of TV," is all she says.

The man lets out a breath like he's made a decision. "OK, then. I was just trying to save you some hassle down the trail when you run into our other teams. We appreciate your time." With that, he steps around Emma. He stops in front of Beans.

"What's your story?"

Beans looks the man in the eye. "I'm with her." He nods in Emma's direction.

The man sighs. "Of course you are." His partner brushes past Daria and Beans, and both men trudge up the trail, rifle barrels shifting above their packs like a tour guide's flag in a museum.

Emma says, "Come on," and continues down the trail.

"Why didn't you tell him you were FBI?"

"Not here." Emma sets a brisk pace, and Daria speeds up to stay behind her. Beans brings up the rear.

Just before the descent from the saddle, Emma pauses. She stands to the side of the trail and looks past Daria back at the giant C of a path they've made. Daria follows her gaze. Beans does the same. There is no sign of the men.

Daria says, "Guess they made it over the ridge."

"Nope," Beans says quietly. "I'm not going to point, but check out the part of the trail where it starts turning east. Right at the curve. Look for the two black spots."

Daria follows his instructions but sees nothing.

"Got 'em," says Emma. "Daria, pretend like the east trail is six inches. Look an inch to the right of the curve."

And there they are. No more than fifty yards from where they first met them.

Daria says, "What's going on?"

"I'm not sure," Emma says. "The only thing I'm certain of is that those men are not TSA."

"Why would they lie to us?" Daria turns to Beans to see if he has any input. He stares at his feet.

"I think the more important question is why they aren't still moving away from us," Emma says. "They're carrying AR-15s. We need to get off this mountain."

17-HAVOC 23

(TWO YEARS BEFORE)

New York to Colorado-August 8, 2020

Figuring out Shavano's code wasn't rocket science. *M1981199.* Once Ethan sifted through all the Army howitzer websites related to M198, and GSA Direct Deposit forms for 1199, the only thing left related to Shavano's number was a Department of Natural Resources website link. He entered the site and found *M1981199* flagged in the same region covered by the L14 map in which Shavano wrapped Doubles' gift. The code was an inactive mine—the Sister Mary O'Malley—just a mile from the historic mining town of St. Elmo.

A month later, Ethan and Doubles fly to Colorado to search for whatever Shavano has hidden. They park outside St. Elmo, less than a quarter mile from the mine, where a faint tree break highlights a potential footpath.

"I'm not sure you really needed me to figure out Shavano's clues," Ethan says, closing the rear hatch on the Jeep Compass they rented at the Denver airport. "You can't tell me you didn't at least plug the mine number into Google."

Doubles shoulders a day pack but doesn't meet his eyes. "I didn't. I was so pissed about the bracelet and figuring out how to give it back that I didn't spend much time thinking about Shavano's stuff." She glances in the direction they will hike. "You want to lead?"

Ethan carries the GPS and the mine coordinates. He considers answering with "Guess I have to" but stays silent instead. He doesn't care whether she already knows Shavano's clues lead to this mine or not. He's just glad to be with Doubles and away from work. Ever since they mailed the unmarked package to the Iraq Museum, a load has been lifted from his conscience. Two months after they sent the package, a newspaper article reported the museum's confusion over the unexpected delivery of the Nimrud relics and no leads on where they came from. If he wasn't crazy about Doubles before, these gifts she has provided—affection, direction, and a sense of integrity he hadn't realized he was missing—seal the deal.

He buckles his daypack belt and chest strap and steps into the trees, locking the rental with the key fob. The SUV beeps and clicks. Doubles glances at him. "You think somebody's going to steal our stuff out here?"

"Nope. But it's a twenty-mile hike back to town if someone decides they like our wheels."

An overgrown but navigable path leads to the mine. Within minutes of leaving the Jeep, they face a cyclone fence framing a rotting entrance to a yawning black hole. The sign hanging from the links reads, DANGER. PRIVATE PROPERTY. DO NOT ENTER. A rusty gate, secured with a shiny Yale padlock, blocks their entry.

Ethan pivots. "Don't suppose Shavano left you a key?"

Doubles shakes her head and scans the fence.

"You game?" Ethan says. "No barbed wire."

"No problem. Let's bring the packs."

Ethan grabs his headlamp and a pair of gloves from his pack. Doubles pats the side of her cargo pants and nods. He pauses to see if Doubles will insist on going first. She doesn't. Getting past the whole pilot-in-command and copilot relationship that they began their friendship with and figuring out how it should change now that they're dating is hard. He's now a pilot-in-command, but she's an instructor and still a couple of years older. That dynamic won't go away, but with everything related to Shavano's legacy, she's been willing to follow his lead.

He climbs the eight-foot-high fence. Doubles makes short work of it as well, and when Ethan reaches for her waist on the mine side of the fence, she shakes her head. "Got it."

They regroup in front of the mine entrance, both donning their headlamps. The slope is steep enough to require a rope. They considered bringing one, but since neither he nor Doubles are climbers, they decided against it. Ethan argued for bringing Horse—heeding what Shavano had written, "Use our crew"—but Doubles vetoed it.

"All he cares about is the money he lost when he sold the ring and any more money he could have gotten from our relics if we hadn't returned them," she'd said.

Ethan surveys the approach. "I'm not worried about getting down—it's not that steep. We can slide. But getting back up?" His headlamp beam bounces wall-to-wall as he shakes his head.

"Look. Steps or something."

Ethan steps around Doubles. Sure enough, horizontal footholds have been dug into the dirt. Chiseled divots in the wall parallel the descent—handholds for the way up and down.

He turns to Doubles, raising his eyebrows. "How about one of us does it and the other stays here in case something happens?"

Doubles shines her light directly into Ethan's eyes, and he flinches, squeezing his eyes shut. "Sorry," she says. "What you're saying. It makes sense."

Ethan nods and steps for the stairs.

Doubles grabs his arm. "But I ought to go."

Ethan hesitates. This one seems like a no-brainer. He's volunteered to help Doubles with this search. He's trying to absolve his guilt over the artifact he accepted. But most of all, this is dangerous. Doubles is his girlfriend, and this is what boyfriends do—they go into dark and dangerous places for the one they love.

"I'm not sure—"

Doubles interrupts. "If you go down there and find nothing, what do you think will happen next?

They'll look somewhere else is Ethan's first thought. "Doubles…" He stops and laughs as he understands. "If I come back empty-handed, you're going to go down there yourself to double-check I looked everywhere."

"Exactly." Doubles moves toward the steps. "So keep your headlamp on. Be back in a second."

Ethan steps to the side. Doubles turns to face him at the slope's edge. She grins, grips one of the side divots, and feels for the first step with her foot.

He gives her a thumbs up. Training his headlamp below, he forces himself not to tell her to be careful. She knows.

It takes Doubles less than a minute to reach the bottom. The chasm veers to her right and Ethan's left. He points his light to help illuminate the path. "What do you see?"

The beam at the bottom swivels. "Looks like it goes straight for about thirty meters then dead ends. Might be a T-intersection. I'll check it out."

"Wait!" Ethan isn't a spelunker or cave expert, but he's read enough survival accounts to know how easy it is to get disoriented underground. "If you start taking lefts and rights down there, you're going to get lost." He pulls his daypack from his shoulders and unzips it.

"Hey PI, I'm the PC, remember? I don't get lost."

"Yeah, right. That's because you always had me checking the map." He pulls a roll of duct tape from the pack. "Shine your light up here. I'm tossing some tape to you. Mark the intersections."

"Uh, Ethan…I don't think tape is going to stick to rock." Doubles trains her light up the steps.

Ethan tosses the roll and it lands at her feet. "Just put it on the ground. Make an arrow out of it. Whatever."

"Got it. You're a smart one. Knew there was a reason I hang out with you."

Her headlamp dims as she walks out of Ethan's sight. She didn't even give him a goodbye. He looks for a spot to sit while he waits for her return. Movement flashes in the corner of his vision on the other side of the fence. He drops to one knee and freezes. Who else would be at this abandoned mine unless they followed them out here? He catches a reflection, then quivering branches through a scrub willow bush on the other side of the chain links. When he discerns the outline of a small mule deer pausing to look back at him, he sighs in relief.

Doubles' determination to return whatever Shavano left behind is inspiring. Ethan is no stranger to the concepts of right and wrong—he's known all along that accepting the knife in Iraq was wrong and that returning it was right—it's the rock-solid resolve to fix a wrong as soon as possible that Ethan lacks. Hiding the knife in his sock drawer was simply easier than confronting Shavano. Way easier than it would have been to tell someone else about Shavano's actions. He was new to the unit. What kind of soldier rats out their friends over something like this? And he had thought it was a dead man's personal items, not some ancient treasure. He can be excused for not taking action earlier.

But Doubles never blinked, considered, pontificated, or delayed. Her one-woman crusade to right the wrong must be some kind of internal code she was raised with. If it had been the Army, why didn't Shavano or Ethan internalize it in the same way?

Doubles' father drove ships in the Navy, and her mom taught school. No brothers. No sisters. Both parents tried to talk her out of the Army, saying the Navy was a better fit for a woman. Ethan's not sure how solid that advice was based on what he's heard about the services, but he can understand their wish for Doubles to follow in her father's footsteps. The devil you know, and all that. But their daughter picked the Army over the Navy for two reasons: the Army had more helicopters, and she wanted to pave her own path.

Ethan hasn't met Doubles' parents, but he knows their family bond is tight. The difference between his upbringing and hers is pretty stark.

Ethan's father built houses by day and stole from them by night. The police caught his father robbing a house when Ethan was six. The subsequent investigation uncovered a string of his prior robberies, and his dad went away for a twenty-year sentence. His mother took her own life a year later. His mother's sister and her husband raised Ethan and his sister. A decent couple, if distant. His father was released seven years later for good behavior, but in the ensuing months, he ended up arrested again for the same crime.

To his aunt's and uncle's credit, they did their duty. A moral choice. If an ethical code comes from nurture, it should imprint.

But it's Ethan's ethical wiring that's off. Just as the aunt and uncle kept their distance when it came to love, so did Ethan and his sister when it came to bonding. Neither could wait to get out of the house and free themselves from their sterile environment and their past. They had little time for each other. His sister double majored in Humanities and Criminology and took a job with a government agency. Ethan's English degree didn't translate into a ready job after graduation. That's how he found himself in the Army.

A whisper comes from below. "I see dead people."

Ethan's heart pounds, and he fumbles for his headlamp. The beam illuminates Doubles standing at the bottom of the shaft, wearing a smile.

"Got you." Doubles switches on her light and focuses the beam on the dirt stairs.

"Empty-handed?" Ethan moves toward where Doubles will climb out of the pit.

"It's a bust. T-intersection. I went twenty feet to the left and ran into dirt blocking the rest of the mine. Made it forty feet to the right and found the same thing. Old dirt. Like it hasn't been moved in a while." Doubles' headlamp beam moves up to the side wall, where she reaches for the next grip. "What's your backup—"

An arc of light momentarily blinds Ethan before spinning across the back of the shaft. Doubles shouts and disappears with the light. Rocks rain down the shaft and a cloud of dust billows from the hole, dimming the beam of Ethan's headlamp.

"Doubles?" Ethan screams. His voice echoes between the mine's walls. "Lisa?"

A low moan floats through the dust cloud still hanging over the shaft.

"Lisa?" Ethan bellows Doubles' birth name with authority like the tone and volume will warn her he's serious.

"Ethan?" Doubles' voice is weak.

Ethan answers, "I hear you. I'm coming down to help."

"Ethan? I need you to go get help. I hit my head. And broke my fucking leg."

Albany, New York-July 10, 2021

"Just like old times, bro." Horse slugs Ethan in the shoulder as they step from operations onto the flight line. "Except Shavano's dead and your girlfriend can't get herself back on flying status. We're the last ones standing from HAVOC 23."

Ethan winces. He's gotten over Shavano's death, but the fact that Doubles' broken leg has prevented her from flying for almost a year isn't anything to joke about. First, the infection. Then, the required re-break of the femur. Eight months later, just a week before she was scheduled to fly, Doubles tumbled from the garage treadmill and busted her arm. She's been working in the flight simulator for the last two months and returns to the flight schedule next month. She's embarrassed at how long it's taken her body to heal. She'll have to go through a proficiency flight evaluation and refresher training to get back up as an instructor pilot in the unit.

"It's not her fault. Recovery's been a bitch."

"It's the Colorado thing. When me, and Shavano, and Kristee Li tried to climb that mountain, we had to get Search and Rescue to help Shavano down. Then you and Doubles go out there and fall in a mine? Another SAR call? Our unit needs to stay out of that state."

"No argument from me. I'm not going back any time soon." That last statement isn't exactly true, but Doubles still doesn't want to bring Horse into the Shavano business. She and Ethan talk about returning to St. Elmo and searching other mines for Shavano's purported relic.

"What were you guys doing out there, anyway?"

"Same thing we were doing last time you asked me that question, Horse. Hiking. Give it a rest."

Horse stares at him like he's going to argue the point. If he asks if the Colorado trip had anything to do with Shavano and their Iraq mission, Ethan's unsure if he can pull off the lie. Instead, Horse pivots to the details.

"When you called for SAR after Doubles fell, did you see Kristee Li?"

"The girl from the funeral?" Ethan hadn't heard the woman's name in two years, except for Horse's mention of her earlier in the conversation.

"Do you know any others?"

"She wasn't there. It's a pretty white county. I would have recognized her." Ethan tilts his head. "Why? You still talking to her?"

"Off and on. More on than off, lately."

"Getting serious? She want to come out for a Tesla ride?" Ethan teases Horse about Kristee but throws in a dig about the new car. He knows where Horse got the money.

Horse shakes his head. "It's not like that. Something's been going on with her recently. That's why I asked if you saw her. I'm trying to figure out what's up."

"Never saw her. Anything I can do to help?" Ethan knows there isn't, but he's just happy the conversation has veered away from Shavano's complicated legacy.

"Not unless you know anything about out-of-the-way places in Asia, visa requirements, and expediting passport processes."

"Holy shit. Did she rob a bank or something? Why's she calling you?"

"You know why. I told you my family's story about getting out of Baoshan when I was a kid."

Ethan wouldn't have remembered Baoshan, but he does recall a drunk night in Cambridge, England, on the way home from Turkey when Horse described his family's secretive flight from China to Myanmar and their ultimate fresh start in the United States.

"You were just a kid," Ethan says.

"That's what I told her, but she won't stop with the questions."

The PI conducting the preflight pauses as he passes them. "You guys going to get this bird ready to fly, or stand around gossiping all day?"

Ethan turns to Horse. "Was I that cocky when I was a PI?" Horse shakes his head and climbs through the side door.

Ethan touches his finger to his forehead in a sarcastic salute. "Roger, PI. We're moving."

18-ZAHN

Salida, Colorado-July 13, 2022

As soon as our captors extract Larkin from the meeting room, the lights below go dark. I pull myself above the two pipes, relieving the strain of keeping my body from crashing through the ceiling tiles. I stay motionless for a full minute, just in case the men reenter the room.

A loud whisper below me penetrates the tiles. "Where's Zahn?"

"Not now," Perez shushes Flores.

I drag across the pipes an inch at a time, resting my chest on the top pipe and using my feet on the bottom conduit for balance and weight distribution. Only two inches in diameter, the pipes might not support my weight for long.

The bullet holes in the ceiling tile mark the doorway. Beyond the entrance joists, light pierces the tile seams, indicating I've reached the main offices. A right turn would aim me toward the front foyer where the men hold Robin at gunpoint. If I continue straight, I'll cross the hallway to the break room. I plan to work toward the far wall of the building and the utility room. From there, I'm only an arm's length from the emergency exit.

But the men holding us hostage aren't stupid, and I suspect someone has an eye on the exit, even though it doesn't have a handle on the outside. Figuring out my next move will have to wait until I'm back on the main floor.

Across the hallway, the pipes jag vertically eighteen inches toward the roof to allow room for the corridor ventilation duct. My foot slips as I scale the obstruction, banging into the duct's side. A muffled boom, like a bass drum, echoes across the ceiling. I freeze in place.

A commanding voice vectors from the front foyer. "Fuckers. Wayne, go check and see what the hell they're doing. Don't shoot any of them, but feel free to show 'em you mean business."

Footsteps pound my way.

The meeting room intercom blares behind me: *Back away from the door.*

A door clicks open, and lights flash in the ceiling tiles behind me. The door closes again.

"Move. Move. Move. Back of the room."

I use the commotion to make my move. Crouching on the pipe before the ventilation duct, I swing onto the other horizontal pipe and scramble across. I swivel my legs across the duct and poke them at the tangle of utilities below to find a toehold. My quick movements make more noise than my previous pace, but it's drowned out by the men yelling in the meeting room.

The tiles to my right cover the break room, which is lit from below. To my left is the dark utility room.

Squad 1, Squad 2.

A man's voice from the foyer answers. "Go ahead Squad 2."

Roger. No progress. Any word from the crash site?

"Their body count was the same as yours. That means one missing. We need you to find him."

Copy. We're working it. I've got Squad 3 working that mining town, then moving south on that trail. We're headed north.

I stop moving, focusing my attention on the radios. Crash site? Mining town? These guys are talking about the helicopter crash.

The man in the foyer radios, "Every other cop in the county has us surrounded here. Just like we planned. We just reestablished contact with the Boss. He wants to know about the locals."

So much for alerting the authorities about our capture. If law enforcement surrounds us, I'll need to be cautious when I bust out the door.

Squad 2 answers. *Tell him from here, it looks like his diversion plan worked. Law enforcement teams are out and about, but no one knows who's in charge. The search guys are just worried about the body recovery. There're some local cops, but they're just bitching about where the Sheriff's guys are. I ran into one Forest Service guy who asked a couple of questions, but that's about it.*

My heart lurches. These sons-of-bitches are holding us here to keep us from something up in the mountains. Something to do with the helicopter. But that's not what has me worried.

Daria and Emma are up there.

I doubt they would delay returning to the trail just because they couldn't contact me. My work phone or personal phone would tell me where they are—if only I had access to either. If Daria and Emma are back on the trail, they're walking straight toward these teams.

Innocent people can get caught in the crossfire. Just look at Robin out there. She has a husband wondering why she didn't come home last night and two middle-schoolers asking why she didn't wake them up for school this morning. She's done nothing to earn an AR-15 pointed at her head.

The foyer guy says, "What did you tell the Forest Service dude?"

I said we were TSA, because of the crash and all that. He just kind of blinked at me and went on his way.

The man laughs. "Squad 2, you need to find this guy. We've drawn some attention over the last hour. Got cars parked outside. A guy on a loudspeaker trying to engage in conversation. The sooner you find him, the sooner we can run our exit plan."

The radios fall silent. I assume a squad must have at least two personnel. Three squads and a boss mean a minimum of seven personnel. Maybe more.

I turn back to my immediate issue: how to get out of the sheriff's office. The utility room ceiling tiles are no different from the meeting room, but I'm uncertain what's below. I slide a panel two inches to the side and wait.

Nothing happens. I grab the tile's edge and pull it to the side. Everything below is black. My flashlight is in my 24-hour pack outside in my truck. My cell phones are in a box in the foyer. I don't smoke. No matter how I drop into this room, it's going to involve jumping into the unknown.

My pulse rate remains amped from my ceiling crawl. The thought of Daria heading out to the mountains makes my mouth go dry. I force myself to take ten measured breaths, trying to calm myself. I need to get out.

The breaths expand my belly against one of the pipes, digging my belt buckle into my flesh and giving me an idea. Locking my feet around the pipe, I pull my belt off and loop it around the lower pipe.

Arranging my feet to drop first, I lower my body from the pipe. I keep my feet away from the pipes and the ceiling structure, trying to avoid any noise but my breath sounds like a freight train. If someone is guarding the exit, they'll bust through the door any minute to see who's hyperventilating in the utility room.

Dropping one hand to the belt from the lower pipe, I slowly distribute my weight onto the length of leather. The pipe flexes, but I'm confident it will hold. I grasp the belt with both hands.

The leather is too thin. My hands slide. I search for any landing spot to break my impending fall. Nothing.

I earned my jump wings in the Air Force and am familiar with a proper parachute landing fall. I also have experience in the wrong ways to fall. None of these experiences occurred in the dark. In the split second before my hand slips off one side of the belt, I stop extending my legs and let them dangle down, forcing myself not to hold them straight. I drop, belt in one hand, concentrating on landing with my knees flexed.

My boots smack the carpet like someone tipped over a bookcase, but I doubt it can be heard outside the door. I roll onto my hip, scramble toward the door on my hands and knees and feel for the handle. If someone checks this room out, I want to be behind the door when it opens.

I catch my breath, my hands resting between my knees, trying not to pant too loudly. A minute passes, and I put my belt on.

Fifteen feet from the building's emergency exit, I mentally map my escape. A hard right out of this room toward the red letters that spell EXIT. A shove on the door bar to get the hell out of the building. Hands up high and wide in case law enforcement has weapons trained on this escape route.

The problem lies between me and the door. What or who is there?

I paw the perimeter of the utility room, taking inventory of what I have to work with. A green glow emanates from a hot water heater. Next to the tank is a sink, and stacked cleaning tools. A broom. A mop. A dank odor wafts from an unidentified bucket. The far wall is shelved. On the first shelf, my hands find an industrial flashlight. the kind with a handgrip on top, large batteries, and, I suspect, a wide beam. I grab it.

A two-foot gap separates the first shelving unit from the second and I find a breaker box. Inside the box, my hands brush over the two columns of circuit breaker switches. A sliver of light under the door leads to the hallway. I rehearse my plan in my head, then shove the flashlight between my legs and use both hands to swipe the switches in each column to the outside of the box. It takes me three swipes to get them all. After the first round, I hear a shout from somewhere in the building. The second swipe turns off the crack of light showing under the door. After the third, I grab the flashlight and move behind the door again.

"Hold your positions at the conference room! Watch that exit!" a voice bellows from the front of the building. "Those guys outside must've cut the power."

"Got it," a male voice calls.

A voice booms outside the door where I stand. "It might be internal. Check the breakers in the utility room."

The door swings open. A figure behind a beam of light steps inside. The beam scans the perimeter of the walls, illuminating the open utility box between the shelves. I allow the man two steps before I step from behind the door, and swing the industrial flashlight, striking the back of his head. No yell, no scream, not even a grunt. The man crumples to the floor, his flashlight rolling toward the left shelf.

I aim for the open door.

"Wayne?"

I enter the hallway, my flashlight weapon at the ready. A beam of light crosses the front of the corridor at the far end of the hall. I drop the flashlight, turn right, and sprint.

The exit light running on battery illuminates my path to freedom. I nail the door's push bar at full speed. Outside, the sun blinds me, but I am singularly focused on putting distance between me and the building. I raise my hands and aim for a row of cars lining the sidewalk. Two steps across the grass and voices pelt me from all sides.

"Freeze."

"Halt."

"Hold your position, or we will fire."

I stagger to a stop, my hands still above my head.

"There's another," I hear a voice from the crowd and sense weapons shifting in front of me. I turn to see the barrel of a gun thrusting from the fire exit behind me.

"That's one of them," I yell. "Give me cover."

I step toward the patrol car in front of me, aiming for the backside so I can put metal between me and the barrel of the gun tracking my direction.

"I said freeze," the officer in front of me screams.

I continue toward the officer, praying he will help me find cover. He raises his hand toward me, and I reach for it.

A loud pop explodes. My body jerks in agony, and I see flashes of light on the inside of my eyelids synched with a tat-tat-tat sound. All my strength drains from my legs. When I open my eyes, all I can see is the sky above me. I remember the rifle barrel poking from the fire exit. The bad guys shot me.

"Drop your weapon," voices scream around me. I'm already dropped. I have no weapon in my possession.

Hands grab me and roll me from my back to my stomach, my face pressed into the concrete sidewalk. They're examining the entrance wound. I try to tell them what happened, but my lips feel like I just left the dentist.

I attempt to move my head, but only my eyes respond. Staring close range at the cement below me, I expect a pool of blood from the gunshot wound. All I see is the sidewalk.

"He's retreating," a voice says.

The sound of a door slamming echoes across the parking lot.

"He's back inside."

The screaming I've heard since I was shot may not have been directed at me, but at the man who shot me. And it doesn't sound like they got him.

Someone grabs my hands and holds them together behind my back. My lips are beginning to function, and I try to speak. It comes out as a grunt. Metal on metal clicks behind me, and the warmth of the officer's hand disappears. He or she has released my hands, but instead of my arms flopping back to my side, they remain behind my back. I'm handcuffed.

Since when does Salida Police, or whoever this is, handcuff gunshot victims? I twist, surprised to feel function returning to my arms.

"He's moving. Roll him over."

Hands grasp me. I see the sky again.

"Holy shit." The voice comes from a silhouette above me.

"What?" A different voice.

"That's Tyler Zahn. From the sheriff's office."

"Tyler...?"

"You know. That dude that falls into all the shit around here? The Dillon Dam? Those kidnapped girls?"

"Holy shit."

I try to speak, but it comes out as a moan.

"How long did he ride the lightning?"

Lightning? I move my lips again. I haven't been shot. I've been tased.

19-DARIA

Colorado Trail near Tincup Pass-July 13, 2022

The descent to the Tincup Pass road takes another hour. While still above tree line, Daria pauses at every switchback, scanning the mountain behind them for rifle-toting, fake-TSA guys. Beans and Emma do the same thing. None of them spot anybody. If they meet any northbound hikers, Daria plans to warn them.

Lightning strikes, hypothermia, and injury lead the list of risks on the Colorado Trail. But women know unwanted advances from men are a danger in remote regions. Less likely than freezing, more likely than lightning. Daria laughs under her breath. A recent poll revealed more than fifty percent of solo female hikers would rather encounter a bear on the trail than a man.

But men packing automatic weapons claiming to be federal agents and refusing to identify themselves?

Daria plans to have a conversation with Emma when they get off this mountain. With FBI agent Emma, not hiker Emma. But Daria wants her father's read on this too. He is on the helicopter crash recovery mission. Maybe he's working with these TSA agents. Maybe they really do work for the government, and Daria and her friends just happened to run into the one super-asshole who can't handle pushback from random hikers.

She pulls up her GPS messages app. Nothing from her dad recently. She tries her phone. No service. She has an app allowing her to type a message on the phone but send it through her GPS, a significant timesaver. The phone has a keyboard with letters she can tap while the GPS has a grid of letters that she has to thumb the cursor over to select.

Dad, are you receiving messages? I want to run something by you.

She hits send. Minutes later, she realizes her mistake. Each one of these messages can take four to five minutes to transmit. She just needs to ask him her question.

We met some guys with automatic weapons on the trail who said they were TSA agents investigating the crash. Do you know anything about that? They wouldn't show us their IDs. Plus they were jerks. Anyway, they were headed the other way (north) on the trail, but I hope we don't see them again.

She sends the second message and tucks her phone back in her pocket. They cross a small feeder creek leading into Chalk Creek and climb the banks to the rocky road that traverses Tincup Pass.

When they cross the road, Daria calls, "Hold up."

Emma turns.

"I'm ready," Daria adds.

"For what?"

"You said, 'not here' when I asked you why you didn't tell them you were FBI. So how about here? Can you tell me now?"

Emma blinks, looking first at Daria, then at Beans.

"Not here."

Daria opens her mouth to protest.

Emma cuts her off, pointing to a stand of trees at an angle off the trail. "There."

They sit among the trees where they can see the road crossing but can avoid being seen if necessary. Emma's hands tremble. Beans' face is expressionless, like he's just along for the ride. As soon as they sit, Beans takes off to relieve himself.

"I didn't tell them because I didn't trust them."

"Because they wouldn't show you their IDs?"

Emma nods. "That's part of it. But there were other things. The TSA doesn't investigate aircraft crashes. I mean, yes, they might get involved if requested. Maybe for a terrorist thing. Or if the investigators thought the thing that brought the plane down might have gotten through airport security. But an Army helicopter crash? I don't think so."

Daria nods but doesn't say anything.

"And I didn't like the way they were acting. If they were actually TSA, I didn't see how me telling them I'm FBI was going to help anything. If I was right, and they weren't TSA, then it could've escalated. And my weapon was at the bottom of my pack."

"Was?"

Emma pats her chest. "Armed up at my last potty stop."

"Does Beans know you're carrying?"

"I don't know." She looks at Daria funny. "Why does it matter?"

Daria's not sure it does, but it feels weird to be hiking together, run into trouble, and not tell everyone in the group you're getting a gun ready—just in case. "What are we going to do?"

"I think we should keep hiking. What do you propose?"

Beans joins them from the woods and both he and Emma wait for Daria's response.

"I sent a message to my dad. I think we should go into St. Elmo, that ghost town you were talking about, and get a ride into town. Tell someone what we saw."

Emma says, "It's not against the law to have those weapons. It's pretty weird to identify yourself as federal agents, but I don't think anybody can arrest them. When we challenged them on it, they backed down." She turns to Beans. "What do you think we should do?"

"Keep hiking. They aren't looking for us, so I don't think we have anything to worry about."

Daria says, "Nothing to worry about?" She turns to Emma. "Is that why you're carrying a gun under your shirt?"

Emma glances at Beans. He looks back and forth between them like he can't figure out what they're talking about. Emma says, "Because you can't be too careful. And your dad would kill me if he thought I didn't have your back."

The men frightened Daria. But Beans is right. They obviously weren't looking for them. And she's hiking with an armed FBI agent. But something feels off. Her instincts tell her they should head into town and regroup. But her ego screams a different message—if she allows herself to be scared off the trail now, she might never return to it.

20-HAVOC 23

(FOUR WEEKS BEFORE)

Albany, New York-Jun 13, 2022

Ethan is almost finished on the treadmill when Doubles bursts into the garage. She motions for him to pull out his earbuds.

"Three more minutes," Ethan pants. "I'm at 4.7 miles."

Doubles flashes him a look of mock horror. The treadmill screen turns black as Ethan staggers to regain his balance. He turns to find Doubles holding the power cord.

He's both pissed and amused. "Wait. Booty call?"

"Dream on, big boy. Better than that. Guess who's going back to Colorado?"

"My sister?" Ethan plays dumb, but it's a partial truth. His sister reached out at Christmas and mentioned she would be hiking in Colorado this summer.

Doubles just stares at him, so he gives in. "How'd you swing a trip to Colorado?"

"Major Fogel got the unit a HAATS slot out in Gypsum—just west of Vail and Beaver Creek."

"Never heard of it."

Doubles breaks into that smile she always gets when she knows something he doesn't. "HAATS. High-Altitude ARNG Aviation Training Site. We used to send crews before COVID. It's a school for helo power management. The theory is that if you can fly a helicopter at thirteen or fourteen thousand feet and manage your power, everything lower than that will be a piece of cake."

"Should I meet you out there? Take another look at the mines?" Ethan lowers his voice like he's afraid someone might hear them. "For Shavano's stuff?"

"I don't want you to meet me out there."

Ethan's shoulders slump. They have tried running the numbers M1981199 backward, and forward, even running them through some of the new artificial intelligence beta apps. They are no closer to finding another place to search than when they failed at the Sister Mary O'Malley mine two years earlier.

And now Doubles doesn't want to meet him in Colorado? He screws up his face, ready to argue. Doubles cuts him off with a laugh.

"You'll already be there, PI."

"PI?" Ethan tilts his head. "I'm going to be your copilot? How'd you work that? I'm an instructor."

"The crew complement is two instructor pilots. Two senior crew chiefs. But since I'm senior to you, I'm having you fly as the PI."

"No way. Major Fogel knows we're dating. Everyone knows. They're going to think we're on a boondoggle." He suppresses a smile.

"So what? Can anyone argue that we're not two of the best pilots in the unit?"

Ethan grins. She's right about that. "What about Horse?"

Doubles' smile disappears. "Not a chance. He already tried to get on the mission when he found out you and I were going. I told Major Fogel I thought Sergeant Hendricks and Sergeant Stepp were the best match for the mission."

"He's going to be pissed."

"He already is."

•　　•　　•

Ethan's waiting in aviation life support for his helmet inspection when Horse approaches him.

"How come I'm not going?" Horse demands, without a greeting.

"Battalion wants the more senior guys to go. Hendricks and Stepp. Talk to Major Fogel."

Horse scowls. "Bullshit. First off, if that bit about experience was true, then you wouldn't be going. I've been in the unit longer than you have."

Ethan shakes his head. Horse holds a different crew position, and he only beat Ethan to the unit by five months. "You and I—"

Horse cuts him off. "Save it. I don't believe that's why I'm not going. You and Doubles heading to Colorado—the last resting place of Shavano." He pauses, checking the room.

Ethan does the same. A lone soldier works the front desk his head bobbing to whatever plays in his unauthorized earbuds.

"Are you guys second-guessing your decision to return your stuff? Looking for more?"

"We don't know—"

"Stop. You guys know something I don't. I think you're heading to Colorado to look for more. And you're cutting me out."

"Right," Ethan says. "We're looking for more, stashed away with Obama's birth certificate and Hunter Biden's second laptop, and the rest of Trump's classified documents." He holds his hands up in surrender. "You got us, Horse."

"Fuck you, Newb," He pokes his finger in Ethan's chest. "I'm on to you guys." Horse storms out of the room.

Ethan is more than a little shaken by the episode. He's urged Doubles to include Horse in their quest to find what Shavano left behind. Mostly because it seems like the right thing to do since Horse was there from the beginning. But partly because Shavano told them to. His directions were to "use the crew."

Ethan's chest throbs where Horse poked him. Doubles' reasons for not wanting to include Horse were valid. All he cares about is the money and anything Ethan and Doubles find without him means he's not getting any. But if Shavano was so hung up about making sure the whole crew reaped the benefits of whatever he left behind, why didn't he say "Share with our crew?" Why the mysterious verb "use"?

HAVOC 23's time in Turkey afforded a unique opportunity to bond. And their mission to Iraq sealed their reputation in the battalion. Five years later, it's still the closest anyone in the unit came to combat since the Iraq War and deployment to Afghanistan.

Ethan's bond with the other three crewmembers is why he uses their call sign as part of his computer login. *0423* The number 4 represents the four of them, and 23 is the call sign. Before the mission, he'd been using his high school football number and his graduation date, more evidence that the mission to Iraq is the most significant event in his life so far.

Ethan eases off the gas and speaks out loud. "Football number and graduation date." A car honks behind him and he accelerates. "Crew members and call sign." Now his heart rate accelerates too. What if that's what Shavano means by "use?" What if "use the crew" means use the number of crew members—four—and add it or take it away from the number he wrote, M1981199? Or something like that?

At home, he bolts through the door, aiming for the extra bedroom he and Doubles use as an office. Doubles calls out from the kitchen as he crosses the living room. "Wings and fries in thirty minutes. I'm using the air fryer so consider it health food night."

"I'll be there. Got to check something on the computer."

Sitting in front of the laptop, he moves his mouse to the browser tab that's remained open since their last Colorado trip. The DNR website highlights the Sister Mary O'Malley mine. He scribbles down the last four digits, 1199, four times on scrap paper and runs his calculations. 1199-4 is 1195. 1199+4 is 1203. He does the same thing with the number 23 from their call sign. When he has the four new numbers, he uses the website's search function to look for results. M1981195 is a bust. *No database match for this query.* M1981203 is a hit. The Tin Star mine, five miles west of St. Elmo, and only three miles from the Sister Mary mine.

Taking 23 away from the original number yields the same no match message. Adding 23 is another hit. M1981222 is another mine, The Chalk Lode. Did Shavano intentionally provide two options? Or does he have stuff hidden in more than one mine?

Ethan jumps as a voice whispers in his ear. "Are you signed up for a math class or writing in code to your other girlfriend?" He whirls as Doubles dances away holding his addition and subtraction problems up to her face.

"Try codes to your ex-boyfriend's treasure hunt. I think I've almost got it."

"You found it?"

"I said almost. I'm pretty sure I've narrowed it down to two locations." Ethan waves at the laptop with a grin. "I'd show you, but you said we've got a wings and fries date. Sorry."

Doubles grabs a chair and pulls it next to Ethan. "Scoot over. Show me what you got."

Albany, New York to Eagle County, Colorado-June 25, 2022
It takes the four crewmembers three days to fly from Albany to Colorado. When the instructors at HAATs ask Doubles what call sign her crew will use for the course, she doesn't blink twice.

"HAVOC 23," she says, before turning to her crew, eyebrows raised. The chiefs shrug and nod. As mixed as their feelings are for Shavano, it's fitting to readopt the call sign that got them into this situation the first time.

The high-altitude power management curriculum is as advertised. HAVOC 23 is on the single-ship track. Three days of academics followed by three days of flights to familiarize the crew with the difference in altitude between New York and Colorado. After two days of mountain academics and three days of mountain flights, the final sign-off item for the crew will be a mission they plan and execute on their own. This last mission will be the only one they will fly without an instructor. They can fly anywhere they want as long as the route includes extended transits above eleven thousand feet. They must select two sites and perform a mountain landing on each.

"We'll use that last flight as part of our search," she explains to Ethan.

He's surprised at this shift in the plan. Their home unit had given the crew permission to take a day off at the end of the course and enjoy Colorado before flying the helo back to New York. Once Doubles informed the crew chiefs that she and Ethan planned on locking themselves in a mountain cabin and not coming out until the next morning, hinting they'd be screwing like jackrabbits, the two enlisted soldiers informed them they would be taking the crew rental car to Cripple Creek and enjoying some high-altitude gambling.

"So we'll just rent our own car and head up to St. Elmo to check out the two mines," Ethan had explained to Doubles after the chiefs left.

"It took us all day to check out the first mine last year. We're not going to have time to check them both," Doubles pointed out.

"Right. We're going to need some luck. Hopefully we'll find what we're looking for in our first mine."

"That's not going to work."

"Why?"

"Because we can't be positive Shavano didn't use them both. I don't want to go to all this trouble and find out later we only returned part of the stuff."

Now Doubles is solving the problem by throwing a helicopter mission into the plan. Ethan says, "What about Hendricks and Stepp? What do we tell them?"

"How confident are you that we're on the right track to finding whatever we're looking for?"

"Above 90%. It's no accident about these numbers."

"Then we'll just tell them we're doing something that needs to be done, and we'll explain later. Don't you think we have enough credibility with our guys for them to trust us?"

"When I go out to retrieve whatever's there, how do I explain what I'm carrying back?"

"You don't. Our mission is to narrow down our ground search after the course. We'll go to one mine. If it's a bust, then when we hike, we'll know to focus on the other one. If you find something too awkward to fly out, we'll come back on foot after the course."

Ethan nods. Doubles has a point. Her plan practically guarantees they can find what they need to find in the time they have after the course. Otherwise, they risk not finding Shavano's stuff and trying to arrange a third Colorado trip.

"I'm in."

· · ·

The three days of academics drag for Ethan. Not just because he's studied all the material before they left New York, but because he can't get his mind off their final mission. He's itching to get out of the classroom and into the air. Doubles must feel the same way because when they climb into the cockpit for their first flight, her enthusiasm is infectious.

"You boys back there ready to rock some Colorado Rockies?" she says over the intercom.

"Ma'am?"

"Ten thousand feet today. It's the real deal."

"We gassed up at Leadville on our inbound leg," Hendricks deadpans. "That was ten thousand feet. We're not going into the mountains today—just runway work. If that's what you mean by rock the Rockies, then yes…woo hoo…we're ready?"

"Fucking smart asses," Doubles retorts. "We finally get off our butts and out of the classroom and now you're going to start playing Debbie Downer with me?" She winks at Ethan.

"No, Ms. Doubles. It's just—"

"Zip it, Elvis. We'll party up front on this mission. No laughing in the back."

The HAATs instructor shakes his head, grinning at the banter. "Starting Engine Checklist," Doubles says.

•   •   •

Unlike academics, the first flying phase ends too fast. The end goal is for both Doubles and Ethan to return to their home unit and teach what they've learned to the rest of their battalion. Same in the back end with the crew chiefs. Every operation the pilot performs on a mission, they do twice: once with Doubles at the controls, and once with Ethan. The crew chiefs swap leads in the back as well.

Walking across the flight line after the third flight, Arnold "Terminator" Smith, their instructor, shakes his head.

Doubles reaches forward and tugs on his helmet bag. "What's up Terminator? Sad to be done with us?"

Terminator turns with a grin. "Actually? Kind of am. Don't let it go to your head, but you're one of the tightest crews I've taught. You get along. You can fly."

Ethan pops in. "HAATS tells the regiments to send their best. You blowing sunshine up our skirts?"

"I don't do it often. You guys got something going. How long have you been flying together?"

Doubles tosses her head back toward the crew chiefs who are still buttoning down the helo. "The chiefs are new to our crew, but we've both flown with them a lot. Ethan and I started off flying together when he first joined up. We did some Iraq time for his first overseas mission back in 2016." She nudges Ethan. "Fun times, right Newb?"

Ethan nods, but he doesn't want to talk about Iraq.

Terminator turns to Doubles. "2016? I thought everyone except the spec ops guys were out of Iraq then." Doubles opens her mouth to answer, but Terminator interrupts her. "Should have known it was you when you asked for the call sign. HAVOC 23—you guys flew the dead Iraqis out of the helo crash near Baghdad, right?"

Ethan cringes. Either Doubles doesn't mind talking about the mission, or she's a good actor. She says, "That was us. Didn't need any of your fancy mountain instruction in the desert. We ran into terrain—canyons, mesas, plateaus—but we were more worried about power management at high temperature than high altitude."

"Right?" Terminator looks at them with what appears to be an even greater amount of respect. "I'm recommending to the boss you guys skip ahead a flight in the syllabus. We'll see if you can do the mountains in two flying days instead of three. Doubt you'll need that third sortie."

Doubles stiffens, probably thinking the same thing Ethan is. Does Terminator mean two days with an instructor, then go home? Or does he mean two days supervised and they still get the "no-instructor" sortie at the end? The one where they plan to check out the mine.

"We don't want to miss any sorties just because we're doing well," Doubles says. "And we heard the last one is the highlight of the course. We want to do the solo mountain flying."

"Everyone solos," Terminator says. "I meant the supervised flights." He claps Doubles on the shoulder. "I won't say anything. But you guys might consider screwing up a little more or your mountain instructor might come up with the same idea I did to get you out of here faster."

Ethan has an idea. "How about we do the best we can and they give us two solo flights? Have you ever seen them do that?" Doubles raises her eyebrows at him appraisingly. She gets it. If they could nab two solo flights, they could check out both sites. Hell, if they got lucky, they could grab whatever Shavano left behind and they wouldn't have to hike at all.

"Not going to happen."

"Why not?" says Doubles.

"The supervised flights are set routes approved by the Forest Service. Mondays we do this. Tuesdays we do that. A blanket approval. But the unsupervised flight is planned by your crew. We don't tell you where to go. And the Forest Service only allows us one day a week for a random flight. That's a long way of saying you're not getting multiple versions of that solo sortie. Nice try, though."

Ethan's perplexed. Why has Terminator gone out of his way to praise their crew, talk about how he's heard of their exploits, and offer to try to help them speed up the next phase? Is he just a nice guy, or does he have an agenda?

Doubles figures it out. "Yo, Terminator. What do you got going tonight? Cub Scout meeting? Date night?"

Terminator's head snaps toward Doubles like he's been hoping for the question. "You guys need help with something??"

Doubles laughs. "Yeah, when the chiefs finish up, we're heading down to the Ice House for a couple of pitchers. It's two for fifteen bucks tonight. But we're not sure our little ol' crew can make it through both pitchers. Could you help us out with that?"

Terminator grins. "See you there." He accelerates toward the HAATS main building, calling over his shoulder. "Got to make a call first."

"How did you know?" Ethan asks Doubles.

"What? Were we just supposed to believe all his bullshit about how great we are?"

"He had me thinking we're the best crew he's ever flown with. How'd you know it was bullshit?"

"I know men. They're after women or beer. I've seen every approach they got. Terminator knows you and me are a thing, so I guessed he wasn't pursuing me." Doubles raises her eyebrows at Ethan. "Although you'd better stick tight to me because if you take off, I wouldn't put it past him." She taps her head. "He must want beer. I bet most of these crews come out here and party by themselves. Leaves Terminator with no one to go out with. I threw him a bone and he bit."

Ethan smiles. Doubles never fails to amaze him.

21-ZAHN

Salida, Colorado-July 13, 2022

The officers who tased me apologized before I left, but only because they knew me. Procedurally, it was probably the smart move. I tried to tell them about the conversation I overheard inside, but they insisted on moving me nine blocks down to the station. Now, I sit across from Officer Joe Nissen at the Salida Police Department, a cup of coffee and an onion bagel untouched in front of me.

"Let's run through this one more time," Joe says. "Just in case you remember something new."

I sigh. "Every minute we waste sitting here discussing my escape is another minute you've got unauthorized armed men crawling around the mountains in your backyard."

Joe shakes his head. "I'm not sure you understand what's happening here. These guys have pretty much captured the entire on-duty county law enforcement team—well, except for you—and are holding them hostage."

"Whoever shot that guy at the helicopter is trying to finish something. And there's a shitload of hikers out there in danger." I slam my palm on the desk. "Including my daughter."

"The feds are racing here to help negotiate this thing. The deputies that were off-shift when they took over the Sheriff's Office can't get their shit together. And you want us to pull resources away from the hostage situation to check out something you might have heard while crawling through the roof?"

I stare at Joe without blinking. "You're making my point."

"What?"

"Why are these guys holding them hostage?"

"Hell if I know. That's why we called in the feds—to find out their demands and do that negotiating thing."

"Assume what I'm telling you is true. These guys have people in the mountains trying to find someone from that helicopter. Now why would they take our guys hostage?"

Joe wrinkles his brow. He's a smart guy. But this is a non-standard situation.

"To occupy our attention?" Joe's voice sounds tentative. "So we don't interfere with whatever they're trying to do?"

"Exactly. Pull from the Buena Vista police—and get some teams in the field. What do you say?"

I'm not expecting Joe to leap from his chair like he's fired up for the second half of the homecoming game, but I am hoping for a little more response than he offers. He eyes me for a moment. I raise my eyebrows. He shakes his head.

"I need to talk to the Chief." He reaches for his phone. "Mind waiting out in the lobby, Zahn? Nothing personal."

I translate this as "I'm going to tell the Chief what you told me. I'm not sure whether he'll believe it or not." Which pisses me off. I've probably been involved in more high-stakes cases in the last three years—even though I wasn't wearing a badge—than Joe Nissen has in his entire career. I emerged from most looking pretty damn smart. Most.

I pat my pockets for my phone on my way out before remembering turning it over back at the Sheriff's Office. I need to warn Daria and Emma what's happening but even if I had my cell phone, it's unlikely my call would connect. Not where they've returned to the trail.

If they returned to the trail. They were thinking of taking a day off. Hope flickers. Maybe they are in Buena Vista. I approach the desk officer to ask to use the phone but shut my mouth when he looks up.

I'm wasting time trying to convince the local police to do something that will take hours to organize and execute. If they even believe me. Meanwhile, my daughter is either at my house preparing to return to the trail or hiking through the area these guys are searching.

"Tell Officer Nissen I had some business to take care of. I'll check in with him later." It's not like they're holding me here.

"He got your number?"

"Yup." I walk out the door, wondering what the bad guys have been doing with all our ringing cell phones.

If I hadn't arrived last to Larkin's meeting, I would have parked in the lot closest to the sheriff's office and been blocked off by what looks like a SWAT unit. They must have brought those guys in from out-of-county.

I climb in my Tundra parked on the other side of the building at the county employees lot and reach for my 24-hour pack in the passenger seat. I press my GPS power button while I motor away. My first instinct is to drive into the mountains, either up Cottonwood Pass or back toward the helicopter crash near Tincup Pass. From either spot, I can hit the trail and talk to other hikers. Find out who might have run into Daria and Emma.

But initial gut reactions aren't always right. Better to mull things over. A mile out of Salida, I pull to the highway's shoulder and grab my GPS. Daria hasn't written to my GPS address. We had been communicating from her device to my email address on my phone and back—not device-to-device. Without my phone, I'll need to use my GPS to send her a message. And I can't even pull up her location.

Where are you at? I ran into a situation and couldn't communicate with you all while you were off trail. I don't have my phone for the foreseeable future. I have information about a threat on your route. If you're off the trail, stay off the trail. If you are on the trail, get off and work your way to BV or Salida—Dad.

The message takes me almost ten minutes to write with the clunky GPS keyboard system and I take a breath before putting my truck in gear. Thumbing out a message on the GPS reminds me it'd be easier on my laptop at home.

Home. I've completely forgotten about Amore. When we lost my friend Kristee on a search and rescue mission over a year ago, I ended up with her dog. Amore was Kristee's dog first, but Amore is now mine. And I'm a bad pet owner. Maybe Daria let him out.

When I park in my Elk Trace driveway, Amore pops up and down in the living room picture window. I press a code into the keypad and burst through the door.

"Daria? Emma? Anybody home?"

I cross the mudroom, leaving the front door open, and kneel to give Amore a quick hug. As soon as I release him, Amore dashes out the open door to take care of business. A quick side-to-side survey of the room surprises me. In my 24-hour absence, I don't see any sign that Amore left any landmines in the house. Either he's hid them well or my dog has incredible control of his digestive system. And it doesn't look like anyone else has used the house either.

My laptop is already powered on, so my inbox is only a click away. I select the messages from Daria's GPS.

Dad, we've decided to stay on trail instead of coming into BV. We're supplied up through crossing Monarch Pass, so we'll plan on seeing you in two days. Hope you don't mind. It was my idea, so don't blame Emma—she's looking forward to seeing you. Me too. Smooch.

My gut churns as the message dashes my hopes of Daria and Emma being off trail. I scroll down.

Dad, are you receiving messages? I want to run something by you.

I continue scrolling. As I read the last message, my fingers quiver.

We met some guys with automatic weapons on the trail who say they're TSA investigating the crash. Do you know anything about that? They wouldn't show us their IDs. Plus they were jerks. Anyway, they were headed the other way on the trail.

Automatic weapons. These guys have to be part of the teams I overheard our captors talking to. My daughter is in danger. I furiously try to recreate the message I sent earlier, adding clarity since Daria now knows the danger.

Dar, hopefully you got my earlier message from my GPS. I'm at the house now. Those are not TSA agents. I don't know exactly what is going on, but those guys are part of something related to the helicopter crash. The crash was not an accident. Get out of the mountains at the earliest opportunity. When you send messages, include my GPS email address because I'm not planning on staying at the house.

Daria's message to me includes a timestamp and coordinates. I cut and paste them into my mapping program. She sent the message two hours ago from where the Colorado Trail cuts across Tincup Pass—just three miles west of where Perez and I climbed to the helicopter crash. Daria indicated they were nervous about the men, but she didn't hint that she and Emma were considering leaving the trail because of it. If they kept hiking, they would be heading south up over a couple of remote passes and descending by the abandoned Alpine Tunnel and Hancock Lakes.

I've got three choices. Drive toward Tincup Pass and try to catch them from behind. Or, I drive most of the way to Hancock Lakes, and hike north on the Colorado Trail to intercept them. The slowest option—but the only one guaranteeing I won't miss them—is to park on Highway 50 near Monarch Pass in the south and back-hike the CT over Chalk Creek Pass. It'll take the rest of the day. I don't have time.

I grab a box of granola bars from my kitchen. My watch reads 15:07. My 24-hour pack is ready to go. My loaded Glock is in the glove box of my truck. I whistle and Amore charges through the front door.

"Sorry, boy." I scratch between his ears. "I know you want to go, but this hike's not for dogs." Amore disagrees, crowding me as I aim for the door. I squeeze out and lock it behind me. Turning and waving will just rile Amore up more. I climb into my truck and jot a message on an index card for my neighbor June.

Got a mission that might put me out overnight. Could you pop in and check Amore's food tonight? Maybe let him out in the yard for a few minutes? Grateful always. Tyler.

June's Honda is gone when I pull up to her house, and I slide my message inside her screen door. Usually, my reasons for asking her to help with Amore are something like this, and I'm pretty sure June likes being a part of our SAR missions. I shovel snow from her driveway and offer to run her trash down to the bins now and then. Which she counters with sourdough bread and chicken soup. It's a never-ending neighbor fest, and I reap most of the benefits from our relationship. She won't know any different.

22-DARIA

Colorado Trail near Tunnel Lake-July 13, 2022

Daria glances behind her. No sign of the fake hikers. The trail behind them follows a meadow down a draw with scrub pine on both sides, a stream running through the center, and wildflowers decorating the sides of the path.

Movement on the western slope catches Daria's attention when she turns to hike again. She stares at the patterned green and catches a flicker of tan. A group of elk dines on hillside grass. She points them out to Emma and Beans. They pause, taking in the beauty of this secluded valley. But Daria can't enjoy it.

She checks her GPS but her dad hasn't answered her messages. The battery indicator reads sixteen percent. She turns it off. They're on the trail. They can't get lost.

They crest a grassy knoll and the trail dips and winds through another valley, this one widening toward St. Elmo. Another elevation peak pokes above the other side, a bit higher than the one they stand on. Daria steps to the side and lets Beans follow Emma down the trail.

"I'm going back to that high point for a picture," she explains.

Beans smiles as he passes. "I'll tell Emma—er, Mud Hen—to slow it up." He doesn't seem to have a hard time remembering Daria's trail name, but she can count the number of times he's used Emma's on one hand.

Daria retraces her steps just short of the saddle and glances down at Beans and Emma. Neither is looking her way. She presses against a boulder to check the trail they just hiked. A half mile back, two figures emerge from the tree line and plod in her direction. She might not be able to pick out the barrels of their rifles, but the color of their clothing confirms her suspicions.

She zooms in with her cell phone, snaps a picture and pushes off the boulder, jogging to catch up with Beans and Emma. She keeps her eyes glued to the rocky trail so she doesn't fall. When she hits a clear area, she spots her hiking partners fifty yards out at the edge of a stream tracking her progress.

"Slow it up, Little Z, slow it up," Emma calls. "We're waiting."

Out of breath, she thrusts her phone at Emma.

"What am I looking at?"

"Zoom in," Daria gasps.

Emma spreads her fingers on the screen and raises it closer. "Shit." Her face hardens and she hands the phone to Beans.

Beans uses his fingers to adjust the range.

Beans lowers the phone, pivoting to scan the final hilltop before the descent past the Alpine Tunnel. The high point parallels the helicopter crash site they've heard so much about.

"What are you thinking?" Emma says to Beans.

Confused as to why Emma cares what Beans thinks—not that every person isn't important—Daria sniffs. She and Emma are hiking this trail together. Beans got picked up along the way and seems pretty clueless. Whether his opinions are valuable or if Beans has any credibility when it comes to danger seems silly. He's the last person Daria would turn to for advice.

"I'm thinking this isn't working anymore." Beans unclips his chest strap and reaches into his jacket.

Daria expects him to pull out a map. Or maybe a satellite phone? Will their unprepared companion suddenly save the day?

What she's not prepared for is the pistol Beans wields.

"Ethan?" Emma says.

"What the hell?" Daria's comment is directed at the weapon, but also at why Emma seems to know Beans' real name—a name Daria doesn't recognize. Have they been having private conversations every time Daria steps away from them?

Beans—or is it Ethan?—half raises the gun at the space between Emma and Daria. "Those men are looking for me. I'm a loose end."

"Not like this. I think—" Emma starts.

"Stop talking. Emma, you're going with me." He tilts his head toward Daria while keeping his eyes on Emma. "She's not. I don't think they want innocent blood on their hands. As long as I'm holding you, Emma, they'll back off."

Daria's mind goes into overdrive. Beans said Emma is innocent—implying he's guilty. But of what?

"You can't leave Daria here," Emma says. "Who knows what they will do to her."

Beans keeps the gun on Emma but glances Daria's way. "Daria, huh?"

Daria glares at Ethan aka Beans. He didn't know her real name either.

"I'm not interested in hurting either of you, but I can't handle two." He steps back from Emma and surveys the sloping valley the creek bisects. "Daria, follow that creek and be out of sight in the next five minutes. Do you understand?"

"No," Daria blurts, but her voice quivers. "Who are you? Why is the government after you?" Her tone hardens. "And leave Emma out of this."

Beans steps back to Emma and grabs her arm while shoving the gun barrel against her side. "No time." He pauses. With a thin smile, he nods over Daria's shoulder. "And they're not government. Not even close." He pushes against Emma. She winces and Daria assumes Beans is digging the gun into her side.

"Move it." He nods toward the creek.

Daria doesn't but Emma mouths the word "go."

Daria shakes her head but Beans pushes Emma down the trail.

Daria runs.

23-HAVOC 23

(TWO DAYS BEFORE)

Eagle County, Colorado-July 10-12, 2022

Ethan's crew doesn't finish the HAATS course a day early like Terminator predicted. On day two of supervised flights, Ethan botches a high-altitude landing. Although he anticipates the power requirement for setting down a helicopter at thirteen thousand feet, he fails to compensate for his sink rate as he lowers to the ground. The instructor pilot—call sign Snoopy for reasons no one on HAVOC 23 has been able to uncover—calls "Abort!" from the jump seat.

Ethan freezes at the command because he assumes he's on target for a spot landing. When Snoopy doesn't see Ethan increasing power, he calls "Abort" again this time in a near scream.

Doubles seizes the collective and pulls. "My controls!"

Even at maximum power, Ethan's downward momentum causes the wheels to slam into the loose shale on the flat ridgeline. The aircraft bounces back into the air both from the rate of impact onto the malleable surface and from the counteracting power Doubles has fed to the engines.

"Shit. I can take it back." Ethan reaches for the controls.

"Goddammit," Snoopy mutters.

Doubles shakes her head. "Take a minute, Ethan. Let's check out what we got."

"Gauges all look fine." Ethan scans the cockpit for warning lights.

"She means the wheel struts, PI," Snoopy calls from behind them. "We need to make sure you guys didn't bust anything outside the helo."

"Fuck." Ethan lowers his head.

"Hey." Something in Doubles' tone makes Ethan look in her direction. Doubles fixes her eyes on Ethan then shifts them toward where Snoopy was standing before he ducked to the rear of the helo to help the chiefs scope out the struts. Snoopy is still plugged in, so Doubles covers her mic with her hand and leans toward Ethan. "Get your shit together. It happened. Nothing we can do about it. So, let's fly."

Ethan stares at Doubles and gets it. Aviation 101. In an emergency, fly the fucking aircraft. He nods. "Got it."

"You ready to take it?"

"I have the controls." He reaches for the collective on his side.

The crew chiefs report back on their inspection. Although the struts can't be checked while airborne, they were able to use a mirror out the side door to examine the landing gear. The wheels appear normal. They recommend checking the struts back at Eagle County Airport.

On the ground, Snoopy rallies the crew on the tarmac before Doubles and Ethan have a chance to inspect the struts. He turns to the crew chiefs. "You two work with maintenance and see what we got. Find out if the aircraft is grounded or not."

Snoopy swings his head back to Ethan and Doubles. "You two. Debrief room, now."

He jabs a shaking finger at the HAATS building. Whether still shaken from the near crash or furious at them, he's trying to hold it until they debrief.

They stride through the lobby. Jenna, the young university student who runs the front desk during the summers, calls out, "How did it go? You're early."

Snoopy doesn't even turn in her direction, aiming for the two briefing rooms at the end of the hallway. Ethan turns to Jenna and shrugs. Doubles gives her a headshake and winks at the young woman. Ethan shakes his head at her optimism. They're in serious shit.

Snoopy holds the door until Doubles and Ethan sit, then pulls it shut. Ethan expects a slam, but instead, there's a firm click, then silence, as if Snoopy is rehearsing what he's going to say.

"Ethan, would you be so kind as to tell me what the fuck that was?" he says.

"It was my fault. I—" Doubles starts.

"Shut up, Ms. Brumstock," Snoopy barks. "We're getting to you. I need to hear from Ethan first."

"I focused on my torque gauges, and didn't scan my rate of descent by looking outside," Ethan offers. "I took it over—to 105%—but it wasn't enough. I should have verified that by looking outside."

"Or, if you were going to fixate on your instruments—which you shouldn't have—you could have checked your vertical speed indicator. But you didn't do that, did you?"

"No."

"One more instrument you didn't check. Any guesses?"

Ethan runs through the high-altitude landing procedures in his head. Out of the corner of his eye, he catches Doubles wiping her brow. Which is odd, because the air conditioning is running full blast. Then it hits him. Temperature. He had chosen his power input based on the briefed temperature rather than the actual temperature.

"It was hotter than we briefed. That's why we needed more power," Ethan says.

Snoopy nods. "And?"

"And if I had paid more attention to what was happening outside the aircraft instead of playing around with power settings inside the aircraft, I could have made all the right inputs without even thinking about the temp or torque. I would have recognized the sink rate and automatically adjusted."

Snoopy shifts his eyes to Doubles. He waits a moment, then says, "Go ahead."

"It shouldn't have gone that far. My job as the pilot not flying is to recognize something like that. Identify it early enough for him to react."

"And?"

"I didn't back him up."

"Not just that, Doubles. You're both qualified as pilots-in-command, but you're in charge on this mission. The orders say you're the one that's held responsible if something goes wrong." Snoopy pauses. "And it went wrong today." He waits another long minute.

Snoopy's pauses are obviously for dramatic effect. Doubles is getting fidgety, like she's too experienced to be treated like a newbie.

"We'll get it right tomorrow," she says. "Then we'll be ready for the independent flight."

Snoopy shakes his head. "There's no tomorrow if the inspection comes back bad. That'll be it."

*   *   *

The inspection results come back that afternoon. No internal structural damage. Ethan isn't surprised. The impact was hard—embarrassingly hard—but it wasn't like they crashed.

The crew is cleared to fly. They skip afternoon beers. No one wants to give the instructors an extra reason to scrutinize them. Everyone's in bed before nine.

Following the morning preflight, the crew rallies near the cockpit to wait for Snoopy.

Doubles raises her eyebrows at Ethan.

"I'm good."

"Hell yeah," says Stepp.

"And bad," Hendricks says.

Ethan turns, and Hendricks quickly adds, "Like a bad-ass pilot, boss. Relax. You got this."

Snoopy approaches the aircraft with a slender, silver-haired man in a blue flight suit with embroidered wings on his chest. As they walk around the nose, Ethan notices a patch on the older man's left shoulder reading "20K." He assumes it means flight hours.

Stepp lets out a whistle. "In a helo? Damn…"

"Doubles. Gentlemen. I'd like you to meet Jake Wagner—the founder of HAATS."

If the two men weren't standing directly in front of Ethan, he'd let out a whistle just like Stepp had. "Wags" Wagner is a legend in the helo community. He pioneered the use of the UH-1 Huey as a gunship in Vietnam, then came back from the war and helped rewrite Army air cavalry tactics based on lessons learned in the conflict. Assuming he was in his mid-twenties in Southeast Asia, Ethan presumes he's got to be at least in his seventies now.

Doubles extends her hand. "It's an honor, sir. Thanks for taking the time to come out and see us off."

Wags steps forward and shakes Doubles' hand before turning back toward Snoopy with a smile.

Snoopy says, "Actually, I'm the one seeing you off. Colonel Wagner will be flying with you today as your evaluator."

Wags winks as he lets go of Doubles' hand.

"Twice honored," Doubles says, keeping her cool.

Ethan swallows. *Oh, shit.*

* * *

Snoopy stands in the exact same spot when they return from their flight three hours later. Ethan smiles. Snoopy's probably thinking the flight was a bust because Wags sits in Ethan's seat while Ethan rides in the back.

As the rotors wind down, Ethan, Doubles, and Wags approach Snoopy, who wears a blank expression. Ethan almost grins at Wags's serious demeanor but manages to keep a straight face.

"You and I need to talk," Wags says to Snoopy.

Snoopy lets out what appears to be a resigned sigh, like he's sure Wags will chew him out for letting the crew advance as far as they did.

"These two are the best sticks I've flown with in the last ten classes. I signed them off." He turns to Doubles. "Ms. Brumstock, you all get your butts inside and start planning tomorrow's mission. Thanks for making my day."

"Thank you, sir," Doubles says. The crew chiefs echo their gratitude.

When Ethan steps forward to shake Wags's hand, the colonel leans in and says, "I mean it when I say you're one of the best I've flown with."

"I appreciate it, sir."

"Don't lose fucking focus ever again. Understand?" Wags's piercing glacial blue eyes garner Ethan's full attention.

"Yes, sir," Ethan whispers.

Doubles strides toward the briefing room. Ethan and the chiefs follow. As he passes Snoopy, he nods. Snoopy doesn't reciprocate, but a smile twitches at the corner of his mouth.

•　•　•

Hendricks and Stepp are already prepping the aircraft when Doubles and Ethan cross the flight line the next morning.

"You sure you still want to do the stop near the mine?" Ethan says to Doubles. "After flying with Wags, I wonder if we've got too many people watching us to pull this off. Plus, we still haven't given the crew chiefs a heads-up." He nods at the two men ahead of them.

Doubles stops in her tracks. "We've only got one day after the course to find this stuff. We'll only have a fifty-fifty chance we're right if we don't do this scouting mission. I want to do it."

He says, "I'm in, then. Just wanted to give you a chance to rethink it."

Doubles tilts her head toward the helo. "Let's go."

It takes longer than they've planned to arrive at their approved operating area in the Collegiate Peaks. The winds scream across the mountains at speeds much higher than forecast. Ethan has to point the nose of the helo into the wind just to maintain course. They've picked their two required landing sites, the first on a knoll near Emma Burr Mountain, and the second, a hundred feet from one of the two mines Ethan suspects holds Shavano's mystery relic.

Doubles low approaches at their first landing site, unable to touch down because of winds. The intended touchdown point is a flat rise they had picked out on the map, a broad expanse of shale with no visible boulders. As they drop between the two elevation peaks on their second try, a gust of wind slams the helo sideways. Doubles corrects and pulls the aircraft higher for a reattempt. As she lowers back down, another wind blast spins the nose to the left. She hauls back again and keys the intercom.

"We're not putting down here. Winds are out of limits."

"Looks like we're done for the day, huh boss?" Hendricks calls over the intercom. "Lunchtime beers?"

Doubles turns to Ethan, her face set. She shakes her head.

Ethan keys his mic. "We're going to try our second site. See if the wind eases up in the valley there. Then we'll head back."

"Just saw another helicopter behind us heading south," Stepp calls. "Everyone's getting out of the mountains. I bet Horse last night after the weather forecast we probably wouldn't finish this mission today."

Ethan glances at Doubles before replying. Her return stare is unblinking. "You bet who?" Ethan calls.

Stepp says, "Horse. You know he wanted to be in on this HAATS gig. He's been texting every day, checking to see how it's going."

"And what are you telling him?" Ethan says.

"Whatever he asks for. He might get selected to come out next year. No hurt to prep him up, right?"

Ethan turns to Doubles again just as the word "Fuck" forms on her lips.

It only takes minutes to fly from the knoll to their destination west of St. Elmo. The landing site they've chosen sits west of the mine, a patch of loose shale jutting in a plateau out from the ridgeline.

The winds are lighter than their first landing site, but not by much.

"You want me to take it, PI?" Doubles asks Ethan, as he jockeys the controls on the approach.

"I got it." Ethan moves his mic away from his mouth and yells over the engine noise. "You just be ready to move. You know where to go?

It's not a timber-lined tunnel like the last one. More like a hole with a pile of rocks next to it."

Doubles points to a cluster of trees near the landing site. "Other side of those, right?" she yells.

Ethan nods.

Two hundred feet above the ground, a radio call interrupts Ethan's approach.

HAVOC 23, HAVOC 23, this is HAATS Command, how copy?

Doubles holds up her hand. Ethan stops his descent.

Go ahead, Command. HAVOC 23 reads you Lima Charlie.

We've had reports of wind gusts up to fifty knots over the Collegiates. Are you seeing that?

Ethan cranks the controls to keep the wind from blowing the helo into the ridge. Doubles keys the mic. *Command, we're seeing wind, but it looks like it's within limits. We're approaching our second landing site now.*

Copy that. If you all are comfortable putting it down, do it. Doubles can you guys maintain your position on the ground when you get there for approximately ten minutes? Wags wants to talk to you and it looks like you're in a good spot for radio reception.

Ethan smiles. Now they don't have to worry about making up an excuse for the chiefs on why they're hanging out at the landing site. He turns to Doubles and gives her a thumbs up. She doesn't return his smile.

Doubles answers. *Roger. We'll set down, and I'll stand by for Wags.*

Doubles is the one that's supposed to check the mine. But she's also the one Wags wants to talk to. Ethan calls out over intercom, "Hendricks, Stepp did you all copy? We're going to put down here for ten minutes or so waiting for a call from Command."

"Copy," answers Hendricks.

"Roger," says Stepp.

"And heads up, I'm going to take a potty break."

Doubles nods.

Stepp answers in a faux southern drawl, "Golly, Mr. Ward. Can't you use the Gatorade bottle like the rest of us?"

Ethan throws it back. "You all didn't bring any wide-mouths. Won't work." One of the chiefs snorts over the mic. "Seriously, I got something going on with my stomach. I'm heading for the trees on the east side of the LZ. Hendricks, can you dig me up some TP?"

"Roger."

Ethan maintains his crosswind controls and resumes his approach, carefully monitoring his descent rate with outside cues. This would be the wrong place to make the same mistake he did two days ago.

The touchdown is smooth, gentle enough for Stepp to exclaim, "Like a baby's ass. Nice put down, PI."

Ethan turns to Doubles. "You have the controls."

Doubles reaches for the cyclic and collective. "I have the controls."

"You have the controls." Ethan raises his eyebrows.

She winks at him. "Hope everything comes out alright." She turns over her shoulder while keying her mic. "Stepp, come sit in the PI's seat while I do this radio call. I need you to guard the controls in this wind."

•　　•　　•

The mine is empty. Technically, "empty" is the wrong word. It's actually full—filled with sand, dirt, and rocks, such that no entry is possible. Ethan scrambles around the red-brown rock searching for an indication that anyone has touched the piles in the last decade. He scrapes back the sandy soil, digging his fingers deep into the dirt feeling for any type of false cover the talus might hide. Nothing.

He climbs from the shallow pit into the howling wind and scans the slope for another option. Maybe there are two mines, and he's picked the wrong one? But this mine opening is the only indentation on the hillside. He whips his head around at the change in the helicopter's engine pitch. Several popping sounds follow on the other side of the trees.

Doubles will be so pissed if he comes back empty-handed. Not at him, but at herself for not insisting she do the checking instead of him. She'll make him sit in the helicopter while she "double-checks" his efforts.

Above the trees, movement startles him. HAVOC 23 lifts into the sky, clipping a treetop with its tail on the way up. Ethan blinks and barrels toward the landing site. Nothing is normal about Doubles lifting off with a crew chief in the seat instead of him. Was it the wind?

He busts out of the trees and tilts his head back. Instead of one helicopter above him, there are two. A red and white Bell 412 turns broadside to HAVOC 23, its cargo side door open with two men crouched behind weapons in the doorway.

HAVOC 23's tail rotor yaws. Ethan braces at the massive gust of wind that causes the Bell helicopter's tail to mimic the Black Hawk's. The wind dies down momentarily, then surges again. The Bell climbs further into the air, but the Black Hawk overcorrects. The Bell helicopter maintains a hover with a box seat view of the impending crash. The Black Hawk's engines whine as Doubles fights to keep the helo in the air. HAVOC 23 is going down.

The woman he loves, his crew, and his helicopter spiral into the side of the mountain. At fifty feet above the ground, the nose pitches forward. The first thing to impact the slope is the cockpit he was sitting in minutes before.

He bolts into a sprint and makes it ten strides before skidding to a halt. The Bell helicopter is in a descent. The two men at the door have their weapons trained on the wreckage of HAVOC 23. The pilots focus on the smoking wreckage as they put the helicopter down. Ethan steps backward, then whirls and runs for the cover of the trees.

He burrows behind a dry log, watching in horror as two men in black flight suits exit and move toward the wreckage, weapons at the ready. Both men aim for the cockpit and Ethan prays he's watching some kind of mistake. That the men are looking for survivors to help, rather than checking to see if they need to finish their work. The men disappear into the front end of the aircraft. Ethan detects movement from the rear. A figure emerges from the billowing smoke, waving a handgun, and staggering toward Ethan. It's Hendricks. Ethan recognizes the grizzled veteran's shuffle.

Ethan pushes up from behind the tree trunk and waves his arms. There is a window of opportunity here, while the two men are inside the wreckage, for Hendricks to make it to Ethan and escape detection. The crew chief's head is bowed, hobbling across the slope. As he steps over a boulder, he glances in Ethan's direction. Ethan waves again. Hendricks freezes, his eyes locked on Ethan. His friend picks up his pace and Ethan can almost feel the desperation in his gait. The wind gusts again in Ethan's face, this time carrying Hendricks's voice.

"They're dead! Both of them are dead!"

Hendricks glances over his shoulder. One of the two men is pointing at him with his finger, while the other aims his rifle. Hendricks momentarily turns like he might fire upon the men, then seems to change his mind, whirling back in Ethan's direction.

He falls like a sack of grain offloaded from a flatbed truck. Ethan staggers back from his cover, his hand covering his mouth. Ignoring the gunmen, he shifts direction and steps over the log to help Hendricks. The bark next to his hand explodes. Ethan whips his head up at the glint of a gun barrel poking from the red helicopter. These men are triangulating on him. He drops behind the log and begins working his way down the slope using the log as cover.

They shot Hendricks.

•   •   •

Ethan slides down the shale on his butt, aiming for the next cluster of trees. He's been spotted.

Why would anyone attack their helicopter? Mistaken identity? But who would go so far as to track down a helicopter crew in the middle of the Rockies and shoot them down? Were they after Hendricks? Is that why they shot him?

He cascades into the basin below, stumbling over logs and crashing through standing water as the ground levels out. By the time he's descended the slope, the answer still eludes him. Is it Shavano's relic? How would anyone else know?

He turns east. After studying each mine's position on the map, the local geography is burned into his brain. The tiny mining town of St. Elmo sits only five miles away. He's uncertain if anyone lives in the town year-round but certainly in the summer someone will be there. And that someone could have access to a phone. Or a computer. Or even a radio.

Keeping the relics under wraps is yesterday's news. He needs to find help. The woman Ethan loves crashed into the side of a mountain. These men swooped in and finished off the only survivor. Now they're looking for him.

Ninety minutes later, Ethan stumbles out of the woods and onto a dirt road. Based on his estimated position he guesses it will take him a short distance north and into the town of St. Elmo. He turns left and picks up his pace.

He rounds a corner of the road. Walking in the opposite direction is a backpacker, about his height and at least ten years younger. The young man wears a beard. He stops in his tracks when he sees Ethan.

"Hey," Ethan calls.

The man lifts his hand in greeting but still wears a stunned-mullet expression. Ethan stops and looks down at his clothes. He's wearing an army-green flight suit, ripped in several places. He touches his face where he stumbled on his way down the mountain. Blood glistens off his fingers. No wonder this hiker appears wary.

"I was in a crash. A helicopter crash. Do you have a phone I can use?" Ethan's voice carries the high pitch of desperation. He has to tell people about the helicopter. And he has to warn them about the gunmen so rescuers don't put themselves in harm's way.

The hiker digs into a pouch hanging from his backpack's shoulder strap and walks toward Ethan. "You can give it a shot, but you aren't going to get any signal out here." He punches a code into the phone and hands it to Ethan. "I'm Taco, by the way." He pauses like he's waiting for Ethan to ask a question.

Ethan doesn't take the bait. He accepts the phone and punches in 911. No ring. No connection. The signal indicator reads SOS. He turns to Taco. "I need to get help. To let people know what has happened."

"Oh, they know. The town back there is blocked off. They've got a guy in tactical gear at each end of town checking people coming in and out." Taco laughs. "Not that there was anyone else but me."

"What do you mean tactical guys? Like cops and first responders?"

Taco shakes his head. "Something else. I'd say some kind of government agency folks. They weren't set up to save people. They're looking for someone." He runs his eyes up and down Ethan's frame. "Someone like you, I guess." He grins. "They'll be happy you made it, dude!"

Ethan absorbs this news. If the men in the town were there to help, they'd be on their way to the crash site, not manning a checkpoint in one of the few exits from this part of the mountain. He hands the phone back to the backpacker.

Taco tucks his phone away. "Good luck," he says and steps away aiming for the direction from which Ethan came.

Ethan unzips his flight suit and reaches inside for the 9mm pistol he carries close to his chest. He pulls it out. "Hey, Taco."

"Yeah?" Taco says as he turns back to Ethan. His eyes widen as he notices the gun. He raises his hands. "Dude. No."

"I don't have a choice, Taco. Those guys are looking for me. I'm a good guy. Give me your stuff."

Taco buries his hand into a pocket and pulls out a wallet. "Take it. Shit all you had to do was ask. I would have helped you out."

"Not your money. I need your stuff."

Taco looks confused.

"Your backpack. Your gear." Ethan points to Taco's head, then his feet. "And your clothes. I'll use my boots."

"Dude…?"

"I don't have time to explain." Ethan uses his free hand to pull out his wallet. While Taco unslings his pack, Ethan holsters his weapon and pulls out a wad of cash. He thrusts it toward Taco while keeping one hand inside his flight suit on his pistol butt. "Take it. And hurry up."

Taco finishes disrobing. He asks Ethan if he can keep a spare set of shorts and a shirt from inside the pack and Ethan agrees. Taco rummages around and pulls out several other items. A cell phone. A baggie of something green. "Phone, and bud. Can I keep this stuff?"

Taco is right about the cell coverage. By the time Taco gets service, Ethan will be long gone. "Yeah, man. Keep it." He stuffs the clothes Taco was wearing in the top of the pack and shoulders it. He needs to put distance between himself and the men blocking the town around the corner. He can change into hiker clothes later.

"Thanks," Ethan turns in the direction Taco was headed when they first met. He points up the road and says, "Colorado Trail?"

"About two miles," Taco says, shaking his head. "Right will take you northbound. Straight will take you south." He pauses. "I wouldn't go south if I were you. That's where the guys in town said they're looking." He points in the direction of the crash. "Head west. You'll hit the trail. Go north from there."

Ethan shakes his head. "I just took all your stuff at gunpoint. Why are you helping me?"

"I don't know what agency those guys work for, but they're not nice. And you can't be all bad if you're just taking my gear and leaving my phone, and my bud. And your cash." Taco smiles. "Good luck, I guess. If you get a chance, my phone number and email address are inside the pack. Let me know when you're done and where I can come get it."

Ethan nods and turns in the direction Taco recommended. Taco continues south. Ethan stops and calls out. "Where're you going?"

"There's a hiker hostel in Garfield," Taco yells. "Only about ten miles. The Butterfly House. They'll have gear I can use. If not, the trail will provide."

Ethan shakes his head. He hadn't expected these hiker types to be so committed.

24–ZAHN

St. Elmo, Colorado–July 13, 2022

Four granola bars later, I pass through St. Elmo. The Buena Vista police have set up a command vehicle for the helicopter crash, and they stop me mid-bite.

The officer walks toward my rolled-down window, palm in the halt position. "Sir, may I ask—hey, Z-man." I recognize Donnie Morgan the same time he recognizes me. "Thought they had all you guys hostage."

"Not me. But I've heard they're still inside." Technically, I speak the truth and I'm not wasting time telling Donnie about my escape when I could be searching for my daughter. "Who's up at the crash site?"

"Feds all over. The FAA. Bunch of Army and Forest Service folks. A three-man Colorado Bureau of Investigation team is covering until the FBI gets here."

"I thought it was an Army Guard helicopter. Why the feds?"

"Cuz the helo is a state and federal asset, and this could be considered terrorism. That's the buzz."

I nod. Donnie's explanation makes sense. How long will it take them to figure out the relationship between the hostage situation in Salida and the helicopter crash? My frustration with Joe Nissen's refusal to push the information up the chain deepens.

"Anybody linking the sheriff's office standoff to this?" I don't need anyone saying I kept information from anyone, so my question is an attempt to cover my ass.

Donnie says, "Why? Do you think there's a connection?"

"How many BV or Salida police officers are searching the mountains for the people who shot the helicopter survivor?"

"None. We don't have enough resources—" Donnie's eyes widen in comprehension. "So, you're thinking…Holy shit."

"Yep." I grimace.

"What's your plan, Z-man?"

"To go look. If you hear about that little situation in Salida resolving, tell my coworkers to join me."

Donnie cocks his head and looks past me to my 24-hour pack riding shotgun. I'm in civilian clothes, by myself, without a weapon in sight, claiming to be on Sheriff's business. He shakes his head. "Radio in if you find anything. We're on BV2. No one is using the Sheriff's frequencies because…well, you know."

"Right."

I park my truck near Hancock Lake and tune my digital radio to BV2. I don my shoulder holster, sling my 24-hour pack over my shoulder, and pull my Glock from the glove box. I consider carrying it in my hand—I'm that worried about who is out here—but unclipping my chest strap on my pack and leaving my fleece jacket unzipped will provide quick access.

I'm a hundred yards from my truck when a voice blares from my radio. I crank down the volume before answering.

Z-man, Donnie, on BV2.

I press transmit. *Go ahead.*

We just got a call from Gunnison Dispatch. They show a GPS SOS alert. Thought you'd want to know.

I scowl. Gunnison's SAR area starts another six miles west of here. And I'm not on a SAR mission. *Roger. Contact the SAR Incident Commander on call and see if they have folks that can help out. I'm out of the SAR loop today.*

Donnie's voice comes back in an apologetic tone. *Gunnison is fielding our 911 calls because our dispatch is, you know, out of commission. An alert pinged five miles from you. You're the closest guy to the coordinates. Take a look while you're out there? Just trying to maximize resources.*

Good call. Give me the coordinates. Does Gunnison have a name associated with the GPS? Normally, I'd consider the odds of the call from Daria to be low, but I've already narrowed her down to this fifteen-square-mile swath of wilderness.

Coordinates are N 38.665528, E -106.428389. I'll ask Gunnison about a name.

I plug the coordinates into my GPS and study the results. The alert is at the top of a creek basin that empties behind me. At the Sister Mary O'Malley mine halfway between my position and St. Elmo.

Z-man?

Go ahead.

You're not going to believe this.

Daria Zahn?

You knew?

I suspected. She's on the Colorado Trail in this area. Tell the SAR guys I'm on my way. I'll approach from the east.

Roger. Keep me updated.

I jog back to my truck and toss my gear in the passenger seat. I make a three-point turn, and a flicker of movement catches my eye in my rearview mirror. Two men climb from the lake shore, each with a rifle barrel jutting from their pack. I brake.

The man in the lead whips his head up as I stop, and holds his hand out to his side, palm away from my truck, signaling his partner to hold his position.

I reach for my Glock. If I exit the truck now, I'll have the jump on them—assuming they aren't packing handguns of their own.

The lead man leans in my direction and unslings his pack. He doesn't appear to be in a rush. His partner does the same.

Four seconds to make a decision. I'm packing my badge. I've got sufficient evidence that armed men in this area are linked to the helicopter crash and are directly involved in the Salida hostage situation. I can take them in to the Salida Police.

One second to act. I ease off my truck's brakes and roll forward, glancing between the road and my mirror to monitor the men. No conceivable scenario here where I leave my daughter thumbing SOS on her GPS. What if she's hurt? What if Emma's injured?

The men's heads disappear behind the knoll as I roll downhill toward the Sister Mary mine.

I check my six o'clock every hundred yards until the road bends and I lose sight of the lake area. Reaching for my radio, I run through what I need to tell Donnie. That we have armed teams roaming the woods. Get up to Hancock Lake and take these guys in.

I key the mic, then release it. Donnie's the only law enforcement officer besides the teams up at the helo crash. If he leaves St. Elmo, he's leaving his post. And he knows nothing about what's going on. Do I really want to send a police officer alone and uninformed into a situation where he's out-manned and outgunned?

I tap my brakes again. Maybe I should turn around and do my duty. Before these guys hurt someone else. These men have murdered a helicopter crew and taken over a town's law enforcement function. Someone has to stop them.

I release the brake, punching the gas pedal, and aiming north toward the mine. That someone is going to have to be someone else. My daughter's five miles away and sending out an SOS.

Nothing will stop me from bringing her home.

25-DARIA

Wildcat Gulch near St. Elmo-July 13, 2022

Daria crashes through the willows, stumbling alongside the drainage that empties into Chalk Creek two miles below, her heart hammering. She wades twenty yards into the tightly woven branches before catching her breath and peering through the brush. Part of her wants to follow Beans—or whoever he is—and Emma so she can report it when she reaches a phone. But Beans will be checking his six, expecting to be tracked. It's not like a person can hide while on the trail. The armed men behind them are proof of that.

Beans says they're after him. He's taken Emma hostage to protect himself. Does that make Beans a bad guy and the gunmen good?

Daria's not trusting anybody with a gun right now.

She moves downhill but jolts to a halt. She needs to hunker down right here, right now. Those men were a half mile behind them. Five minutes for Beans to make his decision to kidnap Emma and ditch Daria. She's been running for two more. If she doesn't stop and hide, the two men will crest the ridge and the first thing they'll see is crashing willows. With her backpack and hiking clothes, they won't mistake her for an errant bear or elk.

Daria slips off her pack, carries it into the thickest part of the willows and stashes it. She lowers herself among the branches. With her eyes barely above ground level, she can just make out the crest.

The men pop into view only seconds later. She forces her breath quiet even though she's certain she's far enough away for them not to hear her. The men pause at the high point and survey the trail ahead. No reason to look in her direction.

But they do. The man who said he was TSA makes a quarter turn in Daria's direction and points. She scrunches her head further into the thicket. The man's face drops from her field of vision, but his finger is not pointed at her. He's pointing to something above her and slightly north. The second man says something indistinguishable. A crackle sounds and Daria recognizes the static of a radio. She breathes through her nose as the two men survey the hillside.

The men disappear up the trail to where she split from Beans and Emma. Daria replays Beans's actions, trying to remember whether they left any sign of their hike breakup.

Three minutes later, a muffled voice carries over the sound of rushing water from the other side of the creek. Daria forces herself to count to a hundred before raising her head. The men are gone.

Time to start crashing toward a phone signal she hopes to find in St. Elmo.

But St. Elmo is hidden by a ridge running east-west from the town. The north side of the ridge is the road to Tincup Pass. The south side is the draw she's hiding in. But the ridge? That's where Beans described the helicopter crashing.

She rolls onto her back and slowly crunches to a sitting position, checking the trail above her first to ensure the men are gone. No one is in sight. She swivels her head and surveys the ridge where the man pointed. At first, nothing but rock fills her vision. But she catches someone wearing orange at the edge of a rockslide. The greenish-gray carcass of what was once a functional helicopter rests above the figure.

On the radio call only minutes before, the gunmen said they were TSA. Were they checking in with the rest of the teams at the crash site? Is she wrong about them being bad guys?

She squints at the figure wearing orange. If they were checking in and letting the investigation team know where they were, why didn't they wave after they made contact? That's what she would have done.

Daria is confident that the investigative team at the site has to be on the up and up. Her dad was with them investigating.

She shoulders her pack. Her GPS dangles from the strap, reminding her of the low battery. Sixteen percent. That's enough to boot up and send an SOS signal. She powers up the device and presses the emergency button on the side of the GPS. An hourglass spins on the screen and a number appears on the screen indicating she has messages. From her dad.

…those are not TSA agents. I don't know exactly what is going on, but those guys are part of something related to the helicopter crash. The crash was not an accident. Get out of the mountains at the earliest opportunity…

Daria's heart pounds. Emma was right. Daria jerks to her feet, ready to get out of these mountains, but her dad—Z-man—is always reminding her to slow down. Think. Sometimes slow ends up being fast when you're working through a problem.

Something related to the helicopter crash.

Daria is wrong about the helicopter site above her. She can no longer assume the people there represent safety. And by pressing the SOS button, she just told Chaffee County law enforcement exactly where she's at. She can trust them, but what about when they page out the 911 call? Her position will be all over the radios. She wants to tell people Emma has been kidnapped. But she doesn't want the wrong people to know where she's at. Because there is more than one set of bad guys up here. Beans took Emma from her at gunpoint. Armed men are looking for Beans. That's her new assumption anyway because why would the men be looking for her or Emma? Her SOS call probably inadvertently helped Beans or the guys formerly known as TSA agents. She powers down her GPS and clips it to her pack.

She waits another five minutes before climbing to her feet and wading downhill. Her breath rips ragged again after only twenty steps. Willow thickets line the creek like patchwork. She focuses on the grassy breaks between each section, desperate to transition from bushwhacking to hiking. At each clear section, she pauses to catch her breath, checking for a glimpse of Beans and Emma—and the men following them—then looks the other way, in case the helicopter recovery teams spot her.

The sun creeps down her back as the afternoon fades. The creek jags to the right ahead of her, into a flat meadow. In the distance, the water returns to its eastern flow, still too wide to jump without getting wet. The terrain on her side has forced the water's shift in direction—she clings to the steep hill to keep from sliding down to the stream below. She falls twice, but stays on her side of the creek. Finally, crossing is her only option.

She spots a potential fording spot. She'll have to take off her shoes, but at least it's shallow enough to keep her shorts dry. She angles her feet sideways to the mountainside and stair-steps toward the water.

A shout echoes above her from the direction of the crash site. She cranes her neck searching for the source. Her feet slip. Her stomach smacks the slope, punching the air from her lungs. She thrusts her hands above her head for something to grab but rakes loose gravel instead. In seconds, she's in the water that creeps up to her crotch and soaks her backpack.

"Shit!" Soaking wet above the tree line with night approaching, she's pissed. She wades to the other side of the stream.

She climbs through the low willows lining the other bank, high-stepping toward a patch of green. When she's clear, she drops her pack. The main compartment's bottom is saturated. Her sleeping bag and tent are in the bottom of her pack but if her dad's pro tip works, she should be okay. She wipes her hands with the wet hand towel safety pinned to the outside of the pack. It would be dry by now but her fall soaked it. Unclipping the pack's crown, and loosening the side straps, she grabs the edges of the trash compactor bag Zahn recommended and extracts it from her pack. Water drips from the bottom as she props it vertically on the grass.

Daria's rain jacket sits on top and it's dry. She spreads it on the grass and pulls out the remainder of her gear. Her pack is soaked. The trash bag's exterior is wet. But her gear is completely dry. She grins. Her father will love hearing he was right about something.

The sun sinks farther below the mountains and Daria shivers. She needs to get into dry clothes and out of these peaks. From the waistbelt pocket of her pack, she pulls out her headlamp and dons it. She stuffs her sleeping bag and tent back into the bag and sits on her raincoat where she can change. The thing she doesn't have is a dry towel to wipe herself with before swapping her bottom layer, but her top half is dry, and she uses her extra shirt.

She's behaving like she's continuing her hike—drying her clothes, concerned about her tent and sleeping bag, but the moment Emma was taken hostage on the mountain trail, Daria's hike ended. When she emerges from this draw, she'll be less than a mile from St. Elmo. She just needs to make it there to call for help.

She struggles to her feet. The sun has set, but she's still hesitant about turning on her headlamp. She'd be visible to both the teams at the helicopter site and the armed men following Beans and Emma.

The meadow ends at the tree line, and the scattered pines morph into a forest. She angles away from the creek. As long as she doesn't start climbing again, she'll make it to the road her map shows at the bottom of the draw. Her pace slows. Without a light, she has to be careful about the deadfall between the tree trunks.

She steps over a fallen log, and when she twists to clear her rear leg from the deadfall, a tree trunk behind her reflects a light. She pulls her leg over and crouches. A headlamp bounces toward her, closer to the river. It will only take a glance in her direction, and she'll be lit up like a deer in headlights. She inches along the log until a stand of trees blocks the light.

Whoever is bushwhacking her direction is looking for something. The hiker pauses every ten seconds or so, surveying their surroundings. Daria edges around the tree stand as the light comes parallel with her, keeping the heaviest branches between the hiker and herself while peering out to watch their progress.

When the hiker stops, the figure's head bows, its headlamp illuminating a GPS. As soon as the beam focuses down, Daria spies a familiar red Chaffee County Search & Rescue North patch.

"Are you on SAR North?" she calls.

The headlamp whips her direction, and she dives behind the branches.

"Daria?"

She lunges from behind the tree, barrels toward the light, and stumbles on a downed tree.

"Daria!"

"Dad?"

26-ETHAN

Colorado Trail near Alpine Tunnel, Colorado-July 13, 2022

"Did you have to pull a gun on her?" Emma almost growls, after Daria's out of sight.

"Hey, I'm making this up as I go." Ethan's not exaggerating. Emma told him last Christmas she had a hike planned in Colorado this summer, but she hadn't been specific. "You'd think siblings would talk more," he adds.

"If you'd just let me tell her what's happening, she'd have been okay when we explained why she had to leave us," Emma says, taking an angry swipe at a willow. "Jesus, Ethan. I told you I'm dating Z-man. That's her dad." Emma tosses an accusatory comment over her shoulder, "Now she's going to find out that we both lied to her."

Ethan moves to keep up. "I'm not okay with *you* getting involved, Emma. They killed my crew. They plan to kill me. You think they're going to let anyone with me survive?"

"I'm not leaving you. And if the roles were reversed?"

Ethan doesn't respond. The right answer is—*I'd try to save you, Emma*—but it's so rare they see each other that he sometimes forgets he has a twin sister. "It's not like we're inseparable, Emma."

"What would you do?" Emma whirls around, hands on her hips and eyes blazing.

Ethan flinches. Doubles and his sister have a moral compass he envies, but he wouldn't leave her. No matter the pain and adolescent crisis they endured growing up, they trudged through it together. He hadn't made it to her FBI Academy graduation ceremony, but that didn't make him any less proud.

Does she feel the same way about his Army service? Maybe what's kept them apart isn't a lack of desire to connect, but their troubled past. An aunt and uncle with no love to spare. A sterile upbringing that left each of them racing to leave it behind, and, in the process, leaving each other.

Ethan sighs. "I wouldn't leave you either." He looks back, scanning the horizon. "We need to move. Those guys will crest that hill any moment. We need to get to tree line up ahead."

Emma turns back to the trail. She hisses over her shoulder, "So what's the plan? I get why you're searching for this thing Shavano supposedly hid. I get why these guys are after it too. But how are we going to get you out of this?"

"I've been thinking about that."

"I'm all ears."

"These guys are basing out of St. Elmo near the crash probably because they think that's where Shavano hid whatever relic he had. Our helicopter zeroed in on that area. They were ready for us. They probably assumed we knew where the relic is. So they're searching for me. Either because they think I have it, or know where it is."

"But you said it's not there. So, we beat them out of the mountains, and you'll be home free. You can come back for it later."

Ethan says nothing.

Emma glances back. "Do you know where it is?"

Ethan nods. "We determined that if it wasn't at the crash site then it was at the other mine. And based on the map you showed me for the southbound route, we're hiking within a half mile of it after climbing Chalk Creek Pass."

"You want to try to get it on the way out?"

"Only if these guys give up on us, which they won't," Ethan grimaces. "But we pick a spot and deviate off trail. We'll let these guys pass us, then we'll grab Shavano's stuff from the mine.

"Then what?"

Ethan juts out his chin. "We do what Doubles wanted. Get it back to Iraq."

27-ZAHN

Near St. Elmo, Colorado-July 13, 2022

Daria stumbles into my arms. I tilt my head skyward, and gasp in gratitude, "Thank you, Lord."

I squeeze her as if this particular hug will be the one that keeps her from ever disappearing again. I want to grab her hand, scramble to my truck and escape the threats lurking in these mountains. Dangers I don't yet understand. Instead, I force myself into SAR mode and switch my headlamp to its red beam so we can talk without blinding each other. "Are you hurt?"

Daria fumbles to turn on her headlamp. "No. But he's got Emma."

Emma! I've been so paralyzed with fear over Daria's safety that I've practically forgotten about the other woman in my life. The woman I might love.

"Who? Who's got her?"

Daria explains the events that led to Beans seizing Emma and leaving Daria behind.

"Dad, what's happening? Why'd he take Emma?"

Daria's story tags with the helicopter crash and the men likely involved in bringing it down, including the team who took over the sheriff's office. None of this makes sense.

"I think everything is tied to this helicopter crash." I describe the wreckage and the crash victims. "Then Perez and I ran into some other issues that kept me from meeting you and Emma when I thought you were coming to BV."

"My feet felt better," she says, with a sheepish grin.

I glance down. "What's wrong with your feet?"

"I had some Achilles tendon issues, but it's going away. I'm fine." She sucks in a breath. "We've got to get out of here and tell the sheriff about Emma."

"That's a problem."

"Why?"

"Because the sheriff and pretty much every lawman in the county are being held captive in a meeting room at headquarters." I fill her in.

"How are you here then?"

"I broke out."

Daria's piercing eyes appear full of skepticism. "Wait. The entire sheriff's office is taken hostage by some kind of elite team with automatic weapons and the only one who makes it out is the middle-aged deputy reserve sheriff who's been on the team for less than a month?"

"I saw an opportunity and I took it. Besides, if I didn't climb through that roof, I never would have heard the conversation tying our captors to the helicopter." I give Daria a thin smile. "And I wasn't about to turn around after hearing that you and Emma could be in danger."

"Well, Emma still is. What's our plan?"

I shine my headlamp directly on Daria. She lowers her eyes. "There's no *our* in this, Daria. You're wet. You're tired. I'm getting you out of here. I'll figure out something on the way."

Daria grabs my arm. "No. We don't know what Beans is going to do. Or those guys with guns."

"Look, kiddo. Neither of us has enough information to make an informed decision about the danger Emma is in, but you're right. That's why I'm getting you out of here."

Daria objects. "But if Emma's in danger—"

"Then, it doesn't make sense to put you in danger as well. If she's not," I take a breath, knowing she won't like it. "Then the time it takes to get you back to town won't matter."

She lowers her beam again, recognizing the "and-that's-final" tone in my voice. We may have been absent from each other's lives for most of her adolescence, but we've also endured quite a bit in the last two years. Adversity that threatened to drive us apart, in the end, strengthened our love for each other.

"Hang on," I say, wanting her to think about what I've said. "Let me call Donnie."

I tell him I've found Daria and to take SAR off standby for a mission. When I finish, I check Daria's face for protest, but she's quiet. "Let's go," I say. "The truck's about a mile down the gully at the road."

The moon tonight is so bright that lights are optional. Last week's local paper mentioned an upcoming "supermoon." We pick our way through the trees and deadfall while avoiding the creek. I follow her, partly so she will feel like she's in control of something, but also out of paternal instinct. I have this irrational fear my daughter might turn around and bolt back to the Colorado Trail.

I check our position on my GPS. We're less than a quarter mile from where I parked the truck. The trees thin as we approach Chalk Creek. I switch my headlamp off. Daria turns. I step forward.

"What's up?" she says.

I lower my voice to a whisper. "I'm a little nervous about just walking up to my truck."

Daria lowers her voice to match mine. "Why? The bad guys are up on the trail. Not here."

"The bad guys we know about. I saw some men with weapons while I was driving here. They didn't look official." I pause. "Bear with me, OK?"

Daria nods in silhouette.

"I'll take the lead. When we get to the clearing, the road is still a hundred yards in front of us. I parked on the far side. You stay in the trees. I'll check out the truck."

"And if everything's alright, you'll start it up and I'll come out?"

"No. I don't want to turn the engine over until we're both inside ready to move. I'll come back and get you if we're good to go."

"You don't think I can walk across a field by myself?"

"No. I have a gun, and you don't."

I deliberately slow our pace because of the dark, checking on Daria only ten feet behind me. My eyes are fully adapted now. She nods in my direction. *Good to go.* The distance between each tree lengthens as we reach the bottom of the draw. A thatch of meadow grass across the stream looks like silvery snow in the moonlight. I raise my palm to Daria like a traffic guard. She freezes in place. I pick a tree and peer around. The road strings across the far side of the meadow, my truck reflecting moonlight on the northern side.

I retrace my steps. "Follow me," I say, retreating into the trees. I pick a deadfall and lower myself behind it, patting the ground at my side. "Sit here."

Daria lowers herself. I turn to the grass meadow behind us and motion for Daria to look.

"Can you see my truck?"

Daria is quiet for a moment. "Got it," she finally says.

"You wait here until I get back. You don't need to watch me. Just hunker down."

"What do I do if you don't come back?"

Daria's question is simple, but I could kick myself for not having a ready answer. She's asking about a Plan B. I'm worried about the truck because someone might be waiting for me. If that's the case, and they get the drop on me, then my plans of returning my daughter to safety are for naught.

"If I don't come back within twenty minutes, I want you to wait here for an hour."

"Why?"

"To be safe. I'll be back in twenty. If I'm not, these guys will be on the lookout for anyone else. Give them an hour to figure out what they're going to do with me, then head toward St. Elmo. You know which direction?"

Daria points past my truck.

I whisper, "Stay off the road. Pick a spot to ford the creek. We've got local police in St. Elmo covering for our lack of sheriff coverage. When I came through, Donnie Morgan was parked at the beginning of town. Look for him or a Buena Vista police vehicle."

"Got it."

"OK. Be right back." I consider hugging Daria or pecking her cheek, but that will probably worry her more. Instead, I give her leg closest to me a quick slap, and crawl from behind the deadfall.

My Survival, Evasion, Resistance, and Escape training from my Air Force days kicks in and I purposely avoid rushing to my truck. Slow is smooth…smooth is fast, is the mantra. After wading across the creek, I deliberately pause every couple of steps, evaluating my approach to the vehicle. Nothing moves in front of me.

At the truck, I scoot around the back, putting the vehicle between me and the road. I peer over the truck bed's edge and scan the interior. Empty. I fish in my pocket for my keychain before changing my mind. Pressing it will make a noise and flash the lights. I could just use the physical key to open the door, but since I've never tried it, I'm unsure how the truck will respond. No one is here. All I need to do is retrieve Daria and we can get out of here.

I edge along the truck but a reflection at my feet catches my eye. Crouching next to the front wheel, I spot a clear glass bottle underneath my front tire. I pull the bottle aside and crawl to the other tire. Another bottle sits behind the tire.

Doubtful a broken bottle would incapacitate my Tundra tires, but it would make noise when I depart. I consider my next move. The road behind me is empty. A bad guy monitoring my truck wouldn't wait behind the vehicle. The logical place to wait is down the road.

I slip into the woods and parallel the route to St. Elmo, while keeping my eyes on the road. It doesn't take long before I spot what I've been looking for. Moonlight reflects off the surface of a dark vehicle parked on the side of the road.

I squat and observe the SUV. I can just make out the silhouette of someone sitting in the driver's seat. The passenger seat appears to be empty. Suddenly, the headlights flash on. I shrink further into the cottonwoods while keeping my eye on the vehicle. The beams illuminate a black shape—no, two black shapes—shuffling across the road. Mama Bear leading her cub across the road. I squint. Although it's impossible to be sure, I feel certain this is the same pair of bears I stopped for two days ago on my way to St. Elmo. As soon as the mother bear is clear of the road, she turns in my direction, huffs and lumbers deeper into the woods. The cub follows.

The only people who know I'm out here are the Buena Vista Police—assuming Donnie called me in—and the armed men at Hancock Lake. The police are the good guys. The SUV isn't law enforcement. So, the bad guys are aware I'm here and want to know when I leave. But they would have been here whether I came searching for Daria or not.

Who else are they looking for? Someone desperate enough to kidnap my girlfriend, perhaps? I've got more questions about Beans for Daria.

I took a chance breaking out of the hostage situation. Now that I have my daughter, I have no intention of putting her in harm's way. We're not getting in my truck.

That leaves two choices: hole up for the night in a location where we won't be discovered or look for Emma Frazier and her captor. But that second option also puts Daria at risk.

That's not happening.

28-DARIA

Wildcat Gulch near St. Elmo-July 13, 2022

"Hole up and hide until morning? While Emma's life is in danger?" Daria hisses.

"Dar, we can't drive out of here without those men spotting us." Zahn has plopped down next to her, his wet legs pressed against hers, hand cupped against her ear. "We can't go chasing Emma. The bad guys outgun us." His whisper is terse but methodical like he's trying to talk her off a ledge.

Daria can't leave her hiking partner in danger. Her decision to hike with Emma had been reluctant. Part of her wanted to prove she could hike the Colorado Trail solo. But now, after all the miles they've put in together—they're close. More than just friends. They've forged a bond, regardless of what happens between Emma and her father.

Somehow, she has to convince her dad to do the right thing. It's an odd position for her to be in. Her dad's proven over and over again that when things get tough, he doesn't look for the easy way out. The only reason he's not going after Emma is out of concern for Daria's safety.

"I'll hide and you go find Emma?" she says, desperate to allay his fears.

He shakes his head. "If I leave you, then you need the Glock, and I won't be able to do anything about Emma."

"I don't need the gun. They won't find me."

"You don't know that."

"Then take me with you. If we find Emma, I'll stay in the background." Daria's whisper is a plea.

Her dad's head shakes no, but his eyes focus on hers.

"Are you going to nag me all night?"

"No," Daria says. "I'm going to wait until you're asleep and go find Emma on my own." She's bluffing, and she's certain her dad knows it. But at least he's listening.

Zahn leans back, studying the sky.

She's pushed him far enough. He's considering her plan. She lets out a puff of air instead of a laugh. Not a real plan, just a proposed action. Chase after her kidnapped hiking partner, find her, and somehow take her away from the man who holds her captive.

Fortunately, if Zahn decides to go after Emma and take Daria along, he won't do it without an idea of how to execute each stage. First, how to search for Emma without being detected. Second, how to approach. Finally, how to rescue her.

Daria waits.

Her dad sighs an exhausted-parent sigh and whispers, "We'll look for her."

Daria pushes from the log, but her father snags her jacket. "We'll look for her. Hopefully, find her. But if we can pin down her location, we'll use my GPS to get the message out to folks who can help, then we're done. Understand?"

Daria doesn't understand. If they find Emma and wait for help, it might be too late. But arguing might change her dad's mind. "Understood."

They pick their way south in the direction Beans and Emma disappeared, Zahn in the lead, keeping the creek between them and the road. The moon illuminates the riverbank. Water tumbling across rocks muffles their footfalls as they plow through the willows. They're aiming for the Colorado Trail, but she's clueless as to Zahn's plan.

When he pauses for her to catch up, she raises her hand.

He moves close to her. "What?"

"Where are we going?"

"South."

"Why?"

Zahn shrugs. "That's the problem. Where do you think he would have taken her?"

"He's hiking the Colorado Trail," she says. "But he's done something wrong because he's worried about the guys that were behind us. I guess he would either hike fast and try to get off at the next road crossing, or he would get off the trail as soon as he could so the guys behind them wouldn't find him."

"Is he really?" Zahn's voice sounds skeptical.

"Really what?"

"Hiking the CT. What kind of thru-hiker takes a hostage? Actually, what kind of guy who's threatened by guys with guns decides to take a random hiker hostage? The guys chasing him don't care about her, and she's just slowing him down."

Daria sighs. "OK. I have no idea, but what are we going to do about it?"

Her dad lays his hand on her forearm and draws her in. "Hey, relax, just trying to explain why I don't have a good plan." He tugs on her arm. "Follow me."

Zahn leads her to a tree, pulls her in among the lower branches, and squats. "Down." He pulls a pair of reading glasses from his pocket and shoves them over his nose. Cupping his hand around his GPS screen, he points to a black arrow on the map. "Here's where we are. Heading south and we'll cross this small stream coming out of Tunnel Gulch."

She pokes at the dashed line on the other side of the water. "And we'll intercept the CT," she says, tracing her finger backward on the trail, "about two or two-and-a-half miles from where he took her."

"Right. And that's where I'm uncertain what to do next." He gently nudges her finger out of the way and points at a label on the map: Alpine Tunnel East Portal. "They could have hidden in the tunnel." He traces his finger to the tunnel's exit.

"Or followed the side trail that goes over the mountain," Daria says, understanding.

Zahn runs his finger along the dashed line toward the black arrow marking their position. "Or they could have just stayed on the CT and passed us already."

Daria nods. "We don't know whether to backtrack on the trail."

"Not just that." Zahn traces the CT past their position. "See the intersections here? They could take the road where I parked my car and head toward St. Elmo. Or they could've stayed on the CT, and are maneuvering over Chalk Creek Pass right now." He points to a bare spot on the map above two lakes. "All switchbacks. If they haven't crossed over, they'll see us coming as soon as we approach the lakes."

Daria says nothing for a moment. No wonder her dad hasn't shared the plan. Just this five-mile stretch of the Colorado Trail requires multiple teams to cover all the possibilities. It's just the two of them. Splitting up isn't an option.

"So, we just need to guess?"

He nods. "What do you think?"

Daria is flattered he's asking her but that's how her dad rolls. He never completely trusts himself. He probes the people around him, wanting their take on any situation in case they might have a better idea.

She remembers Beans and his unfamiliarity with resupply points. "I think he would have kept to the CT."

"Why?"

"He wasn't expecting those guys with the guns. He kept checking our route on a paper map while he hiked with us. He knows the CT. Probably not much else."

"He probably wouldn't take a side trail unless he was confident there was an escape route. So, let's intercept the CT and trail them."

"What about the gun guys?"

"Exactly. If they're still following your guy Beans and Emma, then we've got to watch for them."

He holds a tree branch for her, and they step into the moonlight. Daria doubts she'll be leading. She steps to the side and sweeps her hand toward the south. "After you."

Zahn nods, his smile looking grim. He obviously doesn't like her being here.

They ford a small creek, barely a trickle of water with a boulder in the middle that allows for a two-hop across, and pause at the top of the opposite bank.

Her dad says, "You stay here. I'm going to the edge of the path to check things out. If it's good, I'll come back for you."

He'll do the scouting. Daria will wait.

When Zahn gives her a thumbs up, she joins him, nervous about Emma's fate and what they are trying to do about it. But a small part of Daria considers the bit of trail she's skipped. If she ever finishes the CT, she'll have to hike back in here and finish this segment to truly call it complete. That's how it works.

Zahn keeps looking back at her.

"What are you looking for?" She calls him on it.

"Just making sure no one catches us." The trail behind them is an old railroad bed leading to the Alpine Tunnel. "Even with our headlamps off, the straight path and existing moonlight make us easy targets."

Zahn slows, hugs the right side of the trail, head turned toward the slope. She catches up.

He steps closer to her, keeping his voice low. "They built a new section of the CT here a couple of years back. The old one continues along the old railway bed until it intercepts the jeep roads to Hancock Lake. Hikers were complaining about having to walk on a dirt road."

"And you know this how?"

"A hiker tore their ACL here. She gave my SAR team a history lesson on the CT."

Daria wants to check her trail app but they can't risk the light. "But the dirt road meets back up with the trail at the first lake? Hancock Lake, right?"

"What are you thinking, Dar?"

"Just putting myself in Beans's head and in the heads of the bad guys."

"And?"

"The gun guys didn't know for sure that we're on to them. We didn't jump up and down announcing 'We know you're following us.'"

"OK."

"Beans doesn't want those guys to catch him. And he thinks they will assume we were hiking southbound on the trail."

Zahn nods. He gets it. "If Beans skips the trail turnoff here, he could lose them. He could go straight and turn back south on the road to St. Elmo, or he could hunker down at Hancock Lake and wait for the gun guys to pass them on the trail." Zahn cocks his head. "Nice. I see the logic. Except for one part."

Daria frowns, "What?"

"You said the bad guys would assume that if you didn't know you were being followed then you would stay on the trail, right?"

"So?"

"It circles us back around to the question of why they're following Beans in the first place. When did you say you met Beans?"

"A couple of miles this side of Cottonwood Pass. Yesterday afternoon."

Zahn stares at the ground, his lips moving. He flips one finger out, then another, then another. "Anything unusual about him? Any tells that made him different from other hikers you've met?" He checks over her shoulder again.

Daria relays Beans' cluelessness about resupply points. How his pack is too small for his frame. The fact that his gym shorts don't match his heavy boots.

Zahn continues nodding. "What about his hair? Beard? How long did he look like he'd been out?"

Daria snaps her head up. That's it. Beans' hair was tapered to the skin above his ears. He had the start of a beard, maybe a day or two of shadow.

"He didn't look like he'd been on the trail long."

"He hadn't. Only for a day. And he was carrying someone else's pack."

"How do you know?"

"Because Army helicopter crews don't fly missions with Osprey hiking backpacks."

Daria gasps. "You think he was on board the helicopter that crashed?"

"I know he was."

29-ETHAN

Colorado Trail near Alpine Tunnel, Colorado-July 13, 2022

"We need to turn here." Emma points at a spur trail veering uphill off the old rail-to-trail track.

Ethan's gaze follows Emma's finger. "Kind of obscure, isn't it? I wonder how many people miss this turn, especially so close to sunset." He turns to Emma. "What happens if you go straight?"

Emma studies her phone. "It looks like you can still get to Chalk Creek Pass. It just squares the turn if we stay on this path. If we turn here, it shaves a couple of tenths of a mile because we're aiming straight for the pass." She pauses. "Huh."

"What?"

"Staying on the trail also keeps us away from vehicles. If we follow the old railroad bed we're on, we intercept a portion of an off-road vehicle route."

Ethan peers over her shoulder. He hadn't planned on two options. They can't track the progress of the gunmen behind them if they don't know what route they choose. He explains the dilemma to Emma.

"Then we need to go over the pass." She stabs a point on her cell phone's map. "Watch from the other side once we get back down to the tree line."

Ethan nods. "Even better if we hunker down at the top of the pass. Watch their approach from over a mile out. When they hit these lakes," he points at Emma's map, "we'll let them see us so they know we're still in front. But we'll have a twenty- or thirty-minute lead on them." He studies Emma's phone. "Once we hit tree line, the trail runs through forest to the highway. We can pick any spot and assume they think we're pushing on to Monarch Pass."

They press on toward Chalk Creek Pass. Switchbacks make up the last quarter mile, and Ethan uses the trail turns to scout for followers, checking the junction where the trail meets the lake. He scans beyond for vehicles or people who might have come up on the off-road vehicle route.

Emma points out hikers approaching the lake from the Colorado Trail. "You see those two? Those aren't our bad guys. I can tell from here."

Ethan agrees. "Two women. And behind them is another one. See about a quarter mile back?"

"Got him. Can't tell if it's male or female, but they're wearing shorts."

"Right. Not our guys. So, we'll just sit here like we're taking a break and let them pass."

Emma checks her watch. "It'll be almost dark by the time these guys get up here. What's our plan if we can't see the bad guys coming?"

Ethan had planned for darkness on the other side of the pass at their stakeout spot. Not here. Their pursuers might have more tech than he and Emma. Like night vision goggles.

"We wait until we can't pick out figures anymore and hustle down the other side."

The women hikers cross the pass thirty minutes later. Emma and Ethan trade trail names and updates with the two.

"You guys hiking with whoever that is?" Emma nods at the hiker below.

"Boomerang? Not really, but we're both headed to the Butterfly House for the night."

Ethan shifts his eyes to the ground as he remembers stealing his pack from Taco. The Butterfly House was where Taco hoped to get enough gear to get back on the trail. "Anybody else still hiking tonight? Besides Boomerang?"

The shorter of the two women looks at the other. The taller one shrugs. "We saw some creepy hunter dudes. Have you seen them yet?"

Emma opens her mouth to answer, but Ethan interrupts. He's hoping feigned ignorance might encourage these two to talk more about the men.

"Who?"

"They stopped and asked us questions about whether we'd seen people. We figured they must be hunting because they're going on and off trail a lot like they're looking for stuff to shoot. They've got huge rifles."

The taller one chimes in. "Assholes. All these mountains out here to do your thing on, and you choose the most popular trail in Colorado to hunt?"

Emma piles on to Ethan's strategy. "Damn. Hope we don't run into them. Where were they headed the last time you saw them?"

The shorter hiker says, "You might not see them. We saw them below us when we took the cutoff trail off the railroad bed. They went straight. Either they missed the turnoff, or maybe they're hiking to a vehicle or something."

Ethan looks from the women to Boomerang rounding his second switchback, then down to the lakes. Nothing moves in the quickly disappearing sunlight.

"Hope they took off," Ethan says. "We don't need to deal with that."

The two women say their goodbyes and continue down the south side of the pass. Ethan and Emma have a similar conversation with Boomerang, a hiker with a four-inch white beard and leathery hands who must be approaching seventy.

"I know who those gals were talking about," Boomerang says, pulling on his matching black knee supports. "But I haven't seen them since Tincup. They passed me on the cutoff." He winks at Emma before continuing up the trail. "Good luck."

They wait until they can't pick out trees by the lakes. "Let's head down," Ethan says. "Find a place to hide and wait to see."

"Maybe they turned off at the trail split and went back to St. Elmo."

"Maybe. We'll give them a couple of hours. If they don't show, we'll head to the mine."

"Seems safer to check out your mine after all this drama is over."

Ethan takes one more look down the switchbacks, turns and places his hand on Emma's wrist. "I've got to do it, Emma. For Doubles. I had four years to do the right thing and didn't."

Emma locks eyes with her twin, pulls her arm away, and heads down the pass. "Let's go."

They hike in silence for thirty minutes, headlamps off, slowing their pace at the switchbacks. They skirt two beaver ponds and hop across a rock field. On the other side, tree silhouettes form moon shadows on the water.

Ethan studies the uphill side of the trail. "Start looking for an observation spot about twenty yards off the trail, a little higher than the path." He pauses. "This might work."

"Anything a little farther up the trail?" Emma responds.

"Why?"

"Because I got to use the ladies' tree, and I don't want to spend hours hunkered down wondering if you can smell what I left behind."

Ethan grins, even though Emma probably can't tell. "OK. You take care of business. I'll wait here."

"Settle in. I might be a few minutes." Emma disappears up the slight incline.

Ethan perches on a log beside the trail. He pulls out his cell phone and hovers over it, blocking the light. No service. He flips his light on and takes several steps backward hoping the slight incline will help. Nothing. He doesn't envy Emma's "lights out" bathroom break. Moving downhill, he checks his phone signal again on the off chance the terrain might open up enough to catch a bar or two. Still nothing.

He turns toward his log to wait for Emma. After two steps, he's wrapped in a bear hug and dragged to the ground, a hand covering his mouth. As he lands, he feels hard metal pressed against the side of his head. In a panic, the first thing that runs through Ethan's mind is that the gunmen came from the wrong direction.

"Turn that thing off," a voice hisses in the distance, and Ethan feels his headlamp ripped off, the bright light immediately winking out. Everything is pitch black except for a small green light blinking near his head where the man presses against him.

The man holding him wears night vision goggles. "You see anyone else?"

The hissing voice answers. "Nothing. He's by himself."

"They said he was hiking with two women." The man pushes his lips against Ethan's ear. "I'm going to move my hand from your mouth, and you're going to tell me. Do you understand?"

Ethan nods. The man pulls back his fingers, and Ethan yells "FUCK OFF!" in a voice he hopes is loud enough for Emma to hear. The ache of the metal prodding his temple eases. For a brief moment, Ethan believes the man is letting him up. Then metal crashes down on the side of his face, and Ethan feels like he's been broadsided by a two-by-four. His cheek caves slightly and he hears or feels—he can't tell which—a crunch inside his mouth.

"Well, that ought to shut him up," the hissing voice chuckles. "Not sure you'll get any answers out of him now though."

Ethan's face throbs with pain. He moans. The man presses in and asks, "Want me to do the other side?"

The hissing man speaks in the background. *Boss, this is Team 3 lead. How copy? We got the guy matching your description from your sector. Osprey backpack, combat boots. No women with him.*

The man lying on Ethan turns his head toward his partner. "We saw two women hiking together though about thirty minutes ago. Remember? Right before that old guy?" He presses against Ethan. "Did your hiking partners leave you behind?"

Ethan gives a brief nod. Better to let these guys think the two women he and Emma met on the pass are the same two women the gunmen saw him with earlier in the day. Emma might get away.

"He says those two were the ones," the man on top of Ethan calls.

Boss, sounds like our boy couldn't keep up with the ladies. We met them earlier on the hike up from Garfield. Want us to go back and try to nab them?

If Emma didn't hear him, she'll come barreling out of the woods any second.

The hissing man says, "We're to escort our friend here out to the highway, the way we came up. Boss wants to ask him some questions."

Ethan can only hope that his sis heard that and understands she needs to turn around and get the hell away from these men.

30-ZAHN

Colorado Trail near Alpine Tunnel, Colorado-July 13, 2022
I decide to stick to the Colorado Trail, rather than explore the offshoots. Honestly, I'm more worried about picking the safest route for my daughter than I am about picking the right route. There's no way she's leaving these mountains. So here we are.

I'm terrified for Emma, but my options are limited. We'll look for Emma and her captor while we move, but I'm aiming for Highway 50 seven miles south—the next closest option for getting Daria out of here. A branch off the Colorado Trail runs into Garfield, a tiny town with at least a bar of cell phone signal. I plan on using Daria's phone to make some calls. I need to get a read on what's happening with the rest of my team at the sheriff's office and find out if anyone besides me is concerned about gunmen roaming our mountains.

We hike silently, less because of the exertion required, and more because we don't want to draw attention from anyone else who might be hiking at this time of night. It's doubtful they would be normal thru-hikers. At the junction where the new Colorado Trail segment departs from the old railroad bed, we begin an uphill slog—the first of many choices that might either put us in harm's way or keep us from Beans or the gunmen. Our pace is slower than I'm used to. We've been using moonlight to stay on the trail and the tall forest casts shadows that make footing a challenge.

After multiple switchbacks, the trail levels and curves toward the pass. My map indicates we are pointing toward Hancock Lakes. When we hit the shoreline, we'll exit the last of the trees and begin another slog up Chalk Creek Pass. At least we'll have unobstructed moonlight to guide our steps from the lakes on.

The lake section had provided a respite from the climb, but now we're both breathing hard and we're halfway up the switchbacks.

I halt. Daria almost runs into me. "Break," I whisper, even though the sound of our breathing is louder than the sound of my voice.

"I don't need one." Daria rests with her hands on her knees, using this short conversation to catch her breath.

"I do." I study the uphill side of the path and pick a large rock about five feet from the trail. I step onto it, unload my pack, and sit. Daria sighs, then moves off the trail to join me.

I wait until she's settled before speaking. "What are you thinking?"

"I'm thinking we don't have time for breaks. And I'm thinking you said we're supposed to be quiet."

"We can whisper here. We can see anyone coming from below, and hear someone coming from above."

"Why are we stopping?"

"Because I'm tired. And you're tired. Remember slow is smooth, smooth is fast."

Daria turns toward me. I study her eyes for a hint of understanding. Instead, she wears a look that borders on scornful.

"You weren't a damn SEAL, Dad. You were a transport pilot. You went slow because that's all you could do."

I might have been hurt—angry even—if I hadn't heard this one before. Instead, I give her a half smile. "I fall back on reason number one. I'm tired. Five minutes and we'll hit it again."

We lay back on the rock, staring at the vast expanse above. One of the first things I discovered about living at high altitude in the Rockies was the stars. Front Range city folk can drive outside Denver and survey sights the city's couch potatoes seldom enjoy. Stars sparkling like strands of glitter young girls wear in their hair. But out here? It's a whole new level. At eleven-thousand-feet elevation, the stars are so brightly illuminated and so packed together, the entire sky looks like a slab of mica shimmering in the sunlight. Instead of thousands of stars, the Carl Sagan quote from my youth rings true—billions and billions.

I turn my head to Daria but remain silent. She doesn't want to talk about stars and how beautiful this experience is. But she surprises me by reaching over and squeezing my hand.

"I know," she says.

I turn my eyes back to the sky. A boot scuffs on the slope above. I roll over to my stomach and push myself into a crouch. Daria moves next to me, but I press a hand against her and she freezes.

Above us, a figure moves across the slope parallel to the course we are on. It's someone coming down the mountain. Without a flashlight. I sweep my eyes behind and ahead of them, trying to determine if the hiker is alone. No one else is visible.

I check below. We can't use trees for cover here and the person is too close to outrun. I pull my Glock from its holster and cup my hand against Daria's ear.

"Get behind the rock you're on. Leave your pack where it is. Get as far down as you can."

To Daria's credit, she knows when to argue and when to do what I say. She crawls behind the rock.

I turn back uphill. Nothing moves. I stretch my neck to peer up the trail. The person now walks in our direction. I move to the front edge of the rock and place my feet on the ground. Then I step sideways, building space between my position and where Daria hides.

When the figure is five steps away, I level my Glock and speak evenly. "Hold your position." I expect a reaction. If I was walking alone down a mountain without a flashlight and I heard a voice only feet away, I'm not a hundred percent sure what I would do. Whether I would shout, stop, jump—or all three. Certainly, I'm unprepared for this person's next move.

The shape jinks sideways while crouching, mostly disappearing behind a boulder. A woman's voice comes back in the same even tone I used. "You hold your position. I've got you covered."

"Emma?"

"Tyler?"

"Emma?" Daria's voice rings out behind me and I detect motion from where she had hidden.

I lower my weapon and step onto the trail. Emma stands. I step forward to hold her, but Daria moves past me, wrapping my girlfriend in a hug. "Are you alright? How did you get away?"

Emma meets my eyes over my daughter's shoulders and raises her eyebrows. "Thanks," she mouths. She steps back from Daria and checks her surroundings, looking up the hillside, then scanning the route we climbed. She turns back to Daria. "I'm fine. I need to talk to you and your dad about the getting away part."

Emma steps around Daria and approaches me, but it's suddenly awkward. I'm relieved Emma is uninjured, but I still feel this internal guilt about how I momentarily forgot about her when I found Daria. It feels like Emma knows she's been my second priority today.

Fortunately, Emma seems just as confused. I still have my Glock in my right hand and she has her weapon in hers. She holds out her free hand, but instead of grabbing it, I close my hand into a fist. Emma's face registers momentary confusion, then she closes her hand into a fist and we bump them together. Of all the ways to keep that flame burning, I've chosen the post-COVID, Gen-X greeting I still can't even decide if I like—the fist bump.

"Hey," Emma says.

"Hey."

"We need to talk. Everything's not like it seems."

"We need to get off this mountain and get somewhere with cover. How's it look going back over the pass from the way you came?"

"Bad guys. That's why I came this way. I was heading for St. Elmo," she points down the mountain.

Donnie's likely still parked in town, but the car and the men I spotted on the outskirts of St. Elmo have convinced me the town isn't safe. "There might be bad guys around there too. But I can confirm there's at least one cop. If you saw gunmen south, then I agree. We'll turn around."

We retrace our steps, with my daughter positioned between us. Both of us carry our weapons unholstered, prepared for the possibility of meeting someone on the trail before we hit the tree line.

Upper Hancock Lake reflects the moon off its surface like a searchlight. Once we step from the moon shadow of the pass, it's hard to imagine needing a flashlight. Lower Hancock Lake is visible a half mile away, but Emma points to trees near the water.

"Let's head that way."

"Lead on," I say. The trees take us away from the route to St. Elmo, but Emma seems to have a plan.

As she passes, she mutters, "Trust me."

"I do."

She pauses. "You might not in ten minutes."

I sway slightly. Daria passes me, oblivious to what Emma just said. I fall in behind the two women, my head swirling, trying to figure out what the heck Emma meant.

Emma works her way through the forest. The branches filter away most of the moonlight. She pauses after stepping over a fallen tree.

"Here." She leans against a log blocking her path. I step over the tree, and Daria follows. We both sit.

Emma says, "Like I said, there's more to this situation than it seems. Stuff you don't know."

I'm pretty sure I've figured out her big secret. I can't help myself. "We might have figured it out. Beans isn't a crazy thru-hiker who took you hostage. He's part of the crew that crashed the helicopter." I peer through the darkness, trying to discern if Emma is surprised I know what she's going to tell us. I can't read any expression in her eyes.

"Is that all you got?"

"Am I right?"

"Mostly," Emma says. "Beans is from the helicopter. But he didn't take me hostage. I allowed him to take me so that Daria could get away."

"What?" Daria's voice sounds confused. "I don't understand."

"Beans' name is Ethan Ward. He's my twin brother. He's in trouble."

31-DARIA

Chalk Creek Pass-July 13, 2022

"Your brother?"

With the moonlight glimmering through the swaying pines, Emma's voice barely above a whisper, Daria listens in disbelief. The wind picks up, and Emma's voice oscillates as she shares how her brother ended up on the Colorado Trail. Daria is mesmerized, but Zahn's jaw tightens and settles into a scowl.

"I knew Ethan was training in Colorado," Emma says. "And he knew I was hiking out here. But we weren't planning on seeing each other." Emma lowers her pack to the ground. She turns to Daria. "Remember where I first met Ethan? At the water stop?"

Daria nods, unwilling to interrupt Emma's story.

"Surreal," Emma continues. "Running into my brother, who I haven't seen in years, in the middle of the Rockies wearing a backpack and combat boots. A helicopter crash nearby." She lets out a sigh. "That's why I grilled all the other hikers about the downed helicopter." Emma casts a glance at Zahn before continuing. "When I saw him, I thought maybe he was helping the Army guys investigate."

"Helpers don't take hostages," Zahn mutters. "He's on the run for something he did."

"I resent that, Tyler Zahn." Emma's eyes are unreadable, but her chin remains pointed at Zahn.

Zahn shakes his head. "And the crash? He survives but no one else?"

Emma pauses long enough for Daria to hear her own breath. "He had something to do with it…indirectly. But not in the way you're implying."

"I'm not implying anything, I'm—"

"You make it sound like he killed that crew."

"Tell the damn story then."

Emma sighs. "Fine."

She tells them about HAVOC 23, the helicopter crew in Turkey tasked for a humanitarian mission in Iraq. She describes Shavano, Horse, Doubles, the leader of their crew, and more importantly—Emma explains she sensed this, Ethan didn't tell her—a woman that Ethan cared about. Then she describes the Iraqi mission, the dead bodies, and the bombshell: Shavano's gifts to Ethan and Horse.

"Ethan didn't know what he was doing. He said it was like when someone raises their hand for a high five, it's impolite to leave them hanging. Shavano handed him a knife, and Ethan took it. Shavano gave Horse a ring.

Zahn flinches.

"That mission solidified their reputation in the battalion," Emma continues. "They won awards and advanced in the unit. Shavano and Doubles moved in together. Ethan went on a fast-track qualification to pilot-in-command. Same with Horse as a crew chief."

Emma pauses.

Daria breaks the silence. "What happened to the stuff?"

"Ethan hid the knife away. He knew it was wrong, but didn't know what to do about it."

Daria's dad coughs. "Like fess up and turn it in?"

"We didn't have a lot of role models growing up, Z-man. Daria's lucky to have you."

Daria's eyes widen. Zahn says nothing. Boom—point to Emma for shutting her father down.

Emma continues. "Shavano gets sick with cancer and is dead in a year. He leaves a bracelet from the mission to Doubles. Horse sells his ring and finds out it's an antique from an ancient city called Nimrud, and what they're sitting on—the bracelet and knife—are stolen priceless relics." Emma turns Daria's way, away from Zahn's gaze. "Ethan explained a bit about the history, but I don't remember the details."

"I do," Zahn says. "Nimrud is a famous city from the Assyrian Empire that various people have been digging up for the past century. They've found a ton of treasure, and there are rumors there's more. Those ISIL bastards took over Mosul and Nimrud after the US pulled out of Iraq and razed it with bulldozers." He stares at Emma. "Your brother and his friends stole from ISIL? Stealing is bad, but it sounds better to hear they did it from terrorists."

"No," Emma shakes her head, defiant in the moonlight. "The Iraqi Army took Mosul and Nimrud back. Ethan's crew was returning some of the fallen Iraqi soldiers to Baghdad. Ethan guessed the Iraqis had recovered the treasure from ISIL. And based on where they found the helicopter in Iraq, it looks like maybe the Iraqi crew was trying to keep it for themselves. He said they were way off course."

Zahn eyes lock on Emma.

Emma says, "Doubles finds all this out, and the answer is easy for her. To return the relics to the Iraqi government. They mailed their two items anonymously to the Iraq Museum in Baghdad. I actually read the museum's report back at my headquarters."

Daria can't read Zahn's face. She hasn't heard about the returned relics. It seems like her father would say something if he had.

Emma continues, "But Shavano left behind coded instructions for how to find what he took for himself. The clues indicated he left the item in a mine out here." Emma sweeps her hand indicating the mountains behind us.

"How do you explain the crash?"

"I can't. Ethan couldn't believe they shot his crew chief either. He and Doubles guessed somebody suspected Shavano had something of value. Otherwise, why all this cloak-and-dagger treasure hunt stuff? Someone else knew, and Shavano didn't want them to get it."

"You don't know what Shavano had. Would it be enough to kill for? Innocent people?"

"Ethan wasn't sure that was part of the plan."

"Explain," Zahn says.

"He was there. There was another helicopter. But it wasn't exactly clear the second helicopter brought down the first."

"A bullet in the back of the head." Zahn shakes his head. "Whoever brought it down, killed a survivor. I was there at the crash site, Emma. I saw the entry wound with my own eyes."

"Tyler, I hear you. But I need you to listen. The guys who did the shooting have my brother. His account of the events is all I have."

Zahn says nothing.

"Ethan said he mulled over what happened after he got away. He told me that maybe the crash is what caused the shooting."

"What do you mean?"

"What was the weather that day, Z-man?"

"Clear and a million. No clouds."

Daria interrupts, "But crazy windy, right, Emma?" Daria flashes back to the three hikers leaning against the gale as they came off West Apostle before telling them about the helicopter crash.

"Right," Emma says. "Ethan said the winds were barely within limits to land when Doubles put down and let him off. While he was checking the mine, the winds increased. He thinks Doubles took the bird in the air again because she couldn't control it on the ground. He's not even sure she saw the other helicopter approach."

Zahn appears to consider this explanation. "And once they got it in the air?"

"Ethan said it looked like they were blown right back into the mountainside. The other helicopter was close enough to see it happen."

Zahn nods, picking up on Ethan's theory. "The other helicopter was waiting in the wings for Ethan and crew to pick up whatever treasure they found but might not have known Ethan was on the ground. When Doubles takes off, they assumed she had Shavano's relics."

Emma wears a thin smile. "Then when she crashes, they realize that if they don't land and get Shavano's stash, the crash recovery team will find it, and they'll never have a shot at it."

Zahn finishes, "So, they monitor the crash, and wait for the wind to die down. When it does, they put out a person or people to retrieve it. But why gun down the survivor?"

"Ethan said they came in with guns at the ready. Can you guess what Ethan's crew chief did when he climbed from the wreckage and saw another helo with a machine gun pointed at him?"

"He ran?"

"The crew chief pulled out his 9mm but didn't fire. Why would anyone on the crew imagine they were under attack in a US National Forest? But when he pulled the gun, the bad guys opened up, and Ethan bolted down the mountain."

"Did they see him escape?"

"Yes. They fired at him. When they didn't find the relic, and when they counted up the crewmembers, they knew that someone had made it out. And that meant, treasure or not, they were all in danger of being discovered unless they tracked him down and eliminated him."

"After forcing him to disclose the location of the relic, right?"

"That's what Ethan suspects."

Emma and Zahn both nod as if their investigator brains are running full speed.

Daria struggles to keep up. "So where does that leave us? What do we do?"

"We get you out of these mountains to safety," her dad says.

"We go after my brother," Emma says at the same time.

The two look at each other. Both look hurt, like they can't believe the other's plan.

"Tyler. This is my brother. I'm going after him with or without you."

Zahn leans into Daria, wrapping his arm around her shoulder. "Emma, meet my daughter." His voice is matter-of-fact even though his words are sarcastic. "She's not going anywhere near your brother. Besides, you can't do anything about Ethan if you don't know where he is. And you said you don't know where the other mine is."

Emma's head tilts downward. "I don't. But Daria does."

Daria stands, backing away. "First I'm hearing about any of this."

"The coordinates are on your GPS," Emma says. "Ethan wouldn't give them to me in case we got caught. He waited until we thought you made it to safety and sent them to your GPS."

Daria hasn't rebooted her GPS since she sent the SOS call. She pulls it from her pack. Even in the darkness, she can sense her dad's fury. The GPS shows an hourglass as she waits to confirm Emma's claim.

Zahn's whisper is barely contained. "I'm not exactly thrilled with your brother's decision-making skills, Emma. Stealing artifacts from a foreign country, keeping them when he knows they should be returned, putting his helicopter crew in danger, then—this tops it off for me—sending information to my daughter that puts her life in jeopardy before he knows she's in a position of safety."

"He waited—"

"He wouldn't have even been in the situation if he would have done the right thing from the beginning." Zahn's voice is no longer a whisper. He takes a breath like he's getting ready to launch another volley.

In Daria's opinion, Z-man is uncharacteristically wrong. "Really helpful, Dad."

"What?" Her father sounds incredulous.

"You're always saying to tackle a problem with what you got. If you didn't bring a splint, make one. If you forgot your water, quit bitching and work on fixing it."

"What's your point?"

Daria reins her voice back to a whisper. "Emma wasn't there to influence her brother, so there's nothing she can do about the decision Ethan made." She pauses. "So, your statement is just you being grumpy. It's not helpful."

She sneaks a glance at Emma. Her friend's mouth is curling into a smile. Everyone shifts on their logs, but Daria reverts her gaze to Zahn.

Zahn stands. "It needs to be me that goes after your brother."

Daria smiles.

Emma says, "I don't need you to solve my family drama, Z-man."

Daria notes the switch from "Tyler" to "Z-man" but isn't sure what that means.

"Here's my logic. When that UH-60 Black Hawk went down, our government lost a federal asset. The crash was either directly or indirectly caused by an incident that's federal or international in scope—the theft of Iraqi antiquities. No one knows these things are related except us and the men who are trying to profit from all this. If a deputy reserve sheriff crawls out of the woods talking about priceless artifacts hidden in a mine and a cabal of criminals trying to find it, this thing will take weeks to get rolling.

"On the other hand, if a high-ranking officer in the FBI's Art Theft division brings the facts forward, she's going to get an audience—first because of her credibility, and second because of her relationship to the only surviving member of the helicopter. Her claims will be impossible to ignore."

Emma's head moves in the vertical, centimeters at a time, as if she's slowly understanding Zahn's point. "But I can't ask you to put yourself at risk for my personal issues."

"You're not. My position gives me the authority—actually, the responsibility—to try to prevent your brother from getting killed. If you track down your brother, it looks like a family member making an emotional reaction. If you kill someone, it will be outside your jurisdiction and authority." He glances at Daria and back to Emma. "We've been looking at this all wrong. Time to quit talking about what we want to do, and start doing our jobs. You get me?"

Emma's nod is definitive now. "I have to say one thing, Z-man. And I mean it."

"Go ahead."

"If you find Ethan alive, you need to make sure he stays that way. I need to trust that you won't let my brother die because you're trying to bring these criminals in alive. I'm putting the only family I've got in your hands."

Zahn steps toward Daria and reaches out. She takes his hand, and he pulls her to a standing position, then moves to her side so they both face Emma. He tugs Daria's hand in front of them and places it in Emma's, leaving his hand covering both of theirs.

Zahn says, "That part about trusting me with your family, Emma? I'm putting the same trust in you. Take care of my girl."

32-ETHAN

Garfield, Colorado-July 14, 2022

Ethan stumbles between the two men as they transition from the trail to a two-lane gravel road. Headlights from Highway 50 traffic wink in the distance. A tug from the man gripping his arm rights him. He opens his mouth to catch his breath but the chilly night air sends a jolt through his jaw to the nerve endings where his missing teeth used to sit.

A radio crackles and the men pull Ethan to a halt. The hissing voice speaks.

Go ahead.

Don't bring him out of the forest. When you all get about a hundred yards from the highway, take the road to the left. We're parked back there to give us some cover.

The two men nod at each other and drag Ethan forward. His skull throbs. *Cover? From what?*

They stop at the front end of a pickup truck. Ethan anticipates the next move, waiting for the truck's lights to illuminate and blind him as the questions begin. Instead, the headlights remain off. A door slams.

The man who tackled Ethan releases his arm. "Here you go, Boss."

Ethan lifts his head. A man with a ball cap pulled low and a neck gaiter pulled up to his nose shakes his head. His broad shoulders taper to a narrow waist. Square-toed cowboy boots poke from beneath his jeans.

"Ethan, Ethan, Ethan. Aren't you a slippery one?"

Ethan no longer cares how these mystery gunmen know his name. They've done their research. They know about Shavano, they know what he did, and they're trying to profit from it.

But this man. Something about his voice is familiar. He pictures the airport in Iraq where they delivered the bodies. No. All of those men were Iraqis. He runs through the members of his New York unit. Anybody whom Shavano would have shared his story with.

Ethan considers a response, but the cold air seeps in and he shuts his mouth.

"I guess you know what we need?" The voice scratches at Ethan's memory but he can't quite grasp where or when. The man cups the injured side of Ethan's face, as if he's sorry it all had to come to this. Ethan's sorry too. Sorry he ever let the situation get this far.

The moment Doubles found out about what happened, she committed to righting the wrong. Not Ethan, who sat for years, hiding the problem and hoping it would go away.

His hand on Ethan's cheek, the Boss whispers, "Where'd he hide it, Ethan?"

Ethan shakes his head slowly so as not to aggravate his jaw. The man's eyes are barely visible, but they appear to harden at Ethan's reaction. The man cuffs him with the same hand. Not a punch. Not even a slap. A light tap like two teenagers taunting each other.

But it drops Ethan to his knees with a scream. He clasps his mouth, rocking back and forth. The squared-off toes of the man's boots remain planted below him.

"Do you remember now?" The voice above carries disappointment. Like he's unhappy he's had to resort to such methods.

Ethan wags his head, not in response to the man's question but to try to shake the pain in his jaw away.

"Johnson?" the man calls.

"Yeah, Boss?"

"Can you help me with this?" The boots disappear.

"Thought you'd never ask," Johnson's voice approaches from behind. Ethan shuffles forward on his knees in a futile attempt to build space between himself and another man who means him harm.

A boot kicks Ethan from behind. He reaches forward to keep from falling face-first in the dirt, but the bumper of the truck catches his face. He screams again as his jawbone flames. Men grab his legs and drag him from the truck on his belly.

Rough hands roll him onto his back. A moon shadow covers him as someone bends down toward him. He splays his hands to keep the shape from attacking him. Instead, the figure grabs his hands and yanks him to his feet. Ethan gasps and tries to wrench his hands free. The man switches his grip so that his left hand holds Ethan's right wrist and the other hand holds one of Ethan's fingers in his left hand.

With a quick turn of his wrist, the man snaps Ethans's index finger. The noise pops like the first firecracker on the 4th of July. The men surrounding him go silent.

"Damn," one of the other men says.

A moan escapes Ethan's lips as pain surges from his fractured jaw to his finger.

Johnson releases the finger but retains his hold on Ethan's other wrist. "Ready to tell the Boss what he needs to know?"

Ethan can come up with false coordinates. He might even be able to stay silent and keep these men from finding Shavano's stash. But why? Doubles is dead. His friends from his unit are dead. Shavano is dead. Emma got away—maybe. What exactly is he attempting to prove here? That he's trying to protect some ancient relic for a country he's been to once?

His mouth fills with vomit. He spews on his boots as Johnson steps backward. Ethan tries to speak with the same result.

"Pop the hood."

A chill runs up his spine. Ethan recognizes this voice.

"Wire him up," barks the man who was there at the beginning of this whole thing.

Johnson yanks Ethan's head up.

Ethan gasps. "Horse."

Horse motions to Johnson. "No sense wasting time. Drop his drawers."

•   •   •

Ethan rediscovers his voice in time to tell the Boss, Horse, and the other men what they want to hear. He worries that once he gives up the information, they won't have a reason to keep him around. If they shot Hendricks, why would they bother letting Ethan live?

But his concerns are unwarranted. They don't trust him enough to get rid of him. They zip-tie his wrists behind his back and shove him in the rear seat of the truck while they huddle over a map on the hood. Ethan watches the beams of light crisscross over a paper map spread across the front of the truck. In the glow of the headlamps, Horse—formerly his crewmate, now the man who almost fried his testicles—punches coordinates into his phone. Evidently, he's quicker at determining the mine's location than the other men, because his eyes widen and the other men turn in his direction. The man they call Boss rips his face covering down to his neck. Ethan has no idea what the Boss is saying, but he recognizes him.

It's Shavano's half-brother. The man from the funeral. The one Shavano's mom wouldn't let give a speech.

33-ZAHN

Colorado Trail near Chalk Creek Pass, Colorado-July 14, 2022

I transfer the coordinates from Daria's GPS to my own. Emma peers over my shoulder as I study the mine's location. I tap the minus sign to zoom out. The words "Chalk Creek Pass" and "Mount Aetna" show up on the screen.

"Shit," I say.

Emma stifles a laugh, despite the seriousness of the situation.

"What?" Daria says.

"Your dad just volunteered to climb up the pass again."

I nod. "Looks like the coordinates put us just a mile on the other side and a half mile east of the trail on Mount Aetna's slopes."

"I'm not surprised," Emma says. "Ethan planned to grab the item if we slipped by the gunmen. So, it makes sense we were close to the mine." She rests her hand on my shoulder. "If they're already there, they'll have the high ground. If you beat them there, they'll smoke you out by threatening my brother. What's your plan?"

I'm not up for rehashing the impossibility of rescuing Emma's brother. "What would yours be?"

"Find him. Try to keep them from hurting him." She lets out a sob. "Save him." She throws her arms around me. "Just try," she says as she pulls away. "Let's go, Daria."

"Emma," I call.

She turns.

I hand her my truck keys and tell her about the bottles under my tires. "You need to scope out St. Elmo on foot before you take my Toyota. Make sure Donnie's still parked there and in control of the town."

Emma shivers and turns away.

I whisper at her back, "It's past midnight. If the gunmen are in town, forget about using my truck. Skirt St. Elmo and work your way over to the road."

"Got it," Emma calls without turning her head.

Daria embraces me. "I barely know Emma's brother. I feel terrible for saying this." She sniffs. "Do your best to save him. But don't die for him, Dad. I need you."

I wrap my daughter in a bear hug before stepping back, my hands dropping to her elbows. "I need you too, Dar. Listen. Follow Emma's lead, but back her up as well. You're a smart operator. You might not be FBI or sheriff's office, but you've got a head for this stuff. If you see something off, don't assume Emma sees it too. Help her."

Daria nods. I let go of her arms. She pulls a bag of trail mix from her pack's waist pocket and presses it into my hand. Her eyes flash concern before she turns to catch up with Emma. When she disappears in the trees, I turn toward the pass.

Even though I'm hiking uphill again, my pulse slows. An observer might label me abnormally brave, calming myself as I approach certain danger, beelining for an abandoned mine at night with the intent of finding armed men and rescuing their prisoner. They would be wrong. I'm scared shitless. But moments ago, I was more frightened I'd run into the armed men with my daughter by my side. She's better off with Emma.

The hike to Chalk Creek Pass goes quicker the second time. The steady calm pulse disappears by the second switchback and I'm breathing heavily when I reach the crest. Before continuing over, I stop, scanning the draw pointing toward Highway 50 and Monarch Pass, searching for lights from anybody else this time of night. I spot nothing. I pull my shell from my pack, anticipating the cool air against the sweat

I've produced on my uphill slog. I buckle my waistbelt and check my GPS, orienting it toward the mine coordinates.

The full moon illuminates the steep, talus-covered slopes of Mount Aetna. If I want to avoid descending a thousand feet before turning and climbing back up, I could work my way across the ridge flanking the pass. That would mean more than a mile of rock-hopping above the tree line to reach the mine—a three-hour scramble at best. In this case, the longer route will be faster. I'll stay on the Colorado Trail until parallel with the mine, then make the thousand-foot climb. The downside is that it's likely the same route the gunmen will select.

When I reach the turnoff point, I turn uphill and scramble past the first tree before pausing. As I catch my breath, I listen for anybody below me, in case I've arrived before them. And I listen for noise above, where I suspect the gunmen are. The timing is the issue. Am I following them up? Will I meet them coming down? Or have they already been here and left?

The moon casts jagged shadows as I clamber past the tree line and up the boulder-strewn slope. My breath rasps from the steep vertical climb. Without the aid of a switch-backed trail, I'm back to clawing my way up the mountain like I did when we searched for the helicopter crash—the only difference is I'm catching my breath between massive rocks instead of grabbing at tree roots.

I check my GPS to ensure I'm still on target. The crack of rock on rock startles me. Instinctively, I duck low against an uphill boulder. Another pop explodes, and a trickle of pebbles slides down the slope. A boulder launches off a precipice fifty yards away from me.

I peer over the boulder in the only direction the rock could have originated. Rocks often fall in these mountains, and not just from human interference. Animals, water, wind, and just plain tectonics ensure this barren, seemingly rigid, environment is always changing. Nothing is visible above me. No more rocks fall in my direction. I continue.

A white mass above reflects the full moon like a snow field marking my route to the top. But it's too late in the season for snow, and I'm on the southwest side of the mountain where snow melts the fastest. I catch my breath again and study the color change. I recognize the tailings pile characteristic of mines in this region. On a hillside entrance, miners dig down and rid themselves of the dirt and rock they excavate by spreading it downhill. In time, and with enough dirt, the downhill pile grows in stature, changing the angle of the slope.

I survey the treetops below, letting my peripheral vision scan for movement. Years of night flights in the C-130 taught me the worst way to detect movement at night is to stare directly at what you are looking for.

Nothing moves.

I climb another leg, then pause. If I were searching a mine with a group, I would minimize the number of people I sent down the hole. A mine might be a great place to defend if you don't want people to reach you, but if you ever want to leave the mine, luck won't favor your escape. It's like putting a city under siege in wartime. The advantage goes to the forces surrounding the city—as long as you have the patience to wait.

If these guys are smart enough to bring down a helicopter, take over a sheriff's office, and capture a downed aircrew member, they're probably not stupid enough to allow themselves to be trapped.

I lower myself behind the boulder and survey the tailings pile above me with the same peripheral technique I used to check my six. I wait, but nothing moves. I rest my eyes and scan the pile again. This time, I catch the slightest of movements. The top of the rock pile twists slightly in the moonlight. Instinctively, my eyes fixate on the object, and I force myself to settle my gaze on the side of the pile. There it is again. A small movement that causes the rock-like object to change shade. And this time, I see the rifle barrel.

Where there is one sentry, there is always the possibility of two. Or more. Other gunmen are likely inside the mine. But they probably won't be much longer.

I lower myself between the rocks, ensuring no part of me is visible to the sentry or sentries above. If Ethan's not here, it makes no sense to stop these people from taking whatever they are after. I'm outnumbered, outgunned, and have no stakes in this game. A law enforcement team can pursue these men.

But if Ethan is with them, and I try to save him, neither one of us is likely to come out alive despite my promise to Emma.

My brain says hunker down and reevaluate.

My gut says make a move while at least some of the bad guys are cornered in the mine.

My brain wins. So far, it's kept me alive. I nestle between the rocks and wait.

34-DARIA

St. Elmo, Colorado-July 14, 2022

Daria and Emma trudge toward the outskirts of St. Elmo. The closer they get, the more caution they exercise, moving off trail to monitor the situation. The SUV Zahn spotted between the Hancock Lakes and the mining town is gone.

They maneuver to a group of trees overlooking the gravel road that serves as the main street of the mostly deserted town without glimpsing another soul. Beneath the lone street light, a stationary Ford Explorer with Buena Vista Police stenciled on the side faces the helicopter crash site.

Emma whispers, "Zahn said the sheriff's office is out of commission. The hostage situation, right?"

Daria nods toward the Explorer. "Buena Vista police were monitoring the town when he came through. Not the sheriff's office."

"Something's changed." Emma doesn't move, and Daria assumes she's considering their options. Daria's first instinct is to run to the police vehicle. Zahn said the police helped him after he escaped the sheriff's office. They weren't compromised. They can help.

She opens her mouth, but her friend speaks first, muttering to herself. "If it walks like a duck…"

"What?"

"Sorry. I'm paranoid about that vehicle," Emma says, flicking her eyes toward the Explorer. "Nothing has turned out like we thought in this case. But it's probably the police, right?"

"Right. Donnie Morgan was here when Dad came through."

Emma takes a deep breath. "I want you to wait here. I'm going to approach the vehicle. If we're good, I'll have them flash their brake lights three times for you to come out. Does that work?"

"What if we're not good?"

"That's worst case. You'll know. If I have the upper hand, I'll just yell for you to come out. If I don't, then you need to head east toward Buena Vista. And Daria?"

"What?"

"If it's the worst case, then everything is compromised. Law enforcement vehicles. Chaffee County. Maybe BV police. Stopping a car on the road would be a bad idea. You'll need to find a house on the way down and communicate out of there."

Daria's heart lurches as she imagines trying to hike down this single-road river valley without being detected. "Communicate with who?"

Emma tugs Daria back into the trees. "Type this number in your notes app." She pulls out her cell. "Damn, still don't have service." She reads off the number and Daria punches it into her phone. Emma digs into the side of her hiking pants and pulls out a leather wallet. She flips it open.

"These are my credentials. Snap a pic. If you get somewhere with Wi-Fi, you can send the FBI these as proof I'm involved. If you're just on the phone, then read them this number right here." She points to a stream of digits below her picture. After Daria tucks her phone away, Emma elbows her. "It's going to be OK."

Emma approaches the vehicle from the rear. Daria expects her to close in on the vehicle undetected with her weapon at the ready so she can confirm they are police before she lowers her weapon.

Instead, Emma walks parallel to the vehicle, her hands removed from her pockets, at a normal pace. When she's even with the window of the truck, she freezes and slowly raises her hands. The window of the police vehicle hasn't moved, and Daria can't tell if she's adopting a surrender position preemptively to get the truck's attention, or if the deputy is somehow communicating with her. Either way, Emma no longer has her eyes on the Explorer. She's facing in the direction of the helicopter crash, frozen in place.

Daria follows her gaze. A dark figure wearing a uniform hoofs it down Main Street, a handgun extended in front of him. The scene looks like an old west standoff at the OK Corral, except Emma isn't fighting back.

Emma lowers herself to the street, lying on her stomach, her face pressed to the ground. The Explorer's door bursts open, and another uniformed male, stiff in his movements, steps from the vehicle, a shotgun in hand. He circles behind Emma. The man walking down the street calls to him, and the shotgun-wielding driver moves further around Emma so his line of fire won't take out the other man.

Daria's hands shake as she processes the scene in front of her. The police are taking down an FBI agent. Emma's worst-case scenario is happening right before Daria's eyes.

The man walking draws close and hollers, "Check it, Donnie. I've got you covered."

The officer from the Explorer lays his shotgun on the street and approaches Emma. He straddles her legs, pushing her head down with one hand while digging in her pockets with the other. He pulls out her handgun and holds it up toward the other gunman before shoving it out of Emma's reach. He reaches into her other pocket and discovers her credentials. He flips open the billfold, studies it for a moment, and calls out something indistinguishable.

The man in the street yells, "What?" He steps under the streetlight, his weapon still extended. "Emma?"

Daria gasps, recognizing the deputy. She bolts from the trees, shouting as she runs. "Rick! It's me! Daria."

Chaffee County Sheriff Deputy Rick Perez swings his weapon in Daria's direction, then lowers it as she approaches. A smile tugs at the corner of his mouth.

"Donnie, let Agent Frazier get up," he directs. "Daria Zahn. What the hell are you doing mixed up in all this?"

•   •   •

Perez returns Emma's weapon. She tries to tell him the story, but he's focused on making sure the two women are not injured.

"We'll get to that," he says. He helps stow their packs in the Explorer, then bundles them into the back seat and instructs Donnie to crank the heat. Perez stands next to the open door and studies Daria. The two of them have a history of bad luck together.

Perez says, "You're such a nice young woman, Daria. But you're like a canary in a coal mine. Every time we meet, I know there's trouble brewing somewhere." He glances toward Emma, who doesn't look happy with him. He turns his gaze back to Daria. "Where's your dad?"

Emma lets out a breath. "That's what we're trying to tell you."

Daria is surprised to find Perez here. When Zahn escaped, Perez was still a hostage in the meeting room. "How did you guys get free? Dad said you were held captive down at the office."

"Negotiated release. Sheriff Larkin got pulled out after he got food poisoning and he ended up working out a deal from the outside." He shakes his head. "That whole situation's not over. We've got some of Emma's teammates out here working on tracking them down."

"Out here in these mountains?" Emma says.

Perez looks confused. "In the valley. I doubt those guys would head to the mountains. The FBI is working off the vehicles they departed with and working traffic cams." He focuses on Emma. "What do you know?"

"Thank you." Emma's voice is chilly—sarcastic instead of grateful. She fills Perez in about her brother and the helicopter. Daria relays the part about Zahn uncovering the connection between the bad guys holding Perez and his team hostage and the bad guys out searching for Ethan and Gary "Shavano" Bissonnette's hidden relic.

"Hold it," Perez interrupts. "This Shavano guy's last name is Bissonnette? From Salida?"

Emma nods. "That's how he got the nickname. The mountain, right?"

"If it was daylight, you could see it from here," Perez says. "But Gary Bissonnette died three years ago."

Emma wrinkles her brow. "How'd you know that?"

"He was Sheriff Larkin's half-brother."

Daria gapes at Emma.

Perez furrows his brow

Emma stares down at her feet. "So whoever is behind this not only held you guys hostage in the sheriff's office to keep you from interfering with their theft of any relics, they were trying to keep the one guy who might know what they were up to—Sheriff Larkin—out of the field too." She looks at Perez. "Right?"

"Doesn't make sense," Perez mutters.

"What?" Daria sputters. "The gunmen must have suspected Larkin would figure out their plan."

"No. That's not what I'm saying." Perez turns to Emma. "When the helicopter went down, Larkin never mentioned it belonged to the same unit his brother was in."

"Maybe he didn't know yet?" Emma offers. "Maybe he found out after they pulled him out of the conference room when he got sick."

"If he got sick," Perez says.

"You were there. You said you saw it," Daria says.

"I was. I did. But now when I step back and look at it, something is off."

"Like Larkin was in on it?" Emma says.

"He got pulled out. He got better. He negotiated our release. The three gunmen got away. What does that sound like to you?"

Emma shakes her head. "It can't be that easy. I'll just call my office and have them bring him in for questioning."

"You're right," Perez says.

"What?"

"It's not that easy."

"Why?"

"Sheriff Larkin dropped off the grid about three hours ago. Said he had a family emergency and would be out of contact."

"So, who's in charge of this county now?" Emma says.

Perez meets Emma's eyes. "Me."

35-ETHAN

Mount Aetna, Colorado-July 14, 2022

After surrendering the coordinates, Ethan tries to convince the men that he cannot make the journey with them. They're having none of it.

"You're not leaving my sight until we have what we're after," Boss growls.

The two-hour slog to the mine tests every fiber of Ethan's being. His eyes find Horse, but his former friend strides ahead of the group, as if they never met. When they finally approach the coordinates, after an hour on the trail and another hour scrambling up the mountain, Ethan has no idea if what they've found is the mine. His eyes can barely focus. A mound of loose rock reflects the group's beams of light.

"Set up anchor points here and here," Boss barks. "Horse, get a harness on. You're going down with me."

The guy holding Ethan's arm pulls it up. "What about him?"

"He's going down too."

Horse whispers into Ethan's ear. "Hear that? They're giving you the shaft—no matter what." Ethan doesn't react. Horse hisses, "You and Doubles shouldn't have fucked me over."

Ethan's muddled brain gets that they're going to kill him, but the pain erases any panic. Hands grope at his feet, then straps press against his crotch as someone fits him with a climbing harness. "Sit," a voice commands.

Ethan crumples to the rocks and passes out.

He wakes when the men pull him to his feet. His head lolls and when he opens his eyes, a loop from a double figure eight knot pokes at his climbing harness. They fasten him in with a click of a carabiner.

"Grab the rope," a voice commands. Ethan grabs and misses, pain shooting up his arm from his broken finger. He reaches again, snagging it with his wrist. Ethan twirls in the darkness as the beams of light fade above him. Below him, a faint beam of light increases in size as he descends. His feet finally touch the ground, and he collapses onto the mine floor.

Hands under his armpits yank him to his feet. Boss's voice is quiet. "How far in do we have to go?"

Ethan protests. "He never told me where he hid it."

Horse twists his other arm. "Then how did you know where to go? Tell the man what he wants to know."

"Left clues," Ethan mumbles. "Never talked to him about this."

"Horse, watch him. I'm going hunting." The tall man releases Ethan's arm. "Send Johnson down to help."

"Got it, Boss." Horse turns his head and yells, "Johnson, we need you down here."

A voice echoes down the pit. "On my way."

Boss moves farther into the mine. No one has given Ethan a light. His chances of leaving this pit rely on the two men intent on leaving him down here. After Johnson answers, Horse swings his light back toward where the Boss searches.

A cluster of pebbles rains down behind Ethan, and Horse swings around, his headlamp bouncing off the shaft entrance. A low rumble crescendos.

"Watch out," Johnson calls from the entrance.

"Fuck!" Horse yells. He pushes Ethan into the blackness, and he makes it two steps into the darkness before tripping. Horse tugs at Ethan's arm but when he doesn't budge, Horse disappears into the darkness.

Horse's headlamp blurs and morphs into a yellow glow in the cloud of dust filling the pit. Ethan pushes himself up with his arms just as a massive shelf of gravel and dirt slides from above and buries his legs. Shoving his elbows into the dirt, he tries to extract himself, but the weight of the earth immobilizes him. "Horse," Ethan calls. No one replies. Johnson coughs above him, then calls for help.

"Pull me up! Pull me up! It's caving in."

"We're pulling. Hang on."

Another load of dirt cascades onto the pile trapping Ethan. He pictures Johnson dangling on the rope, kicking the loose scree on the sides of the pit as he tries to scramble back above. The cloud of dust and lack of light prevent Ethan from seeing anything.

The voices ricochet as Johnson spits out obscenities.

Ethan coughs, then spits a mouthful of phlegm from his throat.

"Boss, you guys okay down there?"

Ethan debates whether to answer or not. If he tells them Boss and Horse are OK, these guys aren't going to do a thing. But if he tells them they didn't make it, they might decide to leave him.

Another voice from above. "Horse?"

Ethan calls out. "It's me." He gives up predicting what these men will do.

"What's going on with Horse and the Boss?" the man calls. These men don't know he's incapacitated.

"I don't know. They went further down the mine and the rocks started falling," Ethan calls. "Can you pull me up?"

"Fuck that. The whole wall is about to give away. We're not risking plugging the exit."

"Go check on them," the other voice orders.

"I'm trapped under the dirt that fell. Can't move my legs." Ethan winces, his head throbbing, and he feels nothing from his waist down.

"Sucks to be you," Johnson calls.

Ethan closes his eyes and rests his head on the rock floor, inhaling through his nose to avoid sucking the dust cloud into his lungs. Shuffling sounds force his eyes open, and he blinks at two yellow orbs bobbing toward him.

Two pairs of boots park inches from his face. Ethan squints into the headlamps. The medical bag from the HAVOC 23 mission in Iraq swings between the Boss and Horse.

"Shit. This whole thing is coming down," the Boss says before hollering up the shaft. "You guys ready to bring us up?"

"Yeah, Boss," comes the reply. "But it's dicey."

"I'll go first," Horse says. "Check things out. Hand me the bag."

Ethan opens his mouth. The extra dust makes him cough. "Right!" he gasps.

"You got something to say?" Boss says.

Ethan is desperate. He's not getting out of here. His only plan is sowing seeds of discontent to delay them leaving him alone in this mine. "You think if Horse has the relic and gets out of this pit, he's going to let them pull you out?"

"You really didn't know anything," Boss chuckles. "And I thought you were just full of shit."

"What?" Ethan chokes.

"The way you said 'relic,'" the Boss says. "Like there's only one." He crouches, trains his headlamp on the bag, and unzips it. The gold glitters in the light. "Two necklaces, multiple bracelets. I count four goblets. And one decorative thing—see it in the corner of it down there? The one with the jewels?"

"I told you," Horse laughs. "He and Doubles thought it was a Dirty Santa thing. Shavano just handing out a gift apiece."

Ethan can't read their expressions.

Boss mutters, "He's got a point, though."

"What?"

"Got no problem with you bringing up the treasure. But I'm going up first.

A pair of hands zips the bag, then lifts it beyond Ethan's field of vision.

"See you up top," Boss says.

"What about him?" says Horse.

"Sorry, time to break with tradition."

"What?" Horse is a bit slow on the uptake, but Ethan immediately grasps what the Boss is saying.

"That whole 'leave no man behind' thing."

36-ZAHN

Mount Aetna, Colorado-July 14, 2022

A rumble shakes rocks loose from above my hidey hole. Shouts warn me all is not well in the mine. The armed sentry preventing me from moving disappears. A voice bellows, "Pull me up! Pull me up! It's caving in."

This distraction is my first opportunity to move and I make the most of it, scrambling from below the mine entrance on a circuitous route to a perch above. The men guarding the mine focus on the mishap, but I'm still careful and deliberate, unwilling to draw their attention my way.

From my new viewpoint, I attempt to decipher what happened. The men have recovered one individual, evidently the one who caused a rockslide down the opening. Others remain below. Emma gave me Ethan's description, but it's too dark to distinguish facial features or clothing. None of the men above seem to be under guard. Ethan is likely either absent or down in the mine. I stew on that for a minute. Was Ethan's abduction faked so he could take his sister Emma out of the picture? That would imply Ethan was involved in the search for the relic all along.

The exchanged shouts from above to below aren't collegial. The man at the bottom of the pit is not a friend. Another man yells, "What's going on with Horse and the Boss?"

My heart pounds. Emma mentioned Horse when she related her brother's story about the HAVOC 23 crew. I don't remember all the details, but she was clear about the call signs: a crew chief was called Horse because his last name was Ma, the Chinese word for "horse."

My new position provides the situational awareness I lacked below. If Ethan is inside the mine, I'll see him exit. If the men leave, I can follow them. Worst case, if they try to hurt Ethan, I can attempt to stop them. And their conversations are clearer. The sentry returns to his post but sets up below the mine entrance overlooking my former hiding position. No one's watching above the mine.

"Little further, Boss. Little further. Gotcha."

The talker tugs the man from the hole, helps him to his feet and steps back, giving him room. The Boss scans the area, but I can't distinguish his features.

"We good? Any issues up here?" the Boss says, his voice hoarse.

"No issues, sir. Just the cave-in. Thought we might have lost you guys." The man who helped the Boss looks him up and down. "You didn't find it?"

The Boss chuckles. "Horse is bringing it up. Much more than we thought. Horse underestimated how much my brother pulled out."

My brother? Emma hadn't mentioned a brother when discussing Shavano.

The Boss leans over the hole and tosses a rope below. "You ready, Horse?"

"Ready," the response sounds muffled.

"Shoot him," the Boss calls.

"I don't want to shoot him. He's half-dead already. No one's going to find him."

"Horse?"

"Yeah?"

"Do it."

I stand. The only one I can imagine these men shooting is Emma's brother. I raise my Glock and point it at the Boss, but I don't squeeze the trigger. What good does it do me to kill the man in my sights if the one doing the execution is at the bottom of the mine?

A gunshot booms, muffled like an explosive detonating underwater. I sink into my hiding place, aware I've failed in the one thing Emma asked me to do. Her brother is dead. I practically watched it happen.

A minute later, they rope another man from the mine. I blink, trying to distinguish between what must be Horse and the Boss. It's too dark. One of them hands the bag to the other. Evidently, whatever they found is inside.

I need more light. So far, all I've gathered is Horse's nickname. I'll never be able to pick out any of these men out of a line-up.

The men gather their gear, retrieving ropes and stuffing them into backpacks. They waste no time descending the mountain, leaving me with a dilemma. Follow them so I can help law enforcement track them down later? Or recover Emma's brother's corpse?

I pick my way toward the mine entrance. At the rim, I peer over the edge. A gaping hole lies below, blacker than the surrounding moonlit night.

I check my surroundings to make sure no gunmen have returned. I'm alone. Back at the rim, I flip on my headlamp. The mine drops in a slope with dark dirt slanting to the bottom. The initial ten feet has caved in. At the bottom, the limit of my beam falls upon a splash of color. Something blue extends from the mound of soil at the base. I pick out a white shape at the top of the blue. A face.

"Ethan." My voice carries louder than a whisper but quieter than a yell.

The body doesn't move.

I try again. "Ethan?"

I flip off my headlamp and close my eyes. Not only did I fail to save Ethan's life, but I can't recover his body alone. I'll have to guide a team here after I return to civilization.

I whisper, "I'm sorry, Emma." My wispy lament amplifies down the mine.

A weak voice answers. "Are you the Z-man?"

37-DARIA

St. Elmo, Colorado-July 14, 2022

Once Emma gives him a clearer picture of what's happening, Perez turns to Donnie Morgan. "I want transport up here ASAP to move these two women back to the office. Protective custody until I say otherwise."

"Roger." Donnie returns to his truck to make the calls.

"What about my Dad?" Daria demands. "He doesn't know about Larkin."

"Rick," Emma intervenes, putting a hand on Daria's arm. "What's your plan?"

"Officer Morgan stays here. I'll move a team to Garfield on Highway 50 to block their escape. That's probably where their vehicles are parked. You see any while you hiked into St. Elmo?"

Daria shakes her head. "Just my dad's truck."

Perez says, "Doesn't mean the vehicle Zahn saw isn't still back there somewhere. But it can't get by Donnie here." He studies the sky. "I'll get a helo and see if we can intercept these guys out in the field."

Emma says, "If you have access to air transport, I'm going with you."

"We don't have police helicopters. Reach or Flight for Life might take me. They can't carry both of us unless they drop off some of their crew." Perez gives Emma a thin smile. "Besides, you're out of your jurisdiction and not on duty."

"Screw that. Between the folks we saw and the reports of others, we know there could be six to seven gunmen out there. You plan on taking them all on by yourself in a rescue helicopter with a handgun?"

Perez eyes Emma. Daria can't tell what he's thinking—but Emma's made a good argument about why his Rambo plan sucks. He shakes his head and points to Donnie's truck. "Wait here for your ride. I'm going to coordinate with dispatch. I don't have time for this." He walks away, a handheld radio pressed to his ear.

"Not going to work." Emma strides toward Officer Morgan's Explorer. Daria follows.

Emma taps on the window.

Donnie lowers it. "Climb on in."

"Just a minute," replies Emma. "Why are you parked here?"

"You've seen the map. St. Elmo is the junction for Tincup Pass and Chalk Creek Pass."

"Right. I've seen the map. But why this spot, right here?" She slaps the side of the truck. "You could be a hundred yards closer. Why here?"

"We always park here when something's happening in St. Elmo. The general store there," he points across the street, "has public Wi-Fi. Allows us to access the internet since there's no phone signal."

Emma nods as if she's expected an answer like this. She opens the rear passenger door and turns to Daria. "After you." Inside, Emma taps Donnie on the shoulder. "You have an iPhone charging cord?"

The officer hands the phone end of the charger to Emma. She plugs in and waits for her phone to power on and build a charge.

"Who are you calling?" Daria says. "FBI helicopters?"

Emma smiles. "Not a bad idea, Dar, but no. Not enough time to mobilize. Ethan's training school has a 24-hour number. They're invested. One of their own went down."

Emma works through the phone system, finds a decision-maker, and puts the phone on speaker.

Jake Wagner introduces himself. "I go by Wags. I met your brother. Goddamn unbelievable what happened to that crew. You've made me a happy man by telling me that Ethan made it out alive. The rest of those guys—aww shit. Thought I'd seen it all."

Emma says, "I know you're a training unit, sir. But we need some help to corral the guys who watched your helicopter go down." She pauses. "And murdered one of your students."

The silence following drags on so long that Daria assumes Emma will have to hang up and redial. Finally, Wags answers. "You got it. No questions. I'm going to send you our best pilot. I'll round up the rest of the crew in about fifteen minutes."

"How many can you carry?" Emma says.

"We're bringing a crew of four. I can crowd in eight of you if you're just having us put you down. If you plan on shooting from the helo, then let's just bring four or five of your guys."

Emma and Wags coordinate a pickup location. Donnie keeps turning from the front seat, like he's unsure if he's supposed to be listening to this conversation or if he should be on another line, warning Perez what's happening.

"That best pilot you're sending?" Emma says. "What's the name I should be asking for?"

"I thought I introduced myself already, ma'am. I go by Wags. I'll see you in forty-five."

•   •   •

"You did *what?*" Perez squeezes the window sill on Emma's side of the truck, leaning toward the FBI agent. Emma doesn't flinch, instead leaning toward Perez. Daria's ready to put down money on whether they'll kiss.

"Got us a bigger helicopter," Emma says. "They'll be here in forty-five minutes."

Perez seems to realize how close his face is to Emma's and pulls back from the Tahoe door. "I'm on hold for a Reach medical helicopter. One extra seat. They need two hours to run it up the chain for approval."

Emma nods. She has her back to Daria, so her expression is unreadable. But Perez's face makes it clear he's resigned to accepting Emma's option.

"You packing?" he says.

"Don't leave home without it." Emma pats her jacket.

Perez shifts to the front passenger window to talk to Donnie. "Change of plans. Help us illuminate a landing zone. After we're airborne, maintain ground comms with us and send Daria down with the car we called."

"Got it, boss."

Daria doubts Donnie normally calls Perez "boss." Donnie works for the city, Buena Vista Police. Perez is a county sheriff's deputy. But now that Larkin is suspect, Donnie knows county law enforcement doesn't have a legitimate leader and Perez is filling the gap.

Perez spreads his map across the hood of the car and invites Emma to study the route for their search for Larkin and his men. Certain they aren't going to chase her away, Daria moves in for a closer look.

"The HAATS crew will have night vision goggles. I've got mine in my truck and you can use Donnie's," Perez turns to Emma, "assuming you don't have any in your pack?"

Emma shakes her head.

"Straight over Chalk Creek Pass and down the basin." Perez stabs the map with his finger. "Lights out, with everyone scanning for them. They'll hear us but won't be able to see us unless they're packing goggles too. We can't linger over them. Once we've confirmed they're headed to their cars, we'll move toward the highway and set up an ambush at their vehicles." Perez pauses, turning back to Emma. "Any thoughts?"

"A couple," Emma says. "Where does my brother fit into this? If they have him, an ambush at the cars puts him in danger."

Daria jumps in. "What about my dad? We don't know where he is. He could be captured just like Ethan."

Emma eyes Perez. "Your plan doesn't address the part we care about most. Bringing our family members back."

Perez remains silent, training his headlamp beam on the map. He traces his finger along the route over Chalk Creek Pass and down the other side. Then he jabs his finger on Highway 50 where he predicts the vehicles will be parked. He turns to Daria. "Z-man's the wild card in this."

He pivots to Emma. "And you're not wrong. I can't guarantee your brother's safety if we have a showdown with them. But," Perez returns to the map, "we'll never catch them on foot, so if they have your brother—and if they have your dad—then they're gone. We've lost them with no leads. Hopefully, Z-man somehow got your brother away from those guys, whatever that looks like." He scratches his nose. "If that's even possible?"

Daria's familiar with Highway 50 from ski days at Monarch. They can go east toward Salida. Or southwest toward Gunnison. Perez and Emma are focused on hiking versus flying and how to keep these guys from leaving in their cars. They're missing the big picture.

"What happens if you let them go?" Daria interjects.

"What?" The incredulity in Perez's tone gives her confidence. She's thought of something he hasn't.

"Instead of keeping them from their cars, what if you let them drive away? Unless you know something about Highway 50 that I don't, I think you could use roadblocks miles down either side of the pass just before any side roads that provide an alternative escape."

Perez nods at Daria with a grin. "I'm not even going to pretend I'm not embarrassed." He jabs his pencil on a spot four miles east of Garfield. "One car here." He traces his finger up Monarch Pass and taps it just before the summit parking pull-off. "Another here, with the tactical advantage of being uphill."

Perez spreads his hands over the map and turns toward Emma. "What do you think?"

"Makes sense to me. And the helicopter?"

"Let me coordinate the roadblocks on the radio while we're waiting for the aircraft. Then let's find your brother." He turns to Daria. "And your dad too."

38-ZAHN

Mount Aetna, Colorado-July 14, 2022
I thrust my head over the mine opening. "Ethan?"

"Z-man?" Ethan's muffled voice rises from the pit. "Emma. Told me. Your nickname."

I barely make out Ethan's words. "I thought they shot you. What's your status? Can you move?"

"Can't move my legs. They're buried. My head. Messed up."

I roll away from the opening and shine my light on my 24-hour pack. My previous concerns about the gunmen detecting us disappear in the face of the real emergency. SAR teams don't carry climbing rope unless we're on a high-angle rescue mission. But tucked in the external compartment of my pack are webbing straps, multiple lengths of 8mm rope—almost ninety feet of makeshift rope if I connect them. I guesstimate Ethan's only thirty feet or so down. I'll need the extra length for an anchor. And a way to connect us to my homemade climbing rope.

"Ethan? I'm going to get some gear and come down to you. Hang tight."

"OK."

I retrieve my pack, running through my repertoire of knots I can use to connect my montage of odds and ends together. Although I was a Boy Scout, knots were never my thing. When I flew in the C-130, our loadmasters would try to show me, guiding me through various means of connecting one thing to another, while prepping to airdrop our load over hostile territory. But how to tie the knot—the 1-2-3 of it—lasted only a couple of flights before flitting from my brain like smoke on a windy day.

I execute a sheet bend, the knot I sort of remember for tying ropes of different sizes together, but the result sucks. I rummage in the interior of my pack for an extra rope length, but carabiners rattle on the outside of my bag and spark an idea. I'm moving a guy who weighs less than two hundred pounds. I can make loops with a double figure-eight knot—one of the few I've memorized—and connect my ropes and straps with the carabiners.

Three minutes later, I'm pitched on the mine's edge. I've fashioned a makeshift harness of webbing around my thighs and ass, and rely on an anchor I've set up on a huge boulder. I clip the last carabiner on my forty feet of rope to connect me to it so I can lower myself down the steep slope. "Ethan? Still with me?"

A groan echoes from below.

"Coming down."

I lean back, stepping down the dirt slope. A third of the way down, the pulse of an engine reverberates above. A helicopter. I switch my headlamp off.

Emma said that Ethan saw gunmen exit a helo when his Black Hawk went down, but the sheriff's office also uses rotary-wing aircraft. I need to know who it is. My radio's in the front sleeve of my pack. I've had it turned off while following the gunmen. If the helo belongs to the good guys, they'll have radios tuned to the frequencies I use.

"I'm going back up," I call to Ethan, as I scramble up and belly over the edge. The throbbing rotor beat fades. I unclip from the rope and lurch toward my pack, flipping it and ripping the radio from the front sleeve. I power it up and check the frequency. TAC5. Not the first choice a helo will use. I switch it over to SIMPLEX1, a common frequency helicopters operate on when they have line-of-sight communications.

I pull the radio to my mouth. What do I say? If it's the bad guys, I'm giving myself away. If it's my people, what if the bad guys are listening in?

I lower the radio and pull my wallet from my pocket. I shine my headlamp on the contents and flip through the top row of cards, pulling the last one in the stack. "Please, please." I flip the card to the Morse code cheat sheet. I look for the 'T.' The symbol is a dash. The 'Z' is two dashes and two dots.

I press the transmit button for one second and release. I wait a second and do it twice more, followed by two short jabs on the mic button.

"T" "Z" I jab again, praying I'm on the right frequency and the helicopter is a good guy.

"Tyler Zahn."

39-DARIA

St. Elmo, Colorado-July 14, 2022
Reserve Deputy Scott Powers drives Daria down the gravel road from St. Elmo. They listen on his radio as the HAATS helicopter picks up Emma and Perez. Daria releases a breath when the pilot calls RAZOR 54 airborne.

Powers says, "I'll keep the radio tuned in case we hear more traffic. Probably won't though. They'll be low and between the mountains."

"Thanks." Daria's frustrated she's being shuttled out of the action while Emma heads out on this mission. It makes sense. Daria's just a civilian. But even Perez was surprised when she came up with the idea for the roadblocks.

"What'd your dad think of your decision to hike the Colorado Trail?"

Tense after the last day and night, she almost scowls at Powers's attempt at small talk. How can he talk to her about hobbies when her father is in danger?

Powers keeps talking when she doesn't reply. "Your dad's a good man. Lucky to have him as a reserve deputy."

"How do you know? He just started." Daria's being bratty but Powers is the only one she can take out her worry on.

Powers doesn't seem to notice. "We'd heard about some of the stuff he did before, with Perez. So when he comes in, we all expect him to act like he's some big hotshot. But he does the opposite. He asks a lot of questions, like our opinions really mean something. Did you ever notice that?"

Daria laughs, her anger drying up faster than a T-shirt on a downhill hiking leg. "Yeah. He doesn't like doing things he doesn't understand, so he's not afraid to ask for help."

"It's not just that," Powers says. "The first time I met him, he started asking questions about my family. Asking about my son's school. Whether he likes books. He volunteers at the library, right?"

"That's how he was in the Air Force too," Daria smiles. "Cares about the people he works with." She pauses, not comfortable talking about the years her father wasn't in her life.

"That's why I asked how he felt about you hiking the trail. I'll bet he hasn't slept much while you've been out there."

Another flash of anger ripples through Daria, but fades. It's not about her. He's talking about her dad, and he's right. Family is everything to Zahn now.

Which is why her dad's annoyance with Emma makes no sense. Emma wasn't completely honest with Daria when she met her brother on the trail, and she left Daria alone out there. But it wasn't even four miles from St. Elmo. Zahn's angry because he thinks Emma put his daughter in jeopardy. But Emma's no different from him, willing to do whatever it takes to protect her brother.

Powers holds up a hand. "You hear that?"

"What?"

"That mic keying on the radio. That's Morse code."

Daria listens. She might have picked up the rhythm of the mic clicks as intentional, but she doesn't understand Morse code. "What's it saying?"

"Just two letters. I'm not sure what it means."

"What letters?"

"First one's a T. Then…hang on. Dash, Dash, Dot, Dot. That's a Z."

"TZ! Tyler Zahn," she cries. "It's my dad!"

Powers grabs the mic. "Chaffee Two, Chaffee Two this is Chaffee Seven on SIMPLEX1, how copy?"

No one answers.

Powers repeats himself.

"Chaffee Seven. Roger. We got it."

"Got what?" Daria says. "How do we know what 'they got?'"

Powers replaces his mic on the mount and smiles. "They know it's your dad. They're telling me to shut up."

"How do you know?" She's still worried Perez won't understand.

"Because otherwise, they would have asked what I wanted. Your dad isn't broadcasting with voice. He's using caution for a reason. Perez isn't going to give up his element of surprise by explaining it all to us. Trust me on this one."

Emma, Perez, and the helicopter team are on it.

Daria prays when they say "We got it," that they do.

40-ETHAN

Mount Aetna, Colorado-July 14, 2022

Something nudges Ethan's shoulder. He wills his eyes open. Tyler Zahn stands above him.

"Ethan. Ethan. Hey, you with me?"

Ethan completed the mandatory Wilderness First Aid course before attending HAATS training. The prods and questions are standard operating procedures for testing subject responsiveness.

"Emma's my sister," he whispers, tilting his head toward Zahn's headlamp.

Zahn gives a thin smile. "Something I'd have liked to have known a little sooner. How about we work on getting you out of here?"

"My legs."

"Yep, let me set up some lights and get you out from under this dirt."

Zahn pulls out a spare headlamp, turns it on, and steps to the center of the mine floor, below the opening where he aims it skyward. He tugs off his own headlamp and props it next to the spare, then moves back to Ethan. He scrapes dirt and rock from around Ethan's legs. "The light's a signal. Help's coming."

"Who? What if it's Horse? And Shavano's half-brother?"

"You can trust these guys. But we need to get you out of here—they're coming in a helicopter, and I want to have you up top and ready to load by the time they get here."

Zahn digs out Ethan's legs and has him flex one ankle, then the other. Ethan lets out a huge sigh, swallowing the lump in his throat. He's not paralyzed. He couldn't move because he had a hundred pounds of sand and gravel on him.

Groggy, he pushes partially up, and Zahn helps him stand.

Zahn says, "Lean against the wall while I get you roped up." He brushes the dirt away from Ethan's climbing harness before clipping him in with a carabiner. "What do you got left, Ethan? Can you help?" he says. "I don't have a pulley up there. I don't have a belay device down here."

Ethan hasn't touched the rope yet. Raising his arms is exhausting. But staying in this hole terrifies him. He groans as he reaches for the rope with his good hand. "I'll do it."

"Don't grab the rope," Zahn offers. "I'll go first and gather the slack in the rope as you climb. You weigh too much for me to carry you up. Can you use your hands to scramble up while I hold the tension?"

Ethan takes a breath. "Yeah."

Zahn grabs his headlamp off the floor and snaps it on his head, leaving Ethan's behind. He scrambles ten feet up the steep dirt slope before turning to Ethan. "Come on."

Ethan reaches up for the first piece of rock available. As he pulls himself, the rock ejects from the mine face and falls to his right. He slips, twirls on the rope, then sinks back to the mine floor.

"Again," Zahn grunts, releasing the tension on the line. "When stuff starts falling, just reach up to the next handhold. It's not going to be easy. But you can do it."

Ethan grabs again. The rock he chooses holds, and he stretches with his left hand, groaning as the broken finger radiates pain up his arm. He uses the foothold from where the first rock fell.

"That's it," Zahn says, pulling upward.

Zahn is choosing to rescue him. He doesn't have to. And he's already hinted that Ethan might not be on his Christmas card list next year. No wonder his sister likes this man.

Ethan's reach dislodges another stone. "Rock!" he croaks, scrabbling with the same hand higher in search of another hold.

"Keep going." Zahn's voice rises above the crescendo of falling gravel and sand.

Ethan steps up another few feet and curls a hand over the mine edge, groping for a handhold. He wedges his fist between two rocks, and grunts as Zahn grasps his bad hand and tugs. Ethan squelches a scream of pain and rolls out of the shaft. Lying on his back, he gasps for breath, mouth agape at the stars shining above him.

"Ethan?" Zahn's voice and the hum of an engine jerks him back to reality.

"I hear it. Are you sure about this?"

"It's our guys. I need you to get up."

The throb of the helicopter is close. Zahn pulls him to his feet and switches his headlamp to flashing mode. "Let's move," he calls. He pushes Ethan forward.

"Where? You can't land an aircraft on a twenty-degree slope."

"Near the top," Zahn shouts. The roar is so loud, that Ethan turns to find its source. A mass of black metal stands out from the silver of the moonlit rocks, pulsing up the slope in a slow forward motion. He turns back to Zahn, who points toward the massive rock pile in front of them.

The apex of the pile is the only level point on the entire slope. The question is whether the helicopter can get a wheel on it without its overhead rotor cutting into the side of the mountain. Scrambling in front of Zahn, Ethan claws at the hillside, his pain counterbalanced by adrenaline.

He nears the top of the pile. The helicopter—a Black Hawk—is a hundred yards away, creeping forward in a high-altitude hover, a maneuver Ethan qualified in only days ago. Zahn fumbles to turn off his light so he won't wash out the pilots' night vision goggles.

Zahn ducks his head as the helicopter nears. Ethan drags himself beside Zahn, shielding his eyes with his good hand. The chop-chop of the blades reverberates through Ethan's body as the helo passes overhead, and hope envelops him. Not just that he will emerge from this nightmare alive, but that someday he might pilot a helicopter again.

"Let's go!" Zahn shouts.

The helicopter perches on top of the tailings pile. A figure stands by the door, his boom mic light pointed at the two men. Zahn rises to his feet and grabs Ethan under his armpits.

Ethan pulls away. "I can make it." He steps toward the light.

"Go," Zahn roars, pushing Ethan to the top from behind.

Another figure moves toward the door from inside the aircraft. A brilliant white light explodes near their waist, and the high-power beam blinds Ethan. He crosses his arms over his eyes and ducks, avoiding the spotlight.

A high-pitched scream penetrates the thrum of the blades. "That's him!"

Ethan squints in the glare. His sister's arms reach for him.

41-ZAHN

Mount Aetna, Colorado-July 14, 2022

"Where's Daria?" I shout as soon as I lower myself to the rear bench seat. No one offers me a helmet or a headset, so I have no way to communicate with anyone outside of screaming. Emma grabs my arm, meets my eyes, and nods her head, before joining the crew chief kneeling over her brother's prone body between the seats. Emma's priority is Ethan. But I can't help myself. I tug on her jacket, trying to get her attention.

A man standing between the two pilots turns toward me. He wears a helmet with night vision goggles and carries a comm cord in his hand. He nods at me, before turning back. Everyone's nodding, but no one answers.

Emma turns to me. She also wears a helmet with NVGs. She yells at me, "What?"

"Daria?"

Emma twists so our faces are only inches apart. "Perez sent her back to Salida with Deputy Powers."

She turns back to her brother, but I grab at her again. "The sheriff's office is involved. I'm not sure how deep it goes. We need to find Perez."

A slow smile creeps to Emma's face as she motions toward the man standing between the pilots, then leans toward me. "Who do you think put this whole rescue plan together?"

Perez, the only man I trust unconditionally, pivots, raises his night vision goggles, and shoots me a grin. He kneels down next to the crew chief, checking on Ethan's status. A green Dave Scott headset like I used to wear in the C-130 dangles from the metal stanchion next to me. I grab it.

"—get him to Salida for further evaluation. They might need to take him to Denver," the crew chief says.

"How critical?" Perez's voice barks over the intercom. "Is he going to die in the next hour?"

"No," the crew chief answers. "Not from what I see so far."

Perez raises his eyebrows. "You copying all this Z-man?"

I nod. Perez looks from me to Emma, who seems to know where Perez is going with this.

"He needs medical attention," she says.

"But we've identified the two-vehicle convoy leaving from Garfield. They're heading west toward Monarch Pass. Our guys are going to need air cover."

"Why?" Emma pushes back. "If they're on the move, bring the roadblock patrol cars on the east in behind the bad guys and pinch them off."

"Not sure how many cars the gunmen had. If they split up, then the east side roadblock will need to maintain their position."

Emma turns to me as if I'm a decision-maker, but Perez outranks me and then some. I shrug, and Emma's shoulders sag. She leans over her brother. Ethan grabs her shirt sleeve and pulls her closer.

She shouts, "Are you sure?"

Ethan mouths, "Yes."

Emma gives Perez a thumbs up. "Ethan's good to go." Perez nods.

I key my mic. "Is that all he said?"

Emma glances at Perez and thumbs her talk button. "Those guys, Horse and Shavano's half-brother, they're in on it too."

Perez drops his head. "Shit."

I'm clueless, so I key my mic. "What am I missing?"

Perez is already moving back toward the pilots. "No time, Z-man. I'll catch you up when this is done."

.   .   .

The helicopter U-turns, whipping south to Highway 50. I crowd to the window as we pass Garfield, searching in vain for the unidentified vehicles. The only lights are from the multi-story hotel across the highway and a group of summer cabins lined up in two rows running down the valley.

We follow the highway up the pass. I sense the speed decrease as we approach the coordinates Perez has copied.

I tap Perez on the shoulder. He turns. I pull a cuff from my ear so he understands I don't want to talk on the intercom. "What's the plan?" I shout.

"It ain't fancy." Perez matches my volume. "The roadblock has them stopped right ahead. They came around the bend, spotted it, and retreated around the corner. They've been sitting there ever since. Probably trying to figure out how to get around us. But we've got the advantage of the high ground. Flores thinks the gunmen are going to realize their position sucks and try to skedaddle back down the pass. That's where we come in."

"With a helicopter?"

"Me and Emma have rifles. The plan is to set us up on the ground flanking the helo. If the gunmen start coming down the hill, we'll send the helo at them with a spotlight while we lay down fire. That should stop them in their tracks."

"That's your plan?"

Perez looks annoyed. "The western roadblock guys will be right on their tail. We'll either stop them here or, when they turn around, the roadblock guys will get them. There are no other options."

Perez is a much more experienced law enforcement officer than I am, but I'm uncertain how many missions he's run with air assets. Fewer than me, I'd guess. "Rick, you can't use an unarmed aircraft as a show of force. That's not how it's done."

"I already ran it through these guys. They're pumped up. They never get to do this shit."

"What if the gunmen start firing?"

"They didn't up at the roadblock. We don't think they will. But I've told the crew, if they start seeing small arms fire, they're cleared out."

"Rick—"

The helicopter pulls into a hover. Perez keys his mic. "Wags, Terminator, you hear that? They're coming down." He turns to me and shouts, "Here we go. You stay with the aircraft. You don't have NVGs, and you don't have a rifle. That Glock of yours isn't going to work here."

I've got more to say to Perez about his plan, but he's not listening. All he's given me are the names of the guys flying our helicopter. Wags and Terminator.

Emma unplugs and grabs the rifle lying next to Ethan. She follows Perez to the door, lowering her NVGs and twisting the dials on the lenses. Ethan props up on his elbows, his eyes following his sister's path to the door.

Thanks to the roadblocks, the highway is empty. The helicopter roars in and lowers to the ground with an open rear door on the uphill side. As soon as it touches down, Perez unplugs from his comm cord, and yells, "Go! Go!" He steps from the helo and Emma follows behind. The crew chief follows the two with his headlamp as they clear the perimeter of the helo blades. Behind their retreating shapes, a pair of headlights wind down the pass.

"Clear," the chief calls over the intercom.

The helo lifts airborne, using its forward momentum to clear the trees picketing the highway. Once clear, Wags lines up with the road below, turning the helo's spotlight toward the approaching headlights.

A hand grips my forearm. Ethan's standing next to me looking confused. "What the fuck, Z-man? What's their plan?"

"They're trying to use the helicopter to scare the gunmen into giving up." Ethan is probably the only one on board who recognizes this doesn't really count as a plan.

"All it will take is small arms fire into our engines or the right spot on the rotors. They'll take us out." Ethan's voice is incredulous. He looks at me, and I raise my eyebrows in my best "What can I do?" expression.

Ethan moves to the jump seat behind the pilots. The headlights shine in front of us. They don't appear to move. Ethan turns back and scans the seats, stopping when he spies a helmet rigged with NVGs underneath. He puts it on, plugs into Perez's discarded comm cord, and fumbles for the intercom button.

"Wags. Terminator. You guys are going to get shot."

Terminator whips his head around. "Dude. I thought you were almost dead."

"We'll all be dead if you maintain this position," Ethan says, shifting his gaze to Wags. "Let me see if I got this right, Wags. You need to stop the car?"

Wags doesn't take his eyes from the window but nods as he flicks his intercom switch. "Technically, we're just supposed to keep it from continuing down the pass. But stopping it would accomplish that."

"You do anything like this back in 'Nam?"

"No."

"I have," Ethan says. "It's standard training after the Iraq War."

Wags moves the helicopter closer to the stationary headlights. "You're not getting anywhere close to my controls." He twists his head toward Ethan. "Son, you're not even supposed to be out of that litter."

"I can talk you through it," Ethan says.

"Wags, we got small arms fire from the car," the crew chief shouts over the intercom. "I got sparks off our rotors. They dinged us."

Ethan crouches as Wags yanks the helicopter into a vertical climb. G-forces push me down to my seat. Treetops lit by the car's headlights fade as we elevate several hundred feet in the air.

"That ain't working," Wags says. He turns his head to Ethan. "Educate me."

Ethan describes his proposed maneuver while I regain my feet and search for Perez and Emma. Gunfire flashes on both sides of the road. I assume my friends are flanking the highway, using the guardrails as cover.

Wags loops the helicopter in a broad arc maneuvering in behind the vehicle. As we come in low, Ethan calls out. "Lights off. Don't let him know we're coming in."

"He's rolling!" the chief calls.

Terminator chimes in. "He's taking advantage of us leaving and shooting the gauntlet."

The gunfire brightens as the car moves closer. I picture Perez and Emma swinging their weapons in line with the car as it passes and pray they don't accidentally take each other out.

The SUV's brake lights flash. Wags drops in behind the SUV fifty yards back and I step forward, scanning the windscreen.

Terminator calls out. "Why did he stop?"

"Look in front of the car," Ethan yells.

I peer around Ethan. A bear cub faces the SUV like it's playing chicken.

The SUV brake lights wink out. I key my mic. "He's going to run over the cub!"

Ethan calls out. "Lights!"

Wags illuminates the SUV in blinding white light. The vehicle slams to a stop again. A dark shape lopes across the road and barrels the cub over. The small bear stumbles to its feet and follows its mother over the shoulder.

Terminator calls out, "He's stopped. Move over the top of him."

Wags moves forward. The SUV disappears underneath our helicopter.

"Drop it!" Ethan calls.

Wags settles the helicopter onto the roof of the car.

"Not too much," Ethan directs. "Just enough to keep him from rolling again."

"I've got two guys coming out the passenger side," Terminator calls. "Over the shoulder. They dove over the edge. They're gone."

"That first guy was Horse," Ethan yells. He staggers to Wags's side of the aircraft. "Driver's exiting. He's moving toward the uphill side." Ethan yells. "Hit the lights."

Terminator flips a switch. Wags raises the helicopter and twists it toward the fleeing man. The spotlight illuminates him just as he trips.

Terminator calls, "I see our guys. The deputy sheriff and the FBI gal. They're moving our way with weapons at the ready."

The man on the ground rolls over, shielding his eyes with his hand. He whips his head toward Perez and Emma. Both his hands shoot in the air.

Ethan shouts, "It's Shavano's brother. The Boss."

I crowd to the window for a better view. "What do you mean by 'the Boss?'"

"That's the guy who told Horse to shoot me."

"Holy shit," I say. No wonder Perez didn't have time to fill me in on what must be a long story. Wags, Terminator, and Ethan all turn toward me, so I continue. "I know him as Brad Larkin. The Chaffee County Sheriff."

42-ZAHN

(TWO WEEKS LATER)

Durango, Colorado-July 28th, 2022

The four-hour drive with Ethan to meet Daria and Emma at the end of the Colorado Trail begins in silence. I've found that two men in a truck often makes conversation optional, but in this case, I suspect it's because we both are still shell-shocked by what we've endured. Ethan will carry the scars forever, physical and otherwise.

The three days of interviews and investigation after Perez arrested Larkin and his men allowed Daria to rest her aching Achilles tendons. Ethan was held in custody by order of the FBI until Perez exercised his newly appointed sheriff's authority and talked them into releasing Ethan in good faith. Emma, Daria, and I were under strict orders to stay close to the phone and within the boundaries of Chaffee County until the investigation was over. When the authorities finished their relentless barrage of questions, Daria was ready to hike.

Emma visited Ethan every day while he was detained. Although they had been working toward a reconnection before the helicopter crash, the shared trauma of events brought them closer.

When we crest Wolf Creek Pass, we finally begin talking. Ethan's story of the last six years matches up with what Emma told me on the trail. Not the same choices I would have made. But as Daria reminds me, sometimes my observations aren't helpful.

When Ethan brings up Kristee Li, I swerve the truck and tap the brakes before recovering and regaining my lane at a slower speed.

"Say that again." I glance at Ethan and back to the road. "What Horse said."

"She was asking about out-of-the-way places in Asia, visa requirements, and expediting passport processes. Horse told her about Baoshan, China, where he grew up."

"What were the dates again?"

"Late last spring, maybe summer. I don't know the specific days."

Kristee was in trouble then. Right before she disappeared. But *China?*

After Kristee disappeared, she was all I could think of. Over the past year, I've trained myself not to think about her at all. Now I can't help it.

During the investigation, people discovered Kristee had reasons to want to end it all. But I had believed the opposite—that she had more reasons to want to live. Kristee's sister had discovered a piece of Kristee's gear near the rockslide that indicated she may have been planning to travel. Ethan's revelations about her conversation with Horse have me pondering her disappearance again. Could she have left the country?

43-DARIA

Durango, Colorado-July 28, 2022

Emma snags a table for four at Durango's Whittler's Brewing Company. Daria orders starters before Emma even opens the drink menu.

Despite barreling through the second half of the thru-hike in two weeks, the women had stopped at almost every switchback, catching bittersweet last glimpses of the San Juan Mountains. They'd jog to the next trail reversal and snap photos, both sad and excited to finish their journey. Today's descent to Junction Creek and the Colorado Trail terminus, amid lush forests and vibrant wildflowers, etched itself forever in Daria's memories.

Emma grins at Daria. "Anything fried?"

Daria zeroes in on the menu. "Fried pickles."

Zahn shakes his head.

"Give me a break, Dad. It's not like you paid attention to what you ate until recently."

"I'll have the cheese sticks," Emma says, elbowing Zahn in the side.

"I'll have a light beer," Ethan says, but Zahn fakes falling out of his chair.

"Two IPAs," Zahn says to the server, giving Ethan the stink eye.

Ethan's eye twitches like he's trying to return the gesture, but both eyes close instead. He still has a swollen mouth and black stitches line his scalp.

"When in Rome, Ethan," her dad says.

Emma winks at Daria and orders an IPA as Zahn lectures Ethan on the virtues of craft beer in the Colorado Rockies. Daria grins back and asks the server for a sour.

She's an optimistic person. Her dad says it's a gene thing—that she was born with a propensity to look on the bright side of everything. She disagrees. Her mother and their church were formative in her adolescent years. Her church attendance has tapered since graduating from college, but she has never had a reason to question her faith.

So it's not a stretch for Daria to look back on the events from two weeks ago in a positive light. She might be the only one. The entire county still reels from the revelations that their trusted sheriff collaborated on a treasure hunt gone wrong. One that cost the lives of three service members and the subsequent torture of Ethan.

Worth the cost? No. But it happened. So Daria reflects on the good—Emma and Ethan are reunited, and Emma and Zahn are on their way to reconciliation. Daria questions whether they were ever unreconciled. Love isn't easy. Families are hard.

The relics are on their way back to Iraq.

And Daria is a thru-hiker.

The drinks arrive, and Zahn lifts his glass. "To the crew of HAVOC 23." Emma and Daria raise their pints to the center of the table, but Ethan doesn't join.

"Which HAVOC 23?" he says. "If you're talking about our crew in Iraq, then I can't," he says to Zahn. "Doubles was the only good one. Horse was on that crew. So I'm the only one alive."

Daria never met Horse. He fell to his death after diving over the shoulder of the road at Monarch Pass.

Ethan adds, "If I had done the right thing from the beginning maybe this all could have been avoided." Emma says, "Ethan—"

"I know." He nods toward Zahn. "We talked about it on the way here. I've got to learn to forgive myself, right? I can't drink to Shavano either. He tried to make me believe it was okay to take that knife. He knew the relics were valuable, and he hid them from everyone.

Zahn takes a sip of his beer. "Even Larkin's motive was more noble than that."

Back in Buena Vista, Daria's father had shared information from the preliminary investigation with her and Emma. Larkin's reasons for stealing weren't self-serving. His mother—Mrs. Larkin, not Shavano's mother, Mrs. Bissonnette—was dying of cancer but she refused to move to the Front Range for the necessary treatment. Larkin was spending his savings to bring doctors to her home in Salida to provide treatment.

When his money ran out, Larkin's "posse" stepped in and helped. But when Horse showed up with rumors of Shavano's treasure, Larkin promised those same supporters a cut of the profits if they helped find it. None of them expected the whole thing to career into violence, but when HAVOC 23 arrived on scene, Larkin's men and their borrowed helicopter overreacted to the threat to their potential cash cow.

Daria shoots a questioning glance at her dad. He nods, confirming her interpretation of his toast. He was honoring the HAVOC 23 crew from the HAATS mission, not the crew that flew in Iraq. And he just gave her permission to take over the toast.

She raises her glass. "How about we remember the three who passed away in the crash? To Doubles, and…help me out, Beans."

Ethan gives a weak smile at the use of his short-lived trail name. "Sgt. 1st Class Evan Hendricks. And Sgt. 1st Class Roger Stepp." His eyes well. "And Lisa. Lisa Brumstock. But she would have liked us to call her Doubles if we're raising our glasses at a brewery."

"To Doubles, Hendricks, and Stepp," Daria says. "May they never be forgotten."

"Hear, hear," they chorus. Glasses clink. Ethan gulps his beer.

Emma's eyes linger on Zahn. He smiles and mouths "What?" She just shakes her head.

Daria says, "You two all made up now?"

"There was never a problem," Zahn says.

Emma follows with, "Made up from what?"

Daria laughs. "Right."

Zahn takes a swallow of beer. When he returns the pint to the table, his eyes linger on it. Finally, he looks up at Daria. "OK. Maybe I learned something."

"What?"

"You told me once I was a good judge of character."

"That was the first half of the sentence. Do you remember the second?" Daria smiles at the memory.

"You also said I am sometimes quick to judge." He grins. "You're right."

"Wait. I'm going to need you to say that again." Daria turns to Ethan. "Can you record this?" Ethan attempts to smile and winces instead, the effort too painful to maintain.

Zahn says, "I was too quick to judge during the action. Emma made decisions out of loyalty to Ethan." Emma nods and Zahn smiles at her before returning to Daria. "Every single one of my decisions in those mountains was a direct result of concern for your safety. So, for me to hold a grudge against Emma is hypocritical. And that's not me."

Zahn jerks in his seat and he ducks his head to look under the table. Daria leans back and checks out the under-table action. Emma's foot rubs Zahn's calf.

Zahn reaches across the table with his palm up, resting it in front of her. Emma's smile widens as she drops her hand into his. He gives it a light squeeze.

"It's going to be okay, Tyler." She returns his squeeze.

Daria smiles at her dad.

Emma pulls her hand away and Zahn tugs it back, raising it to his lips and kissing it. "I know."

The interaction between two people she loves warms her heart. Her father had been furious at Emma for leaving Daria on the trail—evidence of how much he loved his daughter—but Emma had done exactly what Tyler Zahn would.

Protect those you love.

Which makes Daria wonder. What will her dad do with the information Ethan shared about Kristee Li?

ABOUT THE AUTHOR

Over a thirty-year Air Force career, author Cam Torrens delivered combat supplies and personnel across Europe, the Middle East, and Africa. He piloted the first mobility aircraft into Iraq during the Iraq War, served as the United States Air Attaché at the US Embassy in Beijing, China, and spent four years as a professor of aerospace studies at Virginia Tech.

A father of six, Cam and his spouse live in Buena Vista, Colorado, where he serves as the vice president of the Central Colorado Writers, volunteers with the Chaffee County Search & Rescue team, and chairs the board for the Buena Vista Public Library.

He's admittedly weird—he likes to count things, like consecutive days running, books read, hiking miles, tennis/pickleball/ping pong matches, jacuzzi use, and so on. *HAVOC* is Cam's fifth book.

NOTE FROM CAM TORRENS

Word-of-mouth is crucial for any author to succeed. If you enjoyed *HAVOC*, please leave a review online—anywhere you are able. Even if it's just a sentence or two. It would make all the difference and would be very much appreciated.

Thanks!
Cam Torrens

We hope you enjoyed reading this title from:

BLACK ROSE writing™

www.blackrosewriting.com

Subscribe to our mailing list – *The Rosevine* – and receive **FREE** books, daily
deals, and stay current with news about
upcoming releases and our hottest authors.
Scan the QR code below to sign up.

Already a subscriber? Please accept a sincere thank you for being a fan of
Black Rose Writing authors.

View other Black Rose Writing titles at
www.blackrosewriting.com/books and use promo code
PRINT to receive a **20% discount** when purchasing.